One
Hundred
Proposals

HOLLY MARTIN

CARINA

This edition is published by arrangement with Harlequin Books S.A. CARINA is a trademark of Harlequin Enterprises Limited, used under licence.

Published in Great Britain 2015
by CARINA, an imprint of Harlequin (UK) Limited,
Eton House, 18-24 Paradise Road,
Richmond, Surrey, TW9 1SR

© 2014 Holly Martin

ISBN 978-0-263-91806-9

98-0915

Harlequin (UK) Limited's policy is to use papers that are natural, renewable and recyclable products and made from wood grown in sustainable forests. The logging and manufacturing processes conform to the legal environmental regulations of the country of origin.

Printed and bound by
CPI Group (UK) Ltd, Croydon, CR0 4YY

Huge thanks to my lovely friend Belinda Jones and my agent, Madeleine Milburn, who encouraged me to write this story; it quite simply wouldn't have existed if it wasn't for you. You both have been my rock through all of this and I feel very fortunate to have you both fighting my corner.

To Kirsty Maclennan and Verity Forbes, who read the first half of the book when I was losing faith in it and demanded that I finish it.

For my mom, my biggest fan, who reads every word I have written a hundred times over and loves it every single time.

To my family, my dad, my brother Lee and my sister-in-law Julie, for your support, love, encouragement and endless excitement for my stories.

To Victoria Stone, who read the finished piece first, for falling in love with it and then screaming very loudly across Twitter and Facebook how much she loved it.

To my best friends Gareth and Mandie, for your endless support, patience and enthusiasm.

The other half of the Gosling Girls, Megan Wood and Laura Lovelock. I love my Gosling Girls so much and I couldn't do it without you all. For the endless promotion, tweets, the blog tour, the videos, the excitement, the gushing and the love. You are amazing.

For my twinnie, the gorgeous Aven Ellis, for just being my wonderful friend, for your support, for cheering me on and for keeping me entertained with wonderful stories and pictures of hot men. Thank you for lending me the beautiful Harrison Flynn for my ice hockey game in Toronto.

For Sharon Sant, for listening to me moan and stress and panic with endless patience and for all your support and friendship.

And some other gorgeous people who have encouraged, supported, promoted, got excited or just listened:
Erin McEwan, Lisa Dickenson, Jaimie Admans, Jack Croxall, Dan Thompson, Sharon Wilden, Kelly Rufus, Pernille Hughes,

Rosie Blake, Simona Elena, Katey Beeden, Maryline, Jo Hurst, Dawn Crooks, Jenny Marston, Kim Nash, Laura Delve, Janet Emson, Pat Elliott, Agi, Becca, Alba, Ana, Jess Bickerton, Kate Gordon, Kiri Mills, Louise Wykes, Stacey Hargreaves, Maggie Woodward, Trish H, Jac and Mark Rumsey, Jodie and James Brown, Arron Davenport and Keith Barrow (for your brilliant proposal video).

To all those involved in the blog tour and cover reveal. To anyone who has read my book and taken the time to tell me you've enjoyed it or wrote a review, thank you so much.

To the wonderful supportive Carina authors, you guys are the very best.

And finally to all at Carina who have helped to bring this book to publication: my wonderful editor, Lucy Gilmour, for making the book so much better; the digital team; Anna and the design team for this incredible cover; and anyone else there who has helped to make this book a reality.

Thank you, I love you all.

PROLOGUE

'Ok, you can open your eyes now,' Harry said.

I blinked in the gloom of the cave. Moonlight tumbled through the opening above us, reflecting off the waterfall as it cascaded into the pool below. We had been in Australia for just a few days but I knew it would never cease to amaze me. Dancing in the pockets of the cave walls were hundreds of fireflies, sparkling like fairy lights.

Nothing could have prepared me for what happened next.

The fireflies started to gather together and slowly a shape was formed. I frowned in confusion and then within seconds the words, 'Suzie, Marry Me,' stood proud against the cave walls, written by the fireflies.

I whirled round to face Harry in shock. 'How did you do that?' I looked back at the fireflies, not wanting to miss anything. Would they perhaps move to form the lyrics of my favourite song? Were they super trained fireflies and in a minute they'd all whip out their mini cheerleader pom-poms and start some kind of dance where they would balance precariously on each other's backs?

'It's some kind of fruit juice, they love it.'

I fumbled in my bag for my camera. 'We have to get a picture for the website.'

I fired off a couple of shots and I could see a few other tourists had entered the cave and were clearly waiting for my answer. They'd be waiting for a long time.

'So what do you think?' Harry said. 'Is this the perfect proposal?'

'It's definitely one of your best, very romantic.' I focused my attention on the photos I was taking. They were going to look fantastic with the waterfall in soft focus in the background and the fireflies in sharp detail set against the inky blue light of the moon.

'But still not the perfect proposal?'

'Not for me, but someone else would love it.' I watched the faces of the other tourists fall at my callous response. 'We're not together, we just work with each other.' One couple looked at me dubiously, so I pressed on. 'Our company creates the perfect proposal, this kind of thing is our bread and butter.'

I resisted the sudden urge to rush over to them and start handing out business cards. As if reading my mind, Harry slung an arm round my shoulder, restraining me with his hand.

I looked up at him innocently but he didn't seem convinced.

The tourists moved further down the cave, leaving us alone.

'You always do that,' Harry said.

'What, promote our business? I know, I can't help it. I'm just so proud of what we've achieved that I want to tell anyone that listens and anyone that doesn't.'

'No, not that. You always say *our* company, *our* business. It's yours, you started it. I'm just the tech guy.'

It was just me to start with. I created the.PerfectProposal. com over two years ago when my boyfriend at the time proposed drunkenly to me over a greasy kebab. It struck me that maybe the menfolk of this world might need a little helping hand to create a proposal their girlfriends would remember forever. Although the greasy kebab is not one I'm likely to forget.

Harry was my web designer. When the business first started he would come by my office, the back bedroom in my home, every day to help update the website with my new ideas, photos and special offers. In the end it made sense to make him a permanent feature. Our website looked fantastic and as an online company this was integral to our success.

But Harry wasn't just the geeky IT guy, far from it. He was the biggest man I had ever seen in my life, with large thighs and big feet. He had stubbly, dark hair and chocolate eyes. But he also had a vivid imagination – where I was organising the logistics for a champagne helicopter trip, he would be the one that would come up with something completely unique like using fireflies.

'And you always put yourself down. We're equal partners now, you helped to make the company a success too,' I said.

He shrugged, never keen to accept that he played such an important part in it. He gestured to the fireflies that were starting to break formation now. 'Is it too sickly?'

I let my camera hang round my neck and leaned into him, I loved the way I fitted against him. 'I love it, I really do, it's… magical. But there's still something missing.'

Was there really such a thing as a perfect proposal? Three months ago, just before Valentine's Day, Harry had made it his mission to provide me with one. But deep down I knew what I wanted and I doubted Harry would be able to deliver it. I should have told him that when he first started this wild goose chase. It would have saved me a lot of heartache.

CHAPTER ONE

Three Months Before

I put the phone down on another excited client and sighed. It was February 11th and we'd had a surge of customers all desperately wanting to propose on top of the Eiffel Tower on Valentine's Day. I felt like screaming. It was only by careful planning that I'd arranged that my customers weren't going to be there at the same time. That's just what a girl wants to feel special, to see other girls being proposed to at the same place and time that she was. Was there no originality anymore? Harry was brilliant at coming up with unique proposals, but no matter how many times I had tried to sell Harry's ideas to them, they wanted the traditional and that was that.

'Another Eiffel Tower?' asked Harry as he absentmindedly uploaded photos to our rolling gallery.

'He wants a dozen red roses delivered to the observation deck at eight.' I rubbed my head in defeat. 'What about something different, going to the ballet or proposing over a bag of chips at the end of Brighton Pier?'

He swivelled in his chair. 'What would be your perfect proposal?'

I looked at him and had a sudden flash of him holding me in his arms and asking me to marry him.

'I don't know, the perfect guy would definitely be a bonus.'

'Ok so you have your perfect guy and it's not greasy kebab boy –'

'Let's be clear, it was the kebab that was greasy not the man.'

He waved away the details. 'So Orlando Bloom or some other non-greasy hunk is asking you to marry him, how would he do it?'

I took a sip of tea whilst I pondered this. If one of my customers phoned up at a loss for inspiration I had a hundred ideas. But for me, my mind was blank.

'I have an idea.' Harry's eyes were suddenly bright with excitement. He whirled round on his chair and started tapping away furiously on his computer. I peered over his shoulder at our website.

Proposer's Blog

How Do You Propose to a Proposer?

Over the next hundred days I intend to find out. I will find one hundred ways to propose to our Chief Proposer Suzie McKenzie, and post the results here for your enjoyment. One thing's for sure, not one of my proposals will be on top of the Eiffel Tower with a dozen red roses.

'You can't put that, we've had fifteen customers who want to propose like that over the last week,' I said, ignoring the sudden thundering of my heart that Harry was going to propose to me.

'Then maybe they'll have a rethink.' Harry was already uploading a picture of a diamond ring onto the blog.

'Or ask for their money back.'

But Harry was still writing.

Day 1: The Traditional Proposal. Location: Our office.

He stood up and got down on one knee – yanking the snake ring off his thumb, he held it aloft to my shocked face.

'Suzie McKenzie, you are my best friend and I cannot imagine finding anyone I would rather spend the rest of my life with. Marry me.'

The world stopped. My mouth was dry. How unfair was it that the one thing I wanted most in the world was happening right in front of me and it was as real as a pair of breasts on Sunset Boulevard.

I wanted to snatch the ring off him, stuff it on my finger and march him down to the nearest registry office. But I didn't.

I cleared my throat of the huge lump. 'Too clichéd, wrong location, wrong ring.'

He grinned as he appraised his ring and stood up, clearly not fussed by this rejection. He started typing.

Crashed and Burned. Apparently a snake ring with evil red eyes and the beige walls of our cramped office isn't good enough for her. I'll try again tomorrow.

Surely not. A hundred days of this torment? I didn't think I could bear it.

He looked at his watch. 'Oh, I've got to go, hot date with Sexy Samantha again tonight.'

Samantha was his first girlfriend in nearly a year. When I first met him he seemed to go through a different girl each week, so I wasn't sure why he'd gone through the sudden dry patch. But Samantha was definitely the type to tempt him out of it.

I'd had the pleasure of meeting Sexy Samantha the night before. Suspicious of Harry's relationship with his best friend, she'd barrelled into my home and demanded that Harry introduce me. I came downstairs in leggings and an oversized black hoodie – I knew I was hardly dressed to impress. And impress her I didn't. The look of relief when Samantha saw me was palpable. She, on the other hand, was a vision of heavenly loveliness. She was almost as tall as Harry, with long blonde hair and curves everywhere. My eyes were immediately drawn to a big pair of breasts, squeezed into an overly tight top. Harry was definitely a breast man. All of his girlfriends were very well-endowed in the breast department. Some of the breasts, I suspected, weren't even real – though Harry didn't seem to mind. I was more in the straight up, straight down department, definitely no curves and not really any breasts to speak of.

I watched Harry log off his computer with haste and obvious excitement about what Sexy Samantha had in store for him that night.

'I have a hot date too,' I blurted out, watching for any flicker of jealousy. Of course there was none.

'That's great Suze.' He looked genuinely pleased. 'You haven't seen anyone since Jack…' He trailed off. My life was defined into two segments. Before Jack and After Jack. I wondered if Jules felt the same. Harry grabbed his jacket, averting his eyes from me, perhaps knowing that he had said something he shouldn't. 'It's about time you got back on the horse again. We can swap notes tomorrow.'

'Or not.' I couldn't bear thinking about that conversation. The literal ins and outs of Harry's date would be something I really didn't want to hear. I'd changed the subject twice that morning already when he started giving me explicit details that would be right at home on the pages of an erotic fiction novel. Sexy Samantha was far kinkier than those baby blue eyes might suggest. Besides, what did I have to contribute to that conversation? My hot date consisted of a tub of Ben and Jerry's and a night in with the beautiful Brad Pitt. I logged off my own computer, keen to show him I also had something exciting to run off to.

'Where did you meet him?'

I racked my brain as I fluffed out my hair in the reflection of a photo showing me and Harry covered in snow and grinning ear to ear after sledging at the indoor Snow Zone. Before Jack.

'Skiing,' I said, then wished I hadn't.

He stopped in his hasty exit. 'Skiing? When have you been skiing?'

'I go every Sunday, skiing lessons, he's my ski instructor.' I was making it worse.

'You hate skiing.'

I had said that, hadn't I. Because this photo was taken when we had our first and last skiing lesson a year before. I had spent forty minutes falling on my bum – as kids as young as five glided effortlessly past me – and the last twenty minutes of the lesson, after Harry had been upgraded to the adult slopes, trying to get up and rolling around on the floor with my skis in the air, looking like an oversized beetle stranded on its back. Harry had felt sorry for me because I had failed so spectacularly and had taken me sledging instead. Much more up my street. There was no skill at all involved in sliding down a slope in a red plastic sledge.

'I like it now. I'm very proficient. Obviously just needed the right instructor.'

'Well that's great, maybe we can go together sometime.'

I fixed a smile onto my face. 'Maybe.'

'What's his name?'

I cast around for a suitable name and a suitable adjective to describe him, something comparable to Sexy Samantha. I had nothing, no names in my head at all. The only name in my head was Harry and that would be too weird. He was staring at me, waiting for me to come up with a name, the silence stretched on. I had to say something.

'Tim.' I almost shouted out with relief. 'Tiny Tim.'

Great. Just great.

Harry's face fell. 'Tiny Tim?'

'Yes.'

'As in…' he waggled his little finger at me.

'No, no, of course not, he's very big in that department. Big all over in fact. Huge. It's kind of an ironic name.'

'Big like me?'

'Well I have no idea how big you are in that department.' My eyes cast down to the sizeable bulge in his jeans and I felt my cheeks burn as he clearly saw me checking him out.

'I meant in height,' Harry said. I'm sure I saw his mouth twitch as he supressed a smile.

'Oh yes, he's very tall.'

'Good. That's good. I have a friend who's a ski instructor at the Snow Zone, he might know your Tim. What's his surname?'

'Timmings.'

I was a terrible liar.

'Tim Timmings?'

'That's right.'

A horn tooted outside and Harry peeled back the net curtain to wave at Sexy Samantha as she leaned on the bonnet of her sexy red convertible. I didn't think I'd ever be so relieved to see her again.

'Well have fun.' Harry threw me a cursory wave as he thundered down the stairs. A second later I heard the front door slam.

I peered out the window, hoping not to be noticed as Harry swept Sexy Samantha into his arms and swung her round as if he hadn't seen her in months. As he deposited her on the floor she waved up at me and I was forced to wave politely back.

With a wheel spin and the stereo blaring out something young and hip, the red convertible roared up the road, taking my heart with it.

I'd been in love with Harry for two long, painful years and we were further away today from getting together than we had been when we first met. We were now firmly in the friend zone and there was never any coming back from that.

Two years was way too long for unrequited love. It was time I moved on with someone else. I would just fall out of love with him, simple as that.

I sighed as I walked into my bedroom and got changed into my cow print onesie. I flicked through some songs on my iPod until I found something suitably rousing and as Gloria Gaynor started belting out '*I am what I am*', I turned up the volume, leapt up onto the bed and danced and wiggled my bum in time with the lyrics. I was highly skilled in the playing of air drums and as Gloria reached a crescendo so did my frenetic drum playing. As the instrumental kicked in I leapt off the bed, doing the splits mid-air. I pulled a muscle in my groin and as I flicked my hair theatrically out of my face I saw Harry's eyes widen in horror as I landed on top of him, one leg somehow hooked over his shoulder as my other foot kicked him square in his crotch.

He screamed in pain. I screamed with embarrassment as he staggered back and landed hard on his bum, my leg still wrapped round his neck.

Gloria was still singing loudly in the background as we stared at each other. Finally I managed to speak.

'What are you doing here?'

'Currently, wondering if I'll ever be able to have sex again. Can you please get off my lap?'

I quickly climbed off him, kneeing him in the face as I tried to stand up. He slowly staggered to his feet, doubled over in obvious pain.

'I forgot my wallet,' he said, by way of explanation.

I swallowed. 'You saw me dance?'

He lifted his head and this time there was no mistaking the grin. 'From the very beginning to the dramatic finale.'

I groaned.

'I better go, Samantha will be wondering where I am. Nice onesie by the way. Does Tiny Tim have one too? A horse or a pig perhaps?'

I stared down at myself, at the pink udders hanging limply from my stomach, and wanted the ground to swallow me up. 'He's not coming round till later.'

'Of course not. And I imagine he thinks you look quite cute in it.'

Cute? Puppies were cute. Is that how he thought of me, as a cute little puppy?

He moved to the top of the stairs and I followed him.

'Do you think I look cute in it?'

He turned and walked back up a few stairs, kneeling on the stair below me so we were eye to eye. 'Yes.'

My heart dropped. I was so far in the friend zone I was now categorised as cute. He'd be patting me on the back next and telling me he saw me like a sister.

'Sexy cute?'

'No.'

My heart sank into my feet.

'I bet Samantha would look sexy in it?'

'I doubt it. I don't think it's possible for anyone to look sexy in it.'

I felt slightly better at this.

'And don't underestimate the value of cute, it's a great quality to have.' He leaned forward and kissed me on the nose. 'And don't stay up too late, I have a big day planned for you tomorrow.'

He ran down the stairs and was gone a second later.

I touched my nose, still feeling the softness of his lips. He thought I was cute. I smiled as I fell in love with him all over again.

CHAPTER TWO

I woke the next day with a start, being quite simply torn from a dream about Jack – a memory of playing with him on the beach as he tried to put wet seaweed down my back. As I became more conscious, the loss of losing him hit me all over again.

I knew immediately that someone was in the room with me. I was face down on my pillow and I leaned up and swept my curtain of tangled brown hair off my face. Harry was sitting next to me on the bed, sipping his coffee and reading my very dog-eared copy of *The Hobbit*.

I scowled at him. I wasn't a morning person.

'Do you not knock?'

Harry's attention didn't even waver from the page he was reading. 'You gave me a key.'

'I could have been naked.'

He put his book down and looked at me. 'All the more reason for me not to knock.'

I blushed and climbed off the bed.

Most mornings I woke to this. I must admit, it was a lovely way to wake up. One night, after these early morning visits had become more regular, I went to bed in my sexiest lingerie in the hope that the following morning he would come in and be so turned on that he might immediately ravish me. But not only did he not even bat an eyelid when he saw me in my black satin nightie, he was more excited about his McDonalds breakfast and the free hash brown he had been given by the girl flirting with him behind the counter than what I had to offer. To add insult to injury, as I tried to arrange myself subtly into a sexy pose on the bed next to him as he chomped through his Bacon and Egg McMuffin, I had simply slithered off the bed into a crumpled heap on the floor. Nowadays it seemed much easier and more comfortable to sleep in my regular pyjamas.

Harry handed me a coffee fresh from the café round the corner. I took a sip – it was made exactly how I liked it, with three sugars and a dash of hazelnut syrup. As I went to take another sip, I realised that a small heart had been drawn in the froth on the top. I smiled and hovered near his side, peering round him to the brown paper bag I could see tucked by his hip.

He was busy reading so I coughed loudly to gain his attention. When he glanced up, I looked deliberately at the bag.

'How do you know this is for you?'

'Because you always bring me nice things from the café. What is it this morning, an apricot Danish, ooh a walnut plait or…'

He whisked it out the bag and showed it to me, and the words dried in my throat. Iced into the top of my favourite cinnamon swirl were the words 'Marry Me.'

I had almost forgotten about this silly hundred proposals thing. I'd hoped he'd forgotten as well. But now it looked like he really did mean to torture me. One hundred days. One hundred different ways to break my heart.

I looked at him and he was watching me hopefully.

'It's certainly unique.' I took the bun from him, and picked a currant out of it, averting my gaze from his.

I forced my voice to sound normal before I spoke again. 'If I bite into this am I at risk of swallowing a diamond ring?'

He shook his head. 'No ring. You said a ring was clichéd. Besides, why propose with diamonds when you can propose with cinnamon and coffee?'

'You should take a picture of it before I eat it. Put it on the blog.' I had a huge lump in my throat.

'Good idea.' He whipped out his phone, pressed a few buttons and pointed it in my direction. I held it out for him to get a good angle and realised my hands were shaking. Harry realised it too. To my shame, tears swam in my eyes.

Harry was off the bed in a second. 'What's wrong, what's happened?'

'Nothing, I'm fine. Just tired.' I stepped away from him but he pulled me back, holding me tight and squashing the bun between us. I breathed him in, his wonderful earthy smell as he started to stroke my back.

'Did something happen with Tiny Tim?'

I couldn't keep up with the lie any longer and it had achieved nothing anyway.

'We broke up,' I said into his chest, hoping that would explain why I was soaking his shirt with my tears.

'Oh honey, I'm sorry.' His hand moved to my hair and my breath caught in my throat. 'Had you been seeing him long?'

Oh what a tangled web we weave.

'A few weeks. It wasn't serious, but I really liked him. But obviously I liked him more than he liked me.'

'Well then the man's an idiot. Who wouldn't love a girl in a cow print onesie?'

I giggled.

He tilted my face up to look at him.

'Right, enough tears. Any man who makes you cry is not worth it.'

If only he knew.

'Anyway, I have a day out planned for you today, so stop moping around and get yourself showered and dressed.'

He released me and we both looked at the squashed bun. Although it looked a bit worse for wear, the words 'Marry Me' were still very obvious on the top. Harry took a photo and I quickly ate it so I wouldn't have to stare at the empty words any longer. It tasted good, despite the fact that with every mouthful my heart broke a little bit more.

'So, as proposals go, is this what you imagined for yourself?' Harry asked, when it was gone.

'Undoubtedly. The perfect proposal. So you don't have to bother with the other ninety-eight different ways now. Write on the blog that you bought me a cinnamon swirl and I caved. I'm a cheap date, easily pleased.'

Harry pulled a face. 'It was a bit cheap and naff, wasn't it? Ok, for my next one it will be something huge.'

'Really, the cinnamon swirl was cute… and don't underestimate the value of cute.'

But Harry was already walking away into the office, scrolling through his phone as he went.

'Harry, are you listening? Nothing says 'I love you' like a personalised cinnamon swirl.'

'Get in the shower, woman, I need to make some calls.'

I sighed. I had to sway him from this path. Ninety-eight heart-breaking days stretched ahead of me like an endless desert, with no respite from the sun.

I got in the shower and stuck my head under the stream.

No, I could do this. Proposals were my entire waking life. My dreams were plagued by them too. Something like this could only be good for business. I just had to become immune to the words. They were empty and meaningless. And now I knew that I was to expect it every day, I could prepare myself for it, pretend in my head the words meant something else.

I got dressed quickly and walked into the office.

'Hey.' Harry was busy typing. 'Our blog has nineteen followers already.'

'Our Proposer's Blog? This hundred proposals malarkey?'

'Malarkey? I'm offended.' He smiled up at me briefly before returning his attention to the screen. 'Yes, I guess they want to see what I come up with next.'

I leaned over him to see what he had written and caught a whiff of his wonderful clean earthy smell. There was the close-up picture of my squashed bun, and another picture I hadn't realised he had taken – of me eating it, my hair a full bird's nest, my face red and blotchy from the tears, dressed in my rather unflattering cow print onesie. Great!

Under the picture was Harry's blog.

Proposer's Blog

Day 2: The Cinnamon Swirl Proposal. Location: Suzie's bedroom (I assure you, nothing saucy going on here).

Is the way to a woman's heart through her stomach?

Our Suzie McKenzie has a very sweet tooth and so I thought to charm her with a sweet proposal of her own. Nadia's Bakery, St Patrick's Road makes the best cinnamon swirls in the world and it's one of Suzie's all-time favourite things to eat for breakfast. So when I explained the situation to the lovely Nadia this morning she was more than happy to provide me with a personalised one along with a heart-topped latte.

So what was Suzie's reaction? She seemed a bit blasé about it actually. Wolfed it down and barely registered the words.

That wasn't true of course, but it was better he wrote that than writing that I burst into tears.

I always thought those proposers that pop the question with a ring at the bottom of the champagne glass were silly – who wants to fish the diamond ring out of the toilet a few days later? Though now Suzie's eaten my proposal, there's nothing left of it apart from the icing on her lips.

I immediately checked my lips and I saw Harry smirk out of the corner of my eye.

Next time, I will do something grand. Something she can't possibly miss. Plus, who would really say yes over a 59p cinnamon swirl?

'That makes me sound shallow,' I said, squeezing past him to log on to my own computer.

'Not shallow, just greedy. And don't bother logging on, we're going out.'

'I can't, it's our busiest time of the year, you know that. Three days before Valentine's Day, all those last minute Larrys will be phoning us up for support.'

'I've already diverted the calls to your mobile and you can still pick up your emails, besides today is completely work orientated – we're sourcing new locations, so stop making excuses and get your boots on.'

When I hesitated, he grabbed my hand and pulled me out of the office.

I laughed. 'Where are we going?'

'First stop, we're going to buy you some decent pyjamas, so the next boyfriend won't be scared off by seeing you in that onesie.'

I stopped dead and when he turned to look at me, his eyes were kind.

'Jack bought it for me,' I said, quietly.

'I know.'

'I'm not getting rid of it.'

'I'm not saying throw it out. But I knew Jack, he had a wicked sense of humour and you know as well as I do that he bought it for you as a joke because you used to take the piss out of onesies and people that wore them. You know that he never intended for you to wear it at all let alone every day since his death. If you want to keep it, keep it. All I'm talking about is options. Something else you could wear that would show off that fabulous figure of yours.'

I opened my mouth to protest as the last words he said slammed into my brain. Fabulous figure?

He moved his hands to my shoulders and when he spoke his voice was soft.

'I know you're trying to keep your brother alive, keep him close, but he would be cringing if he could see you wearing that thing and you know that. Keep him close with your memories of him, not by compromising who you are.'

I blinked. That was very profound for half nine on a Thursday morning.

'I'm just saying, the Suzie McKenzie I know and love wouldn't be caught dead in something like that.'

'I think it's funny.' I knew I sounded like a petulant child.

'Yes, for about five minutes after you opened your present – it's not quite so funny eight months later.'

He had a point. I'd washed it so many times that the white patches were now grey and the udders were looking decidedly limp.

'And while we're on the subject. You can stop wearing black as well. We're not in the Victorian times anymore.'

He pulled me into the bedroom and I followed, still in shock over his brutal honesty. He opened my wardrobe and pulled out my favourite scarlet jumper dress. 'You can wear this today with those purple leggings.'

They would clash horribly. I smiled.

'And you can wear them with those Barbie pink boots you love so much and...' He rooted around in one of my drawers, finally found what he had been looking for, pulled it out and thrust it into my face. 'This. You'll wear this.'

'But –'

'No buts. Get changed. You have five minutes.'

I stared after his retreating back and then down at the black shirt and black trousers I had put on out of habit. In the months after Jack's death my taste in bright and garish clothes had seemed disrespectful somehow. Was one month too soon to return to my colourful spots, stripes and swirls? Was two months? But now it had been eight months and I had seemingly been wearing black ever since. My bright clothes even seemed to have a thin layer of dust on them as they hung forgotten in my wardrobe. Harry had a point. Again.

I came downstairs a few minutes later, dressed in my purple leggings, scarlet jumper, pink boots and my red and gold spotted sequinned beret that I adored and Jack hated because he said I looked like a toadstool. I felt lighter already.

Harry grinned when he saw me. 'You look beautiful.' He offered me his arm. 'Now let's go.'

I leaned into him and walked out into the early morning sunshine.

*

'No way. I'm not doing that,' I said, staring at the scene before me in horror. 'There's nothing romantic about that.'

'Who says proposals have to be romantic?' Harry said as he bent down to forcefully remove my boots.

'It's the rules. Flowers, fireworks, chocolates. A stuffed teddy with the words emblazoned across a red heart. Not this. Never this.'

'I disagree.'

'You would,' I said as Harry pushed me gently but forcibly forwards in the queue.

'I think proposals can be weird, funny or in the case of this little adventure, adrenaline filled.'

I was next.

'If I die –'

'I'll wear a cow print onesie to your funeral. Now get up there.'

My phone rang in my pocket.

'Oh I have to get that, shame I'll miss my turn.'

But to my annoyance, Harry had already wrestled my phone from my pocket and had answered it. He was more than capable of dealing with our customers and he knew I knew that.

'Are you going or what, love?' asked a big gruff man whose face looked like it had been punched several times. His nose was bent in two places and he had a huge scar across his forehead. Had he sustained these injuries doing this? I shrunk back but Harry pushed me forward.

'Yes she is, and send her as high as you can.'

The man nodded, somewhat evilly I thought.

I climbed the steps to my doom and they attached thin rubber cables to my harness. I kept my eyes on Harry as the man bounced behind me for a few seconds, causing me to bounce as well. A moment later I was propelled some ten feet into the air, a scream tearing from my throat. I fell back to the earth but no sooner had I touched the ground than I was sent back into the air again, this time even higher than the last.

We had been walking along the Thames when the sounds of screams had attracted us. As we rounded the corner, we saw the bungee trampolines and watched with amusement as we saw people screaming, being bounced higher and higher in the air. My amusement had quickly turned to horror when I realised Harry had paid for me to have a go, and that we had come here deliberately for this reason.

I screamed again as I flailed in the air, kicking my legs helplessly in the hope that it would slow my descent. Each time I thought I was going to crash into the ground, I came to a slow stop, bounced gracefully off the trampoline and was propelled back into the air again. As I was thrust into the air for the fifth time, a bubble of laughter escaped my throat. It was a rush – a terrifying, brilliant rush. The man bounced with me, sending me higher, and I roared with joy.

All too soon the experience was over, and the man slowed me down and stopped me. He unhooked me and I quickly clambered down the steps and ran straight into Harry's arms, still laughing uncontrollably.

Finally my laughter subsided.

'Thank you.'

'You're very welcome,' he said, into my forehead. 'You see, at this point, while your heart is still pounding furiously and with the grin plastered on your face, I would propose.'

'And I would say yes.'

I felt him smile into my hair.

'So one we can definitely add to our repertoire?'

'Yes, I take it all back. I love it.'

'They're not here all the time, but the guy is going to give me his card as they go all round the UK. We can phone them up if need be and find out where they are.'

'Excellent, it's great to get contacts like this.'

'Are you ready for the next part of our day?'

I pulled back, intrigued. 'There's more?'

'Yes.' He chivalrously picked up the bag containing the pyjamas he had bought me earlier. Very simple, very elegant satin pyjamas. I'd liked the black but Harry put his foot down and we'd eventually agreed on a dusty rose.

'Was the phone call anything good?'

'I've emailed over to him our basic package.'

I sighed. 'That's the fourth today.'

'Hey, the basic package is a good little money earner. You know – on average – half the customers that buy the twenty pound package from us come back and spend ten times that on a big extravagant proposal.'

'I know, but at this time of year I kind of expect to get more big proposals rather than so many basic packages.'

Harry was right, we earned quite a bit from our basic package. For twenty pounds, we sent our customers a brochure of our top fifty proposals. Ideas ranging from the romantic to the ridiculous, top class restaurants to tiny little tucked away cafés strewn with fairy lights. We included days out, fun experiences and romantic getaways. We also included vouchers for discounts and special offers at these hotels and restaurants and if our customers went there, we also got ten percent of their final bill from the companies for introducing our customers to them in the first place. It also gave brief details of more elaborate proposals, something only we could organise, with the promise of a refund of the twenty pounds if they were to book one of the grander proposals with us.

'Romance isn't always about big gestures though,' Harry said. 'Sometimes it's the words the man finds or the effort that he has gone to. It doesn't have to be something expensive.'

'I know that, the smaller gestures are sometimes the best, a message written in the sand on a favourite beach or a personalised cinnamon swirl.' I nudged him as we walked along the road and he smiled. 'But from a business point of view I'm not sure people paying us twenty pounds to send them to propose elsewhere is the best idea. They could spend a hundred pounds or more at these posh places. That's a hundred pounds they could have spent with us.'

Harry switched sides with me and I wondered why as he put himself between me and two men who were arguing, placing his hand on the small of my back as he nudged me round them. I felt embarrassed by the goose bumps that suddenly exploded over my body at his touch.

Harry continued on as if he hadn't noticed my heart leap out of my chest. 'Most people have in their mind what kind of proposal they want to do before they contact us. For most of them it would involve some kind of romantic meal, so they're not likely to spend their money with us anyway. By providing them with a list of romantic places to eat, not only do we get the twenty pounds but also any kickbacks from the restaurants too. We've probably earned more money from the basic package than we have from the big proposals – so I wouldn't knock the smaller gestures if I were you. Come on, through here.'

Harry ducked into a tiny alleyway that wound round the corner out of sight. He knew London like the back of his hand and very rarely went on the underground. There was always so much more to see when on foot. I followed him, his hulking frame almost filling the alley wall to wall. The walls were covered in graffiti and chewing gum, but some of the pictures sprayed on the bricks were very skilful. As we came to an old boarded-up window, he stopped and as I drew near he pulled me to his side, with his hand at my waist, sending delicious shivers down my spine.

'There's a place called Bubblegum Alley in California, and a Chewing Gum Wall in Seattle, where millions of pieces of gum have been stuck on the walls. It's so bright and colourful that what started as something gross has now been declared an official tourist attraction. People travel from miles around to see it and to add their own gum to it. Some have even created little works of art amongst the thousands of globules.'

He stood back a bit and pointed to the wall. There in a heart made from pink chewing gum were the words 'Annie, marry me,' also made from chewing gum.

'Love can be found in the most unlikely of places, you just have to look for it.'

He stared down at me and for a moment I wasn't sure if he was talking about him, or about me and him.

'It doesn't need to be about romance, just little heartfelt gestures.'

I smiled. 'I wonder if she said yes.'

Harry pointed to the green letters written in globules of chewing gum underneath the heart. In big proud letters, the word 'Yes', stood out.

'I like it.' I grabbed my phone from my pocket and took a few shots. I had to put this on the website.

'I knew you would.'

'You see, I don't need big gestures, so whatever you have planned for our next proposal, it doesn't need to be a big yacht or a trip to the moon.'

He walked away, heading towards the sunlight that was piercing our gloom.

'I'll cancel the space rocket then.'

'Harry, I'm serious. Don't waste your money on me.'

He ignored me as we stepped out into the sunlight. He was incredibly generous with his money and he had a lot of it. He didn't get a very good salary from me but he didn't really need it. Years before, whilst travelling around America, he'd had the foresight to invest in a tiny little up-and-coming online social media site called Connected. He'd given a thousand dollars at the time, money he had won at a casino, and years later, when Connected had been the biggest social media site in America and probably the world, he had sold his shares for a huge sum. He'd never told me how much he got from that little endeavour. But it was enough that he could afford the huge house on the other side of the green from me, bought when the property prices had plummeted. And he always seemed to have enough money for little gifts and meals out.

'Spending money on you is never a waste. And we're running late now so we're going to have to run.'

He grabbed my hand and started jogging through the streets, winding his way expertly through the other people.

'We could catch the tube,' I whined, as I tried to keep up with his long-legged pace.

'Running's much more fun,' Harry said, without breaking his stride.

*

The Glade at Sketch was like nothing I'd ever seen before. With its white bricked front, Sketch looked like a simple townhouse – and we'd actually walked past the place before we'd realised it was there. But down the darkened staircase and to the left, a tranquil wooded glade had been transported from some fairy tale forest to this seemingly unassuming restaurant in central London. Trees covered every wall and surface, the leaves of which were painted in every shade of green and gold imaginable. A huge chandelier dominated the ceiling, casting delicate lights over every surface from its tangle of branches. Tiny gold fireflies danced around the walls and floor. Mirrored panels near the roof moved slowly, catching the light from the huge sunroof above us and sending its rays across the room as if the sun was moving through the trees. Wicker chairs, tables and sofas with huge green embroidered cushions were placed casually throughout the room as if they were garden furniture and we were all just simply sitting out in the garden somewhere, enjoying the sun.

'Harry Forbes, we have a reservation for afternoon tea.' Harry said to the beautiful waitress who looked like a woodland nymph with the plaits and twists in her hair, and her floaty dress.

The waitress showed us to our table and we quickly placed an order for tea. Breakfast tea for me, something that sounded like a rare tropical disease for Harry.

'Harry, this place is beautiful.' I couldn't stop looking around, until my eyes met with his and I realised he'd been watching me. 'Thank you for today.'

'My pleasure. I just wanted you to have some fun. You've been so down lately.' He paused, awkwardly, while he rearranged the cups on the table. 'The food here is amazing.'

I reached across and squeezed his hand. 'Thank you.'

The afternoon tea arrived just as Harry was poised to say something else. I reluctantly let him go so there was room for our cake stand on the table.

Harry was right, the food looked and tasted amazing. The sandwiches were all topped with extras like quail eggs and caviar, bringing a simple egg mayonnaise sandwich alive with an assault of different flavours.

There was an array of cakes, all tiny, mouth-watering bites of pure pleasure, some kind of trifle and of course delicious fresh fruit scones.

'So tell me,' Harry said around a mouthful of something chocolaty, 'Tiny Tim, did you and he…?'

Oh God, Tiny Tim was going to come back and haunt me forever.

I picked up some kind of pink meringue that literally dissolved as soon as it touched my tongue. I licked my lips as I played for time.

'Did we what?' I smirked as Harry shifted uncomfortably, waving his hands around in what I presumed was some kind of representation of the act. The man had no problem discussing his sordid sex life but he was still awkward when discussing mine. I wanted to play him at his own game.

'He liked to dress up,' I said as I popped some kind of fruit tart in my mouth. The fruit was crystalized and was like an explosion on my tongue.

Harry's eyes widened. 'Like air hostess, police woman, cheerleader, that kind of thing?'

I shook my head. 'Lots of different things really. One of my favourites was dressing up as a unicorn and he was a lion. He liked to take me from behind and he would roar when he came.'

Harry stared at me, his face unblinking. I picked up a tiny coffee éclair and caught the eye of a tiny little old lady sitting at the next table, her fruit tart poised halfway to her mouth. I blushed, realising she had heard every word.

Still, there was no going back now.

'He liked to dress up as one of the flower pot men, Bill normally, I'm not sure why. I was always the flower, Weed. Then Bill would come at me with his big hose.'

The old lady leaned over to me. 'Dear, do you have the name of the shop where you bought these costumes?'

'I don't I'm afraid, Tim always brought them with him. I will miss his big hose.'

Harry was still staring at me. 'I didn't realise you were into all that weird stuff.'

I licked the icing off the top of the éclair and popped it in my mouth, trying desperately to suppress my laughter but it was to no avail. I snorted so hard that a bubble of snot burst from my nose and I quickly had to wipe it away on my beautiful cotton serviette.

'You're joking?' Harry looked almost relieved.

'Of course I am.'

'So you guys… didn't…'

'It's none of your business. Just because you like to talk about all your sexploits doesn't mean the rest of us do.'

'That's a "no" if ever I heard one.' He smiled smugly. I wasn't going to let him get away with that.

'It's a "yes" actually, but it was just regular sex.' I wanted to expand on that, regular sex sounded so boring. 'Well as regular as three hour sex marathons can be. He had the stamina of a horse. We'd do it all over the flat. On the dining table, up against a wall, in the shower, in the kitchen, on top of the washing machine, backwards, forwards, sideways, doggy style.'

The old lady choked on her fruit scone.

'Sideways?' asked Harry.

'Yes. You should try it, it's great fun. Can you pass the sugar?'

I stared down at my tea. Sideways, how exactly would that work?

'Tell me about your plans for the summer. You said you were thinking about going to New Zealand.'

Harry recovered himself well. 'The land of the hobbits. I would love to. Maybe hire a camper van and drive from North to South. There's so many things I want to do, but it's more fun doing them with someone else.'

'Sexy Samantha not keen?'

'She's definitely not the camper van sort. She's more of the "five star hotel with daily spa treatments" kind of girl. We should go.'

'I would love that, I want to see the world, every tiny little pocket of it, but no girlfriend of yours is going to be happy about you taking another woman off on holiday. Sleeping together in the back of the camper van.' I blushed as Harry's eyebrows shot up. 'I meant actually sleeping – not having sex.'

The old lady leaned in closer again, ready to catch the next instalment in my sex life.

'I should hope not,' Harry said, his tongue licking seductively up the side of his éclair. 'I don't have a lion costume.'

*

I sat back and watched the gold fireflies chase each other up the walls. I was so uncomfortably full, but everything was so hard to resist, that I'd had to eat it all.

We'd had a lovely time, chatting all afternoon, but one of the main topics of conversation from the other guests was the toilets and how funny they were. I had to check them out myself.

I excused myself from the table and, following the directions of the woodland nymph waitress, I walked through another restaurant to a very white room on the other side.

The stairs leading up to the toilets were a brilliant opulent white – looking like they led to somewhere much grander than just some toilets. I walked upstairs to a brightly lit room, the ceiling decorated with beautiful rainbow tiles, but as I reached the top I stopped in my tracks. Several pods sat in a white chamber at the top of the stairs, looking like white cocoons from an alien spaceship. They were about seven foot tall and tapered off like eggs at the top.

I looked around for the toilets but there was nothing else up here. On the other side of the room were several more pods. These pods were clearly the toilets and were obviously the reason for such amusement from the other guests.

I opened the door on one of them, expecting to hear some kind of space age whoosh and was slightly disappointed when I didn't.

Inside was the weirdest toilet I had ever seen. There was no seat at all. I walked in and closed the door behind me. It was obviously some foreign kind of toilet where you stand. A long ceramic oval hung from the wall jutting out at the bottom to catch the waste. I stared at it – how on earth was I supposed to pee in that? Backwards seemed the only safe option. With a bit of negotiating I pointed my bum in the right direction and leaned forward into a sort of half squat. I quickly finished and after redressing I left the pod, dying to tell Harry about the very weird toilets. He was standing right outside and looked shocked to see me coming out of one of the pods.

'What?' I said.

'These are the boys' toilets.'

I laughed. 'No they're not, the waitress pointed me up these stairs.'

'Yes, the girls' pods are over there.' He pointed to the other side of the stairs where several pods were bathed in pink lights in comparison to the pods where I was that were bathed in blue.

Harry peered over my shoulder and burst out laughing. 'Did the urinals not give you a clue?'

I looked back and gasped in horror. I had just peed in a urinal. Now he had pointed it out to me it was obvious. It wasn't some weird foreign type toilet at all, just a bog standard urinal. I felt my cheeks glow crimson.

'I'm intrigued. How exactly did you manage to pee in there?'

I quickly hurried to the sinks and washed my hands. 'I don't want to talk about it.'

I heard Harry go into one of the pods, his laughter so loud I could hear him from the outside.

CHAPTER THREE

I was shaken gently awake the next day. It was pitch black but the hand continued to shake me.

'Harry?' I croaked, though I knew it was him, I could smell his glorious scent.

'Yeah, it's me.'

I leaned over and snapped on the lamp on the bedside table, shielding my eyes from the sudden glare.

'Here, I made you a coffee. The café isn't open yet. It won't be as good as theirs, you don't have any hazelnut syrup for a start, but it might help to wake you up.'

I took the coffee numbly and stared at him in confusion.

'You look good by the way, nice pyjamas.'

I peered over at the alarm clock, blearily. It was four a.m. I put the coffee down and picked up the clock to look at it more closely.

'It's four o'clock!' I said, incredulous. I wasn't even aware that there were two four o'clocks in one day.

'Yes it is.'

'In the morning!'

'How very perceptive of you.'

'Did we discuss this last night?' I racked my brains for any conversation that would have alerted me to the fact that Harry would be disturbing me at this ungodly hour.

After leaving The Glade the day before, we had walked along the Thames as the sun set and the moon danced over the water. It had been incredibly romantic, apart from at the end of our wonderful date, when Harry had rushed off to meet another woman. But I did get a goodnight kiss. On the cheek, but still, a kiss was a kiss.

But as we had chatted, there had been no mention of this ridiculously early intrusion. I would have protested if I'd known.

'No, that's part of the surprise,' he said, pulling the duvet off me. I pulled it back, not ready to face the chill of the morning yet.

'A proposal?' My heart leapt a little. Despite my reticence about being proposed to, I was actually looking forward to seeing what Harry would do next.

'Of course. This one's a good one.'

'Let me tell you, any proposal that starts at four o'clock in the morning is not going to be a good one.'

'You'll love it.'

I threw myself back down on the bed, covering myself with the duvet.

'No, you can't make me get up.'

'Suzie, you have two choices, you can either get dressed now and come with me or...'

'I'll take the "or" whatever it is, definitely the "or".'

'Ok, if you insist.'

'I do.'

There was silence beyond the duvet, and a shifting of weight indicated that Harry had got off the bed. Had I hurt his feelings? Had he gone?

Suddenly the duvet was ripped off me and Harry grabbed my arms, pulled me up into a sitting position and then threw me over his shoulder. He turned and ran for the door.

'What are you doing?' I squealed.

'The "or" was going in your pyjamas.'

Harry ran down the stairs, opened the flat door and ran outside with me still over his shoulder. The street outside was deserted.

'No, no, please, I'll be good, I'll get dressed I promise, just don't kidnap me in my pyjamas.'

Harry lowered me to the ground carefully. 'You promise, you'll go straight back in there and get dressed right away?'

I put my hand up in a Girl Guide salute. 'I promise.'

'Very well, you have five minutes.'

I nodded at him and went back up the stairs, but if I thought I could sneak back into bed that thought was quickly quelled as Harry followed close behind.

*

Harry pulled his car into an empty car park and I looked around blearily. I had dozed in the car, unable to keep my eyes open as Harry's old Beetle, Betty, bumped along the roads. The heating had two settings, scorching hot or off. In the cold winter morning, scorching hot was the only answer but it had made me even sleepier. Harry had tried to placate my frown with a full English breakfast at some greasy spoon road café. It had woken me up a bit.

Harry leaned over to me and zipped up the fleece I was wearing. I had been told to bring warm clothes, but that was the only clue as to what I was doing today.

'Now listen, I had to pull in a big favour for this, and had to tell a whopping lie to get it at the last minute.

You need to humour me in this, otherwise Frank will be disappointed.'

'Frank?' I racked my brain for a Frank but came up with nothing.

'I told him we were a couple, that was the only way I could arrange it so quickly. It takes months to wait for this kind of thing, and Frank was so delighted, after all the business we've put his way, he was happy to help.'

I was stumped, my brain still not firing on all cylinders. Harry got out and held the door open for me, not because he was chivalrous, although he had wonderful manners, but because Betty's door could only be opened from the outside. With Harry's wealth, I often wondered why he didn't buy something better, but he loved Betty with a loyalty that I adored.

He grabbed a cool box from the boot and then took my hand as we walked round some bushes into a field. I had to marvel at how my hand fitted perfectly in his.

The field was lit with muted greys. The sun hadn't risen yet, but it was that time of the morning when the light came with a promise of what was to come. The grass was wet with dew and our breath formed misty shapes in front of us as we walked.

'So we're together, a loving couple?' I nodded, my brain finally waking up as the seed of this idea started to grow.

He grinned as he nodded.

'So as far as Frank is concerned, this is a real proposal?' 'Yes.'

I bit my lip as a delicious thrill ran through me. 'So he'll be expecting a real reaction.'

'Yes. You can tell me what you think about this later, give me a true reaction. It's probably too clichéd for you, but in front of Frank you need to be delighted.'

I could do delighted. I'd seen a few proposals in my time as chief proposal planner; they all ended with kisses. I smiled, I could do that. My heart jolted with sudden fear and excitement. I was going to kiss Harry. It had taken two years but now, finally, I was going to get to kiss him. All thought and reason went out of my head and I had to physically restrain myself from doing one of those little sideways kicks where you click your heels together.

There was a noise up ahead, a roaring, rushing sound, and an orangey glow painted the trees like autumn had come early.

We rounded a corner and I saw it. I couldn't help the grin from splitting my face. In front of me, slowly filling with air, were two hot air balloons.

I shrieked and threw myself at Harry, who managed to catch my flailing arms and legs as I completely took him by surprise.

'I love you, I love you, I love you,' I squealed.

'Wow, that's quite the reaction,' he said, as he tried to gently extricate himself from my embrace. 'I haven't even popped the question yet.'

'It's a yes, it's absolutely a yes. Oh God Harry, how did you know? I've always wanted to do this.'

'You always get so excited about hot air balloon proposals, more so than anything else. I figured it was something that you would want to do yourself.' He pushed me away diplomatically, clearly embarrassed by my reaction. 'Come on, let's go and meet Frank. You must have spoken to the man a hundred times over the years.' He gestured over to the support cars, emblazoned on the side with the name, 'Carlton Balloons.' Frank. Frank Carlton, of course. He was always the first person we contacted for hot air balloon proposals and he almost always fitted us in.

Frank was one of the oldest men I had ever met, his skin looked like the bark of tree. He had three teeth, one on the top and two on the bottom, and the biggest smile I'd ever seen. He was dressed in shorts and a T-shirt, despite the chill of the morning.

'I'm so glad to help you.' Frank said, hugging Harry and then me, greeting us like we were long lost friends, which I suppose in a way we were. 'I was delighted when Harry called. You've made so many people happy over the years, and now you two are together. Finding love amongst everyone else's happiness. I can't tell you how pleased I am. I want you to meet my boys, the ground crew.'

The boys, as it turned out, were three strapping sons in their forties and two other men who worked for him. Frank ran round getting everything ready for our departure, clearly as fit as the men half his age judging by the way he dealt with the preparations with speed, strength and agility. And slowly the hot air balloons started to fill and rise, tugging on their restraints, desperate to be free.

'What bloody time of the day is this?' muttered a voice from behind us.

I turned round to see Badger, Harry's best friend and my cousin, scowling at us. His ginger beard was hidden inside the top of his coat, his eyes peeping out from underneath his blue and white Chelsea pom-pom hat. 'It's bloody freezing.'

I adored Badger. He was one of those solid dependable types that would do anything for anybody. Jack, Badger and I had been quite close growing up, but in recent years we had become even closer after Badger had moved to London too. Jack and Badger went everywhere together, before Jack died. And he was the reason Harry had come into my life, something else to be grateful to Badger for.

I hugged him and he immediately took his hands out of his pockets and hugged me back. Harry hugged him too. Despite the manly size of them both, they always greeted each other with a big hug.

'What are you doing here?'

'Cashing in all of Harry's favours in one day.' He returned to scowling again. 'I was in a wonderful sleep this morning when the alarm went off at some ungodly hour.'

'I needed some help for this one,' Harry admitted. 'And there was only one man for the job.'

There was only one man who would get up this early and drive fifty miles to the countryside to help his friend out. Despite Badger's scowl, I could tell he was pleased about the compliment. Although him being here did put a slight dampener on our nice romantic proposal.

Frank came over to tell us the balloons were ready.

We put the cool box into the basket and Harry helped me in, then held me close like a true boyfriend would do. Though it seemed Badger was to go in the other balloon.

As the cables and ropes were released, our balloons slowly drifted upwards, floating almost aimlessly up into the clouds. It was an incredible experience and I couldn't take my eyes off the receding landscape below us. We were far out of London now. Harry had driven for over an hour, and as far as the eye could see there were just hills and fields in every direction, all growing smaller by the second. Badger's balloon bobbed gently after us, the wind blowing us in the same direction.

We levelled out, obviously reaching the optimum height, and Frank turned the burners off. We hovered there in silence, as if we were hanging from the clouds. We didn't speak, we didn't need to. The world at our feet said it all.

Suddenly a slice of pure gold shot straight from the horizon, lighting up the landscape below us, banishing the remains of the fading night sky and filling the world with a rosy haze. I watched with sheer joy as the sun appeared and for a few moments it wasn't the burning ball of heat in the sky that you can never look directly at, but an orb of muted oranges and pinks, like a light bulb that had just been switched on and was yet to reach its full power.

'It's beautiful,' I gasped, realising that Harry's arm had been around me the whole time and I leaned back into him. I could see Frank watching us out of the corner of my eye, a huge grin on his face.

Harry released me and rooted around in the cool box as I returned my attention back to the landscape below, bathed in great swathes of scarlet and gold.

Harry offered Frank a champagne glass but he declined.

'Frank do you ever get tired of this view, you must see it on an almost daily basis,' I asked, as Harry filled two glasses with champagne.

'Nah, I could watch that view every day, ten times a day and I would never get bored of it. Being up here is the most incredible feeling in the world. If I died now, I would die a very happy man.'

I frowned as he unconsciously rubbed his chest. The inappropriate mention of death coupled with this gesture suddenly had me very alert. 'Are you ok?'

Frank realised what I had been referring to and laughed. 'I'm fine love, just a bit of indigestion. There's plenty of life left in this old dog yet, I want to see my great grandchildren before I die, and none of my grandchildren are even married off yet. No, there's nothing wrong with me apart from my gut complaining about the extra sausage I had for breakfast this morning.'

I smiled, though I was still concerned. Jack's death had given me a bit of paranoia about it all.

Frank switched on the burners and the roar breaking the silence put an end to any further questions.

Harry passed me my glass of champagne and clinked his glass against mine.

'To us,' he said, his dark eyes glinting with mischief.

'To the best kind of friendship.'

As we both took a sip, he didn't take his eyes off me and I wished, not for the first time, I could read what was going on in his head.

I remembered again about the forthcoming proposal and the importance of my real reaction.

My heart slammed against my chest. Just to get one kiss in, albeit briefly, would be an amazing end to this wonderful proposal.

We drifted through the sky, the dampness of the clouds clinging to our faces and clothes like cobwebs. Little beads of water clung to Harry's long eyelashes and I wanted to reach up and wipe them away. But I had to save myself, any inappropriate gestures now could forestall the big kiss I had planned. Would he kiss me back? Oh God I hoped so. What if he didn't? What if he was repulsed by it? If it was to be a genuine reaction, he had to kiss me back. I wondered how long I could drag it on, how long would be appropriate. What if I was a rubbish kisser? Tongue or no tongue? Maybe I shouldn't do it at all. No I had to do it, this was my only chance. My heart was hammering so fast against my chest, I felt sure he could feel it, as he wrapped his arms around me, holding me from behind.

Frank was pulling levers and cords behind us and we started to drop gracefully towards the fields. As we drew closer, I could see the bright colourful cars of the chase crew as they attempted to follow our progress. They were still so tiny at this stage, like toy cars in a miniature village.

Harry nudged me gently and pointed me in the direction of Badger's balloon.

A long banner unfurled from the basket, easily twenty or thirty feet long, and in beautiful hand painted letters – surrounded by flowers, hearts and stars – were the words, 'Marry Me.' Upside down.

'Shit!' Harry said with vehemence, dropping his hands from me like I was a hot potato.

'It doesn't matter.' I said. 'It's lovely, you must have gone to so much trouble for this.'

I quickly grabbed my phone from my pocket and took a few photos.

'No Suzie, fuck!'

I looked around to see Frank on the floor of the basket, clutching his chest, sweat beading on his forehead, his skin turning a very sickly shade of grey.

I knelt at Harry's side as he clutched Frank's hand.

Frank was clearly struggling to speak.

'Phone an ambulance,' Harry muttered, and I fumbled with my phone – hoping desperately that we would get a signal this high off the ground. Thankfully it rang straight through to the emergency services.

I explained the problem and Harry quickly rattled off where we were – though how he knew that, I didn't know. As we were seemingly in the middle of nowhere, I was told an air ambulance would be despatched.

As I finished the call and shoved the phone in my pocket, my ears popped – and Harry's clearly did as well, as with sickening understanding we both suddenly stared at each other. We were dropping, and way too quickly for it to be safe.

We leapt up and to our horror saw the ground coming up towards us at a terrifying speed.

Harry grabbed the valve for the burners, turning them as we'd seen Frank do mere minutes before. The burners kicked into life and with a roar, flames erupted into the balloon.

But was it too late, the speed of the dropping balloon had already picked up too much momentum.

Frank desperately tried to say something to us and Harry knelt next to him again, listening to his whispered instructions.

Harry leapt up and masterfully started turning levers and looking like he knew exactly what he was doing.

'Can I help?'

He shook his head and, trusting he was going to do something to save us, I returned my attention to Frank. He was still breathing but with great difficulty. He was obviously in a lot of pain.

I was panicking wildly, and not just about our impending doom. I racked my brains for any first aid knowledge that could help Frank. Should I put him in the recovery position, perform CPR, lie him down with his legs in the air, his knees up to his chest, should I get hot water and towels?

Would the air ambulance get here in time to save Frank? Would they end up shipping all three of us to the hospital after our crash to the ground?

'Shit Suzie, we're coming in to land. This is it. Hold on – it's going to be rough.'

I grabbed a rope on the side, crouching over Frank to try to protect him. To my surprise, Harry's body was suddenly round mine – protecting me and Frank in a solid cage.

The basket hit the ground hard, jolting my head back into Harry's… and everything went black.

CHAPTER FOUR

My eyes snapped open and I blinked against the glare of the blue sky. Frank.

I tried to sit up but a strong hand pushed me back. 'Stay still, you banged your head pretty hard.'

I looked up into Harry's face, silhouetted against the bright morning sky. 'What about Frank?'

He pointed over to the far side of the field where the paramedics were helping Frank onto the air ambulance.

'He actually seems fine. I don't know whether it was the shock of landing so hard or whether it wasn't even a heart attack to start with, but after we landed the pain just seemed to go away. He even had enough strength to shout at his boys to make sure the balloon didn't get caught up with the burners. He didn't even want to go to the hospital, said it was a whole lot of fuss for no reason, but they're taking him anyway just to be on the safe side. I'm more concerned about you.'

'I'm fine.' I sat up and Harry helped me. As I looked at him, I realised he had two clumps of bloodied tissues stuck up each nostril. I reached out to touch his cheek. 'Are you ok, did I do that?'

'Yes, well more specifically the crash did it. It's ok, just wouldn't stop bleeding.'

One of the paramedics came running over, having safely installed Frank in the helicopter.

'You're awake.' He knelt down next to me and shone a light in my eyes. 'Any dizziness or pain?'

I shook my head. I felt a bit sore but I'd had worse headaches than this before.

'Well, there doesn't appear to be any concussion but just keep an eye on her for the next few hours. If she starts feeling dizzy or blacks out again – take her to the A&E straight away.'

Harry nodded solemnly, though I couldn't take him seriously with his bloodied tissues sticking from his nose.

The paramedic returned to the helicopter and as soon as Frank's sons climbed on board, the helicopter took off, flying over us and then disappearing into the hills.

The two other men that worked for the company were just loading the already packed up balloon into their car and the trailer.

'Where's Badger?' I asked.

'His balloon apparently landed in another field. They're just going to get him now. So as proposals go…?' Harry trailed off, embarrassed.

'Well a near death experience is definitely adrenaline filled. My heart was pounding, there was close, physical contact. It's not a proposal I'm likely to forget.'

Harry laughed.

'In all seriousness, the banner was beautiful, it must have taken you ages.'

'I didn't actually see it before Frank keeled over. Did you take some photos?'

'Here.' I yanked my phone from my pocket and showed him the photos. His face fell.

'It's upside down. Oh I'll kill him.'

'It's an easy mistake to make.'

'I don't care, I'm going to kill him. So apart from the near death experience and that your proposal was upside down, would it have been the perfect proposal?'

'I loved it – the scenery, the views, the champagne, the banner, that anyone would go to that much trouble to propose to me would be amazing. If you wanted a real reaction, I think you would have got one.'

Harry scowled and then stood up and helped me to my feet. 'Come on, let's go home.'

Proposer's Blog

Day 3: The Hot Air Balloon Proposal. Location: Over the fields of Hertfordshire.

I know the consensus will be split down the middle here, with half of you thinking 'Awww, a hot air balloon proposal, how romantic,' and the other half thinking 'how clichéd, he might as well do it on top of the Eiffel Tower if he's going to trot out these old fashioned proposals.' I'm not sure where Suzie stands on this issue. I knew she had always wanted to go in a hot air balloon, and I want to make her dreams come true, but ultimately I know she's looking for something unique. So I tried to balance this out with my proposal written on a hand painted banner as we floated majestically above the sun-kissed fields. It was perfect. Well, at least in my head.

Things started well, better than well actually. When Suzie realised she was going hot air ballooning, she threw herself into my arms, shouting for the entire world to hear how much she loved me. Now for all you would-be proposers out there, I imagine hearing the words 'I love you' are quite pivotal when you're about to propose.

Who would have thought it – Suzie Mackenzie, champion of the extraordinary proposal, was won with a simple hot air balloon proposal. She really is an old romantic at heart.

But never in my wildest dreams did I imagine it going in the direction it went next. For one, my beautiful proposal was upside down thanks to the uselessness of my ex-friend Badger. For personal reasons, I can't tell you how badly it went wrong after that – matters beyond anyone's control.

But Suzie did seem very impressed by the amount of effort involved in this one. I don't think a proposal has to be expensive, but the amount of effort involved is clearly, in the eyes of the woman anyway, directly proportional to how much the man loves them. Obviously this is the way I'm going to have to go from now on.

I finished reading the blog. Harry had rewritten it three times. There was so much we couldn't put in. We couldn't possibly damage the reputation of Carlton Balloons for something that was quite clearly not their fault. How many people would want to book balloon flights with them if they knew there was the possibility of crashing? Frank had been flying balloons for around sixty years. He had a spotless record, and many customers commented on how gentle the landings were in comparison to other balloon pilots. There was no way we could tell the truth.

We had heard back from Frank's family a few hours before and he was fine. The doctors were keeping him in overnight to do more tests, much to Frank's annoyance, but his son said they were confident that he'd be allowed to go home tomorrow.

'Is it ok?' Harry asked, after returning with two teas from the kitchen.

'It's fine, but I don't know about the extra effort thing. As we said yesterday, the small proposals are sometimes the best.'

'I thought you would like it, it might encourage our customers to go with some of our more extravagant proposals.'

I smiled. After my moaning the day before about how many basic packages we had sold, Harry was trying to rectify it.

'Oh, so this hundred proposals is all tactical then, it's not about finding me the perfect proposal at all, it's just a business stunt?'

Harry completely missed the tone of my voice. I was joking, but his face fell and the look of hurt on his face was like a punch to the gut.

'Is that what you think?'

'I was joking, I'm sorry – I didn't mean it.'

'This wasn't about the business at all, I thought you knew that.'

'I honestly don't know why you're doing all this. No one has ever gone to this much effort for me before and I don't understand why you are?'

He stared at me and it was clear that he didn't want to say why. I waited, watching him.

'I wanted to cheer you up. You've been so down since Jack died, I wanted you to have something to look forward to every day.'

I felt like I'd just been hit by a bus. My lip wobbled, an actual wobble, and I looked away as tears filled my eyes. Harry quickly moved to hold me. Again. It was not actually possible to love this man more than I loved him right now.

'Oh God, Harry,' I whispered into his shirt, as he held me tight against him.

'I'm sorry, I didn't mean to make you cry.'

'They're happy tears, I promise.' I pushed him gently away and he stepped back to look at me with concern. 'I'm just lucky to have you.'

He smiled, with relief, then moved to look at his computer, clearly embarrassed.

'Sixty-one followers on our blog so far. That's amazing.'

I smiled at the change of subject.

'That's fantastic.'

'Yes. And after mentioning Nadia's Bakery in yesterday's blog, I've had emails from quite a few places begging us to use them in my next proposal.'

I moved closer as he scrolled through his emails.

'Anything interesting?'

He quickly minimised his email screen. 'Nosy, aren't you? I don't want to spoil the surprise.'

He logged off his computer and any hints at what was to come vanished into a screen of blue. He checked his watch and pulled on his jacket.

'Hot date with Sexy Samantha tonight?'

'No, I'm meeting Badger for drinks and a few games of pool. Any hot plans for you?'

'Dinner with my lovely sister-in-law.'

'Excellent, have fun.' He planted a quick kiss on my cheek and left. If this goodbye kiss was going to become a regular feature, I could get used to it.

*

A splat of something green and foul-smelling hit the side of my cheek.

Bella giggled and laughed as the green mush slid down her face too.

'Is your niece causing a mess again?' shouted Jules from the kitchen.

I scooped Bella up out of the chair and plonked her on my lap, hoping to minimise the splatter damage if I was behind her. 'No she's just perfect, aren't you, pumpkin?'

Bella chuckled and wiggled her legs as I wiped her face and firmly took the spoon from her sticky grasp. I leaned into her soft, warm head as I spooned up some more of what Jules had told me was pureed broccoli and cauliflower. She smelt amazing, like milk, talcum powder and baby lotion. Her hair was dark just like Jack's, the same nose, the same eyes, the same chin – there was no getting away from the fact that she was his daughter.

Jules walked in carrying two glasses of wine and passed one to me. She was wearing a bright yellow top today, one that I hadn't seen on her before. Her hair was freshly dyed with warm honey coloured highlights and she was actually smiling. It had been a long time since I'd seen her smile. Maybe she'd been given a proverbial kick up the bum as well as me. I liked it, life was for living.

'You look good.'

'I feel good. Bella's sleeping properly at night now and she is such a delight during the day. And I know I shouldn't be glad of this, but Jack's insurance money has meant that I haven't had to rush back to work. I get to spend all day with her and I love just being a mum. Jack didn't want me to work again after she was born anyway, so he'd be happy that I'm taking care of her.'

'You're doing a wonderful job, she's such a happy child.'

Jules smiled fondly at Bella, smoothing out her wayward locks. Her eyes moved to mine.

'You look happy too. How's Harry?'

I failed to see how the two were connected. 'He's good, gave me a good talking to yesterday about not clinging to the past, hence I'm back to my colourful clothes again.'

'I've always loved your sense of style, or lack of it.' She smirked mischievously. 'And I hear he proposed.'

Back to Harry again. 'Not properly.' I laughed at the thought. 'Just, you know, business.'

She peeled a banana and passed it to Bella's eager hands. 'I like Harry.'

'I like him too.' I jiggled Bella on my lap, deliberately trying to avoid Jules's eyes.

'And you two have never…'

'No not at all, never. We're friends. He doesn't see me like that. Plus his reputation with women is hardly squeaky clean. He used to be with a different woman every week. The man's a complete tart.'

'Maybe he's just looking for the right woman. Jack was the same, you know that. Famously sleeping with two different women on the same night.'

'Whoa, I knew he had lots of girlfriends, I didn't realise he'd had a threesome.'

Jules spat out her wine and Bella giggled, blowing raspberries with her own lips.

'Not a threesome. Just slept with one girl, she broke up with him and by the end of the night he was in another woman's bed.'

'How do you know this?'

'I was the other woman.'

I felt my mouth fall open. 'And didn't it bother you that he'd been with someone else hours before?'

Jules shrugged as she mopped up the wine. 'He wasn't anything serious, not for me. And his ex-girlfriend at the time was a complete cow so I was just pleased to get one over on her. Then we started seeing each other, just the odd night here and there, and then those odd nights became every night. He didn't look at anyone else after that.'

'Weren't you worried that he would stray?'

Jules smiled hugely. 'I don't want to sound big-headed, because the feeling was entirely mutual, but I could see your brother was head over heels in love with me. That look never faded in all the eight years we were together.'

I smiled.

'Harry's probably the same. He's looking for The One.'

'I don't think he is. He doesn't actually believe in love or The One.'

'Oh that's rubbish. I know he was hurt badly when he was a kid, and he's holding back from falling in love in case he gets hurt again, but when he finds the right woman, he's never going to let her go.'

I felt myself go very still.

'What do you mean he was hurt as a kid?'

Jules went very pale. 'I thought you knew.'

'He told me he didn't believe in love, not long after we first met. I thought he'd just come out of a painful break up. What do you know that I don't?'

Jules turned away and started picking up Bella's toys. 'I shouldn't have said anything. You and Harry are so close, I thought you knew.'

'He hasn't really told me anything about his past. I know he doesn't speak to his parents.' I swallowed. 'Did they hurt him?'

'No, he wasn't beaten or abused, it wasn't like that. It's not my place to say. I only know because Badger accidentally let it slip to me once. Just forget I said anything.'

As if I could. Although I didn't feel I could push Jules into telling me. If Harry wanted me to know then he would have told me.

Jules threw the toys into a big chest and picked up her wine glass, swirling it around and studiously staring at the contents. 'You know he was offered a job.'

My wine got stuck in my throat and I coughed to release it. She seemed very caught up on her gossip, especially Harry gossip.

'Where, when?'

'Last week. It would have paid very well. I don't know what you're paying him but I doubt it would come close to this. Company car, pension plan, private health care plus lucrative shares in the company.'

I gaped. 'He doesn't like big companies and office politics. He's always said he'd never go back to working somewhere like that. Remember that job he turned down in America?'

'His dream job?'

'It wasn't his dream job.'

'He sure did talk about it for months, about how excited he was.'

It was true that when Harry first came into my life there was a big plan to move to New York and the great job he was going to be starting out there. But one day he'd told me he'd had second thoughts.

'Apparently people weren't happy with the merger that was taking place and the new CEO. He didn't want to get involved in all of that. As I said, he doesn't like office politics.'

'Didn't he cancel the contract around the same time that Jack died?'

Words dried in my mouth. No. He couldn't possibly have cancelled the contract because of me, to be there for me. Not if it really had been his dream job.

'I'm just saying, he keeps being offered these fabulous opportunities and he keeps turning them down. His Connected money isn't going to last him forever, especially considering how generous he is with it. It would be hard to turn down that kind of salary.'

'What kind of salary?'

She told me and I felt the blood drain from my face – it was nearly five times what he was on with me.

'So the question is, why would he stay?'

'He likes working for our company. It's his now too, he's built it up to what it is.'

'Ok, I can see he would have some kind of loyalty towards you and the company, but I think there's another reason.'

She stared at me, her pale blue eyes unblinking.

'Well it's not me, is it?'

She stared at me. Thankfully, then the timer on the oven went off indicating our pizza was cooked.

Jules smiled as she got to her feet. 'Just think about it.'

She went into the kitchen. As if I could do anything but think about it.

*

I sat on the tube, staring at my bag, feeling the envelope burning through the leather onto my lap. My mind had been filled with Harry all night, and why he would turn down such an opportunity and the job in America, but all thoughts of him had been wiped clean when Jules handed me this envelope at the end of the evening.

The train rattled to a stop at another underground station.

A letter from Jack. Jules had found it amongst his things. There had been one for her and one for Bella too.

She hadn't opened it, of course, she gave it to me to read at the end of the night. She obviously wanted me to read it then and there but I wanted to be alone for that. I promised to tell her what it said after I'd read it.

Now my hands were itching to tear it open, but not here, not with the late night Friday drunks and party goers. I just wanted to get back home as quick as I could to my little flat to be alone with Jack's words.

What had he wanted to say to me all those months before? Why didn't he say it in the last few days? Everything had happened so quickly. From the time he was diagnosed with leukaemia until the day he'd died had been just six months. But he had been fit, strong and laughing almost to the very end. He had never let it get him down. The last week had been awful, when he had deteriorated before our very eyes, but even then, even in the last few days he had still kept his humour. We had been with him at the end, all of us. Mum and Dad had flown over from New Zealand, me, Jules, Harry, Badger and a huge number of his friends had stayed with him as he just went to sleep and never woke up.

And now, here was a message from him.

My train arrived at my stop and I hurried up the steps and along the streets. It was quiet in this part of town, even though we were very central. The old Victorian style street lights lit the way ahead with sporadic puddles of light. The green was deserted but I looked over to Harry's house, as I habitually did, as I walked down the opposite side. The downstairs light was still on, but then he was always a night owl. I ran up the steps to my front door and then up the stairs to my top floor flat, whipping out the letter as I closed the door behind me.

I stared at the letter in my hand. I wanted to open it and devour the words inside that Jack had written eight months before. But I was scared as well. I started pacing the lounge. Suddenly I didn't want to do this alone. I grabbed the phone and dialled Harry's number. It was late but he was still clearly awake.

It rang several times before he answered. He sounded croaky.

'Hey.'

'Hi, are you busy?'

He paused for a moment before he spoke. 'Are you ok?'

I was silent. It was pathetic really, needing Harry to hold my hand as I read the message from beyond the grave. But I knew that opening this letter would unleash a whole heap of emotions, and I didn't want to be alone when that happened. But Harry had been there for me so many times over the last few months – at the funeral and afterwards – just holding me when I would suddenly burst into tears, and the lovely day out he had taken me on the day before just to cheer me up. I was suddenly hesitant about asking him again.

Though my silence spoke volumes.

'I'll be round in two minutes.'

I tried to protest but it was quite clear Harry was no longer there.

There was a muffled noise and Harry obviously hadn't realised he hadn't hung up properly.

'Don't look at me like that. I know you were warm and cosy but Suzie needs me,' Harry said to someone, probably Sexy Samantha. I winced.

I didn't know if she said something to him or was just giving him the evil eye but Harry carried on talking, clearly as he was getting dressed.

'I know, I know! I'm sorry. You know you're the most important woman in my life, heck the world. I know

I need to get my priorities sorted, but Suzie is pretty damned important too.'

I smiled, hugely flattered, although that wasn't going to go down well with Sexy Samantha.

'Look, just make yourself comfortable and I'll be back real soon.'

I heard him give her a quick kiss, then another muffled noise as he no doubt picked up his phone.

I heard his footsteps run down the stairs and his front door slam and the phone went dead.

Crap. The last thing I wanted was to come between him and his girlfriends. He would be pissed off when he got over here to find the only thing that he had left his hot girlfriend for was a stupid little letter.

I heard the key in the lock and then his footsteps as he ran up the stairs towards me. Crap, crap, crap.

He appeared in the lounge, took in my worried face and in a second was across the room and holding me in his arms.

'Oh Harry, I'm really sorry, I shouldn't have called,' my voice was muffled as my face was pressed into his wonderful hard chest.

'Yes you should. You always should.'

'I didn't realise I was interrupting a night of passion.'

He pulled back a bit to look at me in confusion.

'I heard you on the phone, talking to Samantha.'

He laughed. 'I was talking to Jemima.'

For a second I wondered if he had moved on already from Samantha to a new woman – it wouldn't be the first time – then I remembered his beloved cat.

'I was asleep, she was lying on my chest. She wasn't impressed about being moved.'

I laughed. 'Well, please send her my sincerest apologies. And I'm sorry to you too, I didn't mean to wake you.'

'Oh, don't worry about it.' He shrugged.

'It's nothing though, nothing serious.'

He was going to hate me.

'It's obviously something or you wouldn't be calling me.'

I sighed and pulled away completely. I picked up the letter and showed it to him. 'It's from Jack.'

Harry's eyes widened. 'Now that does sound like something serious.'

Oh God, I loved this man.

'Have you read it?'

'No, I wanted you to be with me when I did.'

He smiled. 'I'm honoured you would think of me. Where did you get it?'

'I had dinner with Jules tonight, she found it amongst his things.'

He pulled me down next to him on the sofa.

'How's your gorgeous niece?'

He was delaying, trying to distract me, and I let him as I curled up at his side, the letter in my hand.

'Beautiful, getting more beautiful each day. God she looks like Jack. The same dark hair, the same eyes. Even the same feet. It breaks my heart that she'll never know him. He would have made a wonderful father.'

'He met her though. Got to hold her. And when she's old enough you can tell her all about him. Play all the practical jokes on her that he played on you.'

'I'd like that.'

He looked at the letter. 'Do you want me to read it to you?'

'No, I want to read it.'

I stared at it. He stared at it. It would have been so much easier if the letters were like the Howlers in Harry Potter, where the envelope would simply shout the contents at you, whether you wanted to open it or not.

'Come on love.' Harry put his arm round me. 'It's a big deal, I get that. But are you not dying to see what he says? I know I am.'

I quickly slid my thumb under the flap and ripped open the envelope. The letter inside was small, so no huge reams of big brotherly advice then.

I pulled it out and opened it. Harry respectfully waited for his turn to read it. As I started to read, Harry's fingers stroked the back of my neck.

CHAPTER FIVE

Dear Stinky,

Stinky Sue, his childhood name for me that had stuck and was subsequently shortened to Stinky, or rather childishly Stinky Poo, or even just Poo. I smiled. I loved my brother so much.

So I'm dead, that kind of sucks. And I had the best practical joke to play on you too. Took months of planning and I was just about to spring it on you when the whole leukaemia thing took over. I've asked Jules to finish it for me, so I'd watch your back if I were you.

My biggest regret about dying is not being able to whip your arse on Mario Kart again. You know that I was the better driver and that last time we played you won purely because I was tired from the chemotherapy. But if I thought you were going to go easy on me because of my condition, I was sadly mistaken. I don't know how you can live with yourself, beating a dying man at a video game. You could have let me win.

I laughed at this.

Know this, as revenge, I put my toe nails in your bed and hid several more around your flat. I know toe nails freak

*you out. Every time you find one, think of me, and know
that I'm watching you. And not in a big brotherly protective
way, but in an evil, stalky kind of way. If I can, I'll rattle
my chains and moan a lot now and again just to scare you.
I swear, if I can come back and haunt you I will.*

*Ok now for the serious bit. I talked about this with Jules
but with everything else that happened in the last few
weeks we just never got round to talking about it with you.
I want you to be Bella's godmother. She needs a wonderful
aunt and I know that you will always be there for her, with
trips to the zoo and sleepovers and I know you will spoil
her rotten. But also I know that if anything were to happen
to Jules there is no one else in the world but you that
I would want to raise my daughter.*

I swallowed a lump in my throat.

*I love you and I'm so very proud of you. I want you to be
happy. I know you so well and I bet any money that Harry
is sitting next to you whilst you read this, probably holding
your hand. Tell him I said hi, and that Chelsea sucks, that
will piss him off.*

'He says to say hi to you,' I said.

'He mentions me?' Harry smiled proudly.

'Yeah he says Chelsea sucks.'

The smile fell from his face at the slur on his beloved
football team. 'I'll give him Chelsea sucks. He's only
saying that because he's dead and he knows I can't argue
back.'

'He loved to wind you up.'

Harry smiled, fondly. 'What else does he say?'

'Here.' I leaned into him so he could read the letter too.

And one more thing I want you to do for me, my dying wish – and you can't refuse a man his dying wish. Tell Harry you love him, that you've always loved him and always will be in love with him.

I gasped with horror and snatched the letter back from Harry.

'What's wrong?'

'How far did you get?'

'The bit about the toe nails, let me read the rest.'

'NO! No way. It's private.'

I leapt up out of his reach.

'We don't have secrets from each other, we tell each other everything.' Harry stood up, his eyes dark with mischief. 'Don't make me take it from you.'

'It's nothing, just… it's private.'

Harry leapt forward and I turned to run but he caught me around my waist, pulling me back against him. He snatched the letter from my hand and held it up high so I couldn't reach.

'Harry, no.' I leapt up to get it but failed.

'Now let's see what little sordid secret you're keeping from me.'

He started skim reading out loud. 'Aw, he wants you to be Bella's godmother, that's sweet. And he says he loves you, that's nice, he says hi to me, Chelsea sucks…'

'HARRY, PLEASE!' I screamed with such desperation that Harry stopped reading and looked at me.

'You really don't want me to read this do you?'

I shook my head frantically. My cheeks were burning and I could feel tears of humiliation pricking my eyes. 'Please don't read it, I'm begging you.'

He released me and handed me back the letter without another word. I grabbed it, nearly sagging with relief.

'Is it something horrible?'

I moved away from him, sitting on the other side of the room, and tried to calm down my heart.

'No, something that Jack only wanted me to know. Something private for him.' I couldn't look at him in case he saw the lies.

I straightened out the crumpled letter on my lap and carried on reading.

Tell Harry you love him, that you've always loved him and always will be in love with him. I bet you all the money in the world that he says it right back. There has been no one for you since he came into your life and if he doesn't feel the same way at least you'll know, at least you'll stop wondering and maybe, finally you can move on. Regardless of his feelings, he will always be your best friend, nothing will change that. Tell him now or I will haunt you every night, slamming doors and turning on taps and I'll invite all my ghostly friends round to haunt you too. Tell him Suze, what have you got to lose?

Love you always
Jack
(Mario Kart World Champion)

I stared at the treacherous words. If he knew Harry would be sitting with me, why would he write that, knowing full well that Harry could read it too? And how the hell did he know? No one knew about my inappropriate crush on my best friend. I had never told anyone, least of all my indiscreet blabbermouth big brother.

I looked up at Harry, who was obviously hurt that I didn't want to share the letter with him.

'It's nothing.' I repeated.

He wasn't convinced.

I stood up, folding the letter carefully into my pocket. I walked over to him and hugged him.

'Thank you for coming over, everything seems easier when you're with me.'

He reluctantly hugged me back. 'Except anything that's private.'

I made up my mind there and then. 'I'll tell you one day, I promise. I'm just not ready yet.'

This seemed to mollify him as his hug tightened. 'Do you want me to stay for a while?'

I nodded.

'Do you want to play Mario Kart?'

I smiled. 'How did you guess?'

'I'll set it up, go and get some beers,' he said as he crouched down by the TV.

I went into the kitchen and leaned against the fridge as I re-read the letter again. I heard the Wii spring to life in the other room.

I would tell him – if that's what Jack wanted, then I would do it. But it was going to take a hell of a lot more than cheap Bulgarian beer to find the courage to do that. I tucked the letter back into my pocket and walked back into the lounge.

Harry passed me a remote and I swapped it for a beer.

'I'm not going to go easy on you,' Harry said.

'I wouldn't expect you to.'

'This one's for Jack.'

'He'll like that, especially if you win.'

'I'm not going to lose.'

I took a swig of beer as I looked at my best friend. 'We'll see.'

*

I woke the next morning feeling like my head had exploded. It had been a long night, carrying on to the very early hours of the morning. We had drunk, played multiple games of Mario Kart and then other games that required skill and balance that neither Harry nor I could achieve after several bottles of beer. At some point I had fallen on the sofa, too tired and too drunk to move. I wasn't really aware of anything after that.

There was a heavy weight on me and I couldn't move at all. I opened one eye and saw Harry lying on top of me, snoring loudly. I closed my eye against the early morning sunshine that penetrated the room painfully. The feel of his snores vibrating through me was nice, like a cat purring. Harry didn't snore so it was obviously an adverse effect of the drink. I smiled to myself. Waking up with the man I loved wasn't a bad start to Valentine's Day.

I lay with my eyes closed for a moment, wondering if I could go back to sleep. Suddenly my eyes snapped open as I realised where Harry's hand was. Why hadn't I noticed it before? I looked down and sure enough his hand was gripping my left breast like his life depended on it. God, even in sleep he was a breast man.

Seeing his hand around my breast like that did things to me, a twist of desire lancing straight through my stomach. Though he would be mortified if he woke and found his hand there. Carefully, I tried to prise one of his fingers from my breast, but he was gripping it quite hard and he was so strong even the muscles in his fingers were not something I could fight against. I tried to push my hand between his hand and my breast but to no avail. As I lay there trying to decide my next course of action, Harry stirred and woke up. He looked down at me and smiled sheepishly, still currently unaware of where his hand was. This could go either of two ways. He could realise where his hand was, realise he liked it there and plant the other hand on my other breast, then it could lead to the places of my deepest, darkest fantasies. Unfortunately for me, it went the other way.

Harry looked down, saw where his hand was and leapt off me with a definite 'Urgh'. Revulsion hadn't been high on my list of possible reactions. He glared at me.

'Don't look at me like that, I didn't put my breast in your hand. You were still standing and playing on the Wii when I passed out last night. What you did after is your business.'

'Sorry, I would never – '

I stood up. 'I know you would never. Never, ever, ever – right? Not in a million years.'

I flounced out the room straight into the bathroom, locked the door, quickly undressed and stepped straight into the shower.

When I came out it was quite obvious that we were never going to speak of it ever again.

'Two hundred and three followers, Suze, that's huge,' Harry shouted from the office. I walked in. He didn't look up from his screen and I could see his cheeks blush as I looked at him. 'And some magazine called Silver Linings is going to call me on Monday with regards to featuring our blog as some sort of column.'

'Whoa, that is huge.'

'I know.' He grinned up at me, obviously relieved we weren't going to talk about 'breastgate'. 'Look, I better go, I'm supposed to be seeing Samantha today. I'll see you Monday.'

Two days off from being proposed to. There was a brief oasis in the desert. And after the massive proposal the day before, he'd earned a few days off.

*

Waterfalls, emerald green rainforests, turquoise seas, koalas, kangaroos, crocodiles and white sandy beaches all assaulted me from my computer screen. Australia was a beautiful country and I wanted to devour every single part of it.

Even though it was the weekend, I was still answering emails or doing research for the.PerfectProposal.com. I'm not sure when it had become my life, Before Jack or After Jack, but it had become something of an addiction now. Every spare minute I had was spent researching new locations, new proposals. I loved it. It made me so happy to think of couples getting engaged in these places and that in some small way we were helping them to start their life together.

One of my clients was taking his girlfriend to Australia this summer and wanted some ideas for romantic places to propose. Maybe I had taken a little bit more interest in researching Australian locations because I'd always wanted to go.

My friend, Peri, had emigrated there two years before to marry some beach bronzed Adonis called Brad. Her emails and Skype calls ever since had been filled with details of beach barbeques, surfing, sunshine, scuba diving, water skiing and the incredible beauty of the Australian east coast.

I was living in her tiny flat, on permanent loan from her and the only way I could afford such an affluent, central location. But despite my house sitting duties, Peri tried to convince me to move out there with her every time we spoke.

When she was first set to move there, she desperately tried to persuade me to go with her. With my parents over in New Zealand, and most of my friends scattered to the four corners of the world, there didn't seem a lot to hang around for. I'd always wanted to live abroad, somewhere hot or maybe a big city. Then Harry had come into my life and all thought of leaving Britain had quickly vanished.

But I wanted to visit. I was desperate to experience some of this sunshine bliss for myself and had set about saving for it. My savings account, renamed 'Aussie Dreams', currently had a huge total of two hundred and forty six pounds in it. I had a long way to go.

My computer pinged to indicate I had a message just as I was looking at pictures of the beach paradise at Tangalooma.

I closed down my web browser and opened up my email. I frowned with confusion as I read the notification. Harry's Proposer's Blog had been updated. The followers our blog had all registered so they would be notified when the next blog went live. For some reason, Harry had included me on this notification as well. But what new updates would Harry have now? He hadn't proposed to me today. He was supposed to be with Sexy Samantha. I clicked on it and my confusion deepened.

Proposer's Blog

Day 4: The Self-Humiliation Proposal. Location: Trafalgar Square. Date: Valentine's Day. Time 1pm.

My dear would-be proposers, nothing says 'I love you' like some toe curling humiliation. If you are prepared to go to any length necessary to declare your love for your woman, no matter how embarrassing or degrading, then that surely can't be a bad thing.

Join me, if you can, for my special Valentine's Day proposal. I'll be near one of the four lions. I'll be the one dressed in black and white.

I stared at the words. I looked at the clock. It had just gone twelve. I stared at the words again. Then quickly grabbed my bag and coat and ran out the door.

*

Trafalgar Square was packed, as it was at all times of the year, despite the cold weather. Pigeons fluttered about, scrabbling for any kind of leftover food that the tourists may have discarded.

Four big bronze lions stood proud in the middle of the square as I cast my eyes frantically around for Harry. He'd said he was going to be wearing black and white, did he mean a tux? My heart leapt at the thought of Harry looking delicious in a sexy tux.

There was quite a crowd around one of them so I headed in that direction.

I saw Badger first, his bright ginger hair welcoming me in like a beacon. He greeted me with one of his huge bear hugs.

'Hey, Badger, how much did Harry pay you to be involved in this one?' I could see people giggling and laughing at something on the other side of the lion that I couldn't see.

'Are you kidding, I wouldn't miss this for all the tea in China.' He nodded his head behind him and I followed his gaze.

As the crowd parted slightly, I saw Harry dressed in a very tight cow print onesie that was clearly several sizes too small for him.

My eyes temporarily dropped to the significant bulge, shown dramatically because of the tightness of the onesie. I dragged my eyes away from it to look at Harry as he approached me, holding a single yellow rose.

He looked ridiculous.

'Hi,' he said, passing me the rose.

'Hi.' There were no other words in my head.

He bent his head and whispered in my ear so only I could hear him. 'I wanted you to know that I loved Jack almost as much as you did. So this one's for him.'

I smiled with love for him.

'And you have to have a special licence to perform anything here so I don't think we're going to have long before the police descend. If it all kicks off, just run.'

He stepped away. Police? What on earth was he going to do that would bring the police down on us?

'What? Harry, wait…'

He let out an ear piercing whistle. Music started from the other side of the lion and the immediate crowd fell silent.

The music was classical, possibly Tchaikovsky.

'You wanted the ballet and a bag of chips.' Harry said as Badger plonked a bag of slightly cold chips in my hands. 'Well, there are the chips and here is the ballet.' He raised his voice. 'Ladies and Gentleman, may I present to you the National Ballet's version of Cow Lake.'

Laughter erupted as the crowd parted. From behind the lion danced twelve big burly lads holding hands and kicking their legs about in some very bad attempt at ballet. I burst out laughing. I instantly recognised them as being from Harry's rugby team. They were all wearing cow print onesies and pink tutus over the top. Harry joined on at the end, seamlessly, as they danced inelegantly from side to side, kicking their legs out, kicking each other, stamping on each other's toes. This clearly had not been practised and it made the crowd laugh even more every time they hurt each other. I was laughing so hard that my face was aching. The music gained in speed and they broke off in pairs, lifting each other off the ground as their partners kicked their legs in the air. It was a mess but the crowd were lapping it up.

The music reached a crescendo as Badger started signalling frantically to wrap it up. They quickly formed rows – two rows of five, one row of two – as Harry broke away and moved to stand in front of me. As the music stopped they all turned around to reveal a letter on each of their backs. In foot high sequinned letters, the words 'Suzie Marry Me', were clear for everyone to see. With a final dramatic pirouette, Harry came down on one knee with a huge grin on his face and clutched my hand.

The crowd broke into spontaneous applause.

Badger interrupted the romantic scene before my eyes with a sudden shout. 'RUN!'

The cows leapt up and dispersed into the crowd. Harry stood up and kissed me on the cheek before he disappeared into the crowd too. Within seconds, my own personal Flash Mob had vanished, leaving behind only a cold bag of chips to show any sign that it had actually happened.

I casually ate a chip as I sauntered away, hoping I was pulling off the nonchalance I was going for. Though the police were clearly not that bothered. They ambled over to see what had caused the great crowd but when they saw it was over, the last thing they were going to do was give chase to thirteen burly cows.

My phone buzzed in my bag and I fished it out from amongst the tumble of rubbish. It was Harry.

'Hey. Meet me by the fountain in five minutes. I just need to get changed.'

I was still giggling when he came jogging over, thankfully dressed back in his jeans and T-shirt.

'Well?' He sat next to me and stole a chip. He didn't seem bothered at all that it was now stone cold.

'I loved it.'

He laughed and slung his arm around me. 'Happy Valentine's Day Suzie.'

'Aren't you supposed to be with Sexy Samantha right about now, instead of entertaining me?'

He shrugged. 'She's not returned my calls.'

A flash of hurt crossed his face but it was gone so quickly I thought I might have imagined it. This wasn't normal. He used to go through so many women when we first met, but he never grew attached to any of them.

'So, no hot plans tonight?'

He shook his head.

'Surely not. Harry Forbes alone on Valentine's Day night.'

'Ah you know me, Suze, I don't believe in all that rubbish anyway.'

'You mean love?'

He nodded.

I frowned. To close himself off from the possibilities of love meant closing his heart to happiness. I understood he was trying to protect himself but not moving on at all didn't sit with his happy, spontaneous demeanour. I decided to push it.

'I don't see how you can say that, considering the line of business we are in. We've seen so many happy couples get together, get married, live happy lives with each other.'

'Loving someone means trusting them.' He looked at me in a rare moment of seriousness. 'I learned many years ago that I couldn't trust anyone.'

What was he hiding? I knew so little about his past. I'd asked but he always gave me the vaguest of information then changed the subject. I'd stopped pursuing it in the end.

He took my hand. 'I trust you, you're my best friend. You're the only one I do trust.'

Though not enough to tell me why he had these issues in the first place.

He picked up a chip and offered it to me, deliberately prodding me in the nose when I leaned forward to take a bite. I giggled and I sensed the moment was over.

I loved this man. He made me laugh, he made me cry, he was there for me in every possible way that he could be. Who went to that much trouble for someone they just liked? What if… he *had* found love… with me? The only one he could trust.

Jack's letter dug into my back pocket, almost burning me with my brother's final wish. I would tell him. In fact I would tell him tonight. I would never hurt him, he must know that and if he didn't feel the same way then at least I would know, one way or another.

CHAPTER SIX

I stood at the bottom of Harry's steps willing myself to do this. Jack was right, I had to tell him. I couldn't go on like this, loving him from afar. Yes it would be weird between us, especially if he had no inclination in that area, but it wouldn't affect our friendship. And if it did… I swallowed. If it did and he didn't think he could be friends with me anymore then maybe without his constant presence in my life I could finally move on.

I looked down at myself. I was dressed ok, my best jeans and a pretty flowered top. It wasn't over the top. If I chickened out, he would never know what I had come here for tonight. We had done Chinese and movies a hundred times before, this would be totally normal at first. Then with a few glasses of wine inside me, I would simply tell him. I could do this. My heart leapt. I couldn't do this.

I sighed. One thing was for sure, if I didn't go up the steps now and knock on his door, the Chinese was going to get cold.

I walked up the steps with renewed determination. I was going to tell him. I rang the bell.

There was no answer at the door, and no sign of movement inside. I could hear music coming from the lounge so he probably hadn't heard me. Carefully, I leaned over the bannister, putting my hand on the windowsill for balance and peered through his window.

Harry was there, sitting on the sofa with no shirt, intently watching something I couldn't see, though it wasn't the TV – it was the wrong place for that.

I raised my hand to knock on the window when a movement caught my eye. A woman. Sexy Samantha. Dressed only in her underwear, she walked towards Harry with two glasses of champagne, she passed one to him then straddled him. I watched him smile as he moved his hand to her waist. She took a sip of her champagne then kissed him.

I couldn't move. I was frozen in shock. It had taken me hours to summon enough courage and Samantha was in there with him doing exactly what I wanted to be doing. I'd thought they had broken up. I watched with a huge wave of disappointment as she ran her hands down his chest to the buttons on his jeans.

So that was it. The conversation, the words I'd spent ages practising faded from my mind.

It was stupid to think that Harry could ever feel that way about me, not when he seemed to have a huge collection of girls on tap. I had to go quickly before he saw me.

I pushed myself off the windowsill, but my foot slipped off the step behind me. I head-butted the window hard, toppled over the bannister and fell into the bush below. A second later the red sweet and sour sauce, the noodles and Harry's favourite prawn with cashew nuts emptied their contents all over me. The bag of prawn crackers fell at my feet.

I stared morosely at the mess, wondering if I could still use the prawn crackers to mop up the sauce.

To make matters worse, I wasn't alone. Jemima, Harry's cat, stood unblinking at me from the depths of the bush.

Then, almost as if she shrugged, she stalked towards me and proceeded to lick the sauce off my face.

If Jack was here now, if somehow he had been brought back to life, I would wrap my hands round his throat and kill him all over again. Immediately guilt lanced through me at such a horrible thought and coupled with the crashing disappointment of seeing Harry with Samantha, I pulled Jemima tightly against me and cried into her fur.

'Hello, who's there?'

Harry's angry voice came from up above me and I froze, trying desperately to stifle my sobs.

'Bloody peeping tom,' I heard Samantha say.

Footsteps came down the steps towards me.

'There's someone in the bushes,' Harry hissed.

'Shall I call the police?'

Oh God, could this situation get any worse? Although maybe the police taking me away would be better than having to face Harry and Samantha.

'Get my baseball bat,' whispered Harry. I heard her footsteps run back inside the house.

What was he going to do with the baseball bat? Ok this was getting out of hand. I stood up, popping up out of the bush like a jack in the box.

'Hi.'

Noodles slowly moved across my forehead and down my cheek, thankfully my tears seemed to be lost in the sweet and sour sauce.

Harry, still without his shirt, looked at me and slowly broke into a huge smile.

'Hello.'

Jemima was still licking my face.

'I brought Chinese.' I held up the now empty bag. 'I thought we could watch the latest zombie film. Though

I see you are already set for entertainment tonight so I'll leave you to it.'

I climbed out the bush as gracefully as I could, but Harry was already coming down the stairs towards me.

'So the noodle hair, is this a new look you're trying out? I think I prefer the onesie.' He picked a clump of noodles and beansprouts from my head and threw it on the floor. Jemima treacherously leapt out of my arms and started eating the remains. 'I'm presuming none of this is blood, are you hurt?'

My pride and my heart were definitely. Though any external pain I'd received from the fall had yet to catch up with my brain. I shook my head.

He had the most glorious body, he was so big in every sense and I just wanted him to wrap his arms around me and hold me like he did the other night. But clearly that wasn't going to happen with Samantha, ready, willing and able, waiting for him inside.

'Oh!' Samantha's voice sliced through the air above us. 'It's you.' The disappointment was evident. I looked up at her and saw her shifting awkwardly, not least because Harry hadn't taken his eyes from me. She was dressed just in his shirt, it swamped her but with her hair tousled and her lips red she looked every inch the sexy girlfriend.

'I'm sorry,' I mumbled to Harry. 'I didn't realise you had company when I came over. Don't worry about me, go and have some fun.'

I took a step away from him but he caught my hand. 'Don't go.'

'What are you suggesting, that I join you for a threesome?'

He laughed. 'I don't think I could cope with that. You naked in my bed…' He rubbed his hand across his eyes as if to dispel that image from his brain.

I was mortified. 'Right well on that rather unflattering note, I'll leave you to it.'

Harry caught my arm. 'Wait, I didn't mean…'

I pulled my arm from his grasp. 'I got it.'

'I don't think you do…'

I turned and walked away. Could this evening get any worse?

'Hey, wait up.' I heard Samantha's voice call out to me. Oh apparently it could get worse. I turned to see her running across the green towards me, Harry was standing at the top of his steps watching us curiously.

'Look, Harry told me about your brother, I'm very sorry to hear that.'

'Erm thanks.' Where was she going with this?

'Harry's a great guy.'

'He is,' I said, cautiously, painfully aware of what a mess I looked like in comparison to her effortless beauty.

'I know he's been there for you a lot since James died.'

'Jack.'

'He feels sorry for you. He told me.'

Wow. That hurt a lot more than it should.

She stared at me, her eyes were honest and clear. 'I like you Suzie, and I don't want to see you getting hurt. Just… don't confuse pity and kindness for love, because it's not that. If he wanted to be with you, he would be with you.'

Talk about brutal honesty.

'Samantha!' Harry called. There was a warning edge to his voice. He didn't like that she was talking to me, or warning me off more like.

Samantha smiled at me. 'Have a good night.'

I watched her turn and run barefoot across the grass and straight into Harry's arms. With a last look from Harry they disappeared into the house.

Samantha was right. Harry wasn't shy. If he had any feelings for me he would have told me by now. And, after the quick dismissal of the idea of me in his bed, I wanted to get down on my knees and thank the powers that be that I had never declared my undying love to him that night. He wouldn't have told me quite so bluntly but the conversation would have been mortifying.

I turned away and didn't look back. Yes it hurt, but to finally have it confirmed was like a weight off my shoulders. I was free, there was to be no more wondering if his kind actions or words had some ulterior motive, no more thinking that one day we would fall into each other's arms and live happily ever after. That was never going to happen now. For the first time in two years, I could finally move on.

*

I knocked on Jules's door early next morning. She'd be up, Bella always woke up ridiculously early.

I had lain awake most of the night thinking about Harry and I needed some kind of distraction from him today.

Jules opened the door looking very dishevelled and her eyes widened when she saw me.

'Did I wake you, aw sorry mate, I thought you'd be up by now, with Bella.'

I kissed her on the cheek and pushed past her into the house.

'Bella's still asleep.'

'I thought we could go out today, maybe London Zoo. Bella loves the animals.'

'Great idea. I'd love that. But I have some things I need to take care of this morning. Why don't I meet you there about twelve?'

'Cool.'

'And I'm running late so… well not meaning to be rude or anything but…' she grinned at me good naturedly.

'Well why don't I get Bella up and dressed for you. I can give her breakfast whilst you have a shower and get dressed yourself.'

I moved to the stairs.

'NO! I mean, Bella's a bit grouchy in the morning. She doesn't like being woken up by anyone other than me.'

'She knows me, I'm sure she'll be fine.'

I walked up the stairs.

'Suzie please. I…'

A very loud male yawn interrupted whatever she was going to say next. I stared at her, willing my ears to have picked up a neighbour's yawn or perhaps a TV. I felt sick.

'Jules, where are you? I have something for you, something big.' A male voice floated down the stairs.

It was a friend, a brother, her father. It had to be. He had a big present, that was it. It was all perfectly innocent. I ignored the voice in the back of my head that told me I knew that voice.

I raced up the stairs, ignoring Jules's desperate pleas behind me.

I pushed open the door to her bedroom and stared at Badger, lying stark naked in Jules's bed with his huge erection in his hand.

His eyes widened when he saw me.

'Shit, Suzie, wait I can explain.' Badger scrabbled out of bed towards me and I lurched back away from him. This was a horrible nightmare, one that I wanted to wake up from at any minute.

I looked at Jules, waiting for any kind of explanation that would make this all right. She was leaning against the wall with her head in her hands, looking like The Scream by Edvard Munch. I probably had the same expression.

'I'm sorry, I'm so sorry. I never wanted you to find out like this.'

'It's true? You've been sleeping with Badger behind my brother's back?' The inaccuracy of the words punched me in the stomach. 'It's been eight months.' I quickly rectified. 'My brother has barely gone cold and you're screwing around with his cousin already. I suppose I should be grateful that you're keeping it in the family.'

'Suzie, it's not like that.' Badger was quickly doing up his jeans.

'And you, how could you betray me like this? We're supposed to be friends. You were supposed to be Jack's friend.'

Bella started crying and as Badger stepped towards her bedroom to soothe her, a new horror hit me. Badger raising my niece, Badger being the only dad that Bella would ever know.

Tears welled in my eyes and I ran down the stairs and out onto the street.

I could hear Jules chasing after me.

I managed to get two houses away before she caught my arm and pulled me back.

She was crying too. 'I'm sorry, I never meant for it to happen, but it did and I'm so sorry. I know this probably won't help, but I'm not just sleeping with him, it's not sex. I love him.'

My stomach lurched.

'You loved Jack,' I spat. 'How can you love someone else so soon after his death?'

'Do you think I have any control over it? I felt so guilty, I still feel guilty, but I can't go on punishing myself any longer. I can't deny what I feel for Steve, I'm sorry.'

Steve? Who the bloody hell was Steve? Someone else she was sleeping with? Then I remembered that that was Badger's real name.

Badger came running out of the house, carrying Bella on his hip as if she belonged there. Bella had stopped crying and was clinging to Badger's hair as he unconsciously stroked her back. Bella saw me and broke into a huge smile, her hands reaching out to hug me.

'How long has it being going on?'

'Steve has been coming round ever since Jack died.'

'Thought you could jump into the marital bed whilst it was still warm did you? I hope you at least changed the sheets before you got in.'

'It wasn't like that. How could it have been? I was a mess after Jack had died. Steve helped me, he did the cleaning, the washing, he cooked meals for me. It was just nice to have someone to cry on. You know what that was like, you had Harry. I had no one.'

'You had me.'

'You had your own grief to attend to. Steve and I were friends, it was never anything more than that.' She sighed heavily. 'The first time we slept together was four months after Jack's death.'

'Four months!' I wanted to slap her. I had to physically stop myself from doing just that.

'We were both drunk, we never meant for it to happen,' Badger tried to explain.

'Oh so you just tripped and your dick fell into her repeatedly.'

'Dick.' Bella gurgled, happily. Any other time it would have been funny.

'I cried for days after, I didn't want anything else to do with him. I refused to see him again. But I missed him so much. We didn't do anything again for weeks, months, though we started seeing each other. I suppose we've been a couple for two or three weeks now.'

'I love her, Suzie, I hate that we've hurt you like this, but this is more than just fooling around.'

The words of togetherness sliced through me. Bella leaned into Badger's shoulder affectionately.

'And how do you think Jack would feel about this?' I gestured to the little family unit.

Fresh tears filled Jules's eyes. 'I would hope that he would see I was happy and would be pleased for me. I hope, in time, you'll be happy for me too.'

'Don't hold your breath.'

I walked away and managed to turn the corner before I burst into tears.

*

I sat staring at the small stone fountain as water gushed from the top like a bubble. St Dunstan-in-the-East was an oasis in the middle of all the noise of the city. Amongst the high rise buildings and busy roads sat this tranquil hidden garden. The twelfth century church had been bombed in the Second World War and was never repaired;

it had then been made into a public garden. Trees grew from the walls, vines crawled through the empty windows as if they were tentacles trying to suck the church back into the ground. Wild flowers grew from little borders round the edge of the church. Weak, winter sunlight streamed through the open roof, glinting off the water of the fountain. I was alone, which I was thankful for.

Though as a huge shadow loomed over me, blocking out the sunlight, I knew straight away who it was.

Harry sat down next to me and put his arm round me.

'Badger called.'

'Did you know?'

'Yes.'

I glared at him. 'And you didn't tell me?'

'It wasn't my place to tell.'

'You're supposed to be my friend.'

'I am, you know that I am. But this was their thing. They had to figure it out for themselves. I didn't want to get in the way. Telling you would have interfered. Jules feels guilty enough about this as it is without factoring you into the equation.'

'You should have told me.'

'So you could have stopped it?'

'Yes. She doesn't love him. This is grief, pure and simple.'

'Then you should be happy that she has found some comfort, that someone was there to help her pick up the pieces.'

'She slept with Badger four months after my brother died. Four months. Do you know how that makes me feel? Jack would be heartbroken. He loved Jules so much.

Jack and Jules, Jules and Jack. Then Bella. They were the perfect little family, the perfect happy ever after. And four months after he died she was sleeping with someone else. So maybe she never really loved Jack at all.'

'That's rubbish and you know it.'

I stared at him, stung at the betrayal. 'You're supposed to be on my side.'

'The side of stupidity, I don't think so.'

I stood up. 'You think I'm being stupid.'

He sighed and rubbed the back of his neck. 'I get that you're hurt. It must hurt to see Jules move on, to see Badger watching Bella grow up when Jack will never see that. But surely you don't want Jules to be on her own for the rest of her life.'

'I expect her to grieve over Jack a darn sight longer than four months.'

'Four months was an accident. Two people who loved Jack, still grieving over him and seeking comfort with each other. We never slept together, I mean actually had sex, but there was many a night after Jack had died that we slept in the same bed, that you clung to me as you slept. You sought comfort with me. Them sleeping together isn't that far removed from what we did. People grieve in different ways.'

'And now grief has turned to love. I don't think so.'

'You should be happy for her.'

'Happy?'

'Say if Jules was one of your friends, not your sister-in-law, and she started seeing someone else after her husband had died. Wouldn't you be happy for her, that something was finally making her smile again?'

'It's too soon.'

'I imagine a lot of people would think that. But do you think you have any say who you fall in love with and when? Do you think she has any control over it?'

'What about Bella?'

'What about her? She needs a dad.'

My fists clenched. 'Badger is not her dad.'

'He loves her, Suzie, loves her like she's his own.'

'He has no right to love her.'

'That's a bit selfish, isn't it?'

'So I'm selfish and stupid now.'

'Jack wanted Jules to be happy again, to find love again, he said so in his letter to her. Yes, it's happened a lot sooner than any of us expected, but you have to take happiness now, while you have the chance. I think Jack would be delighted that Jules has found happiness with someone who loves her and Bella so much. That's all he could ever hope for, someone that treats them right, who would go to the ends of the world for them. You know Badger as well as I do. I can't think of a better bloke for Jules to end up with. He deserves happiness too.'

I was hurting so much inside right now. It wasn't fair. None of it was fair. Jack should still be here to raise his own daughter, to spend the rest of his life with the woman he loved, who loved him. And Harry should have been mine. There were no happy ever afters.

I wanted to run away from all this. From seeing Harry every day, from Badger and Jules. Suddenly the answer was obvious.

'I'm thinking of emigrating.'

'That's a bit of an extreme reaction to all of this.'

'I have nothing for me here anymore.'

'Thanks very much.'

'I'm in your way. The third wheel. I don't want to come between you and Samantha. If I move to Australia, you can get that well paid job, you can stop dropping everything for me and running every time I hurt – and I won't have to watch my niece being raised by another man.'

The idea was suddenly growing on me. Those beaches, waterfalls and rainforests. A new life.

Harry stood, looming over me. 'You listen to me. You have never and will never be in my way. Meeting you was the best thing that ever happened to me. Not only do I now have the best job in the world, helping other couples get together, but I also have the best friend. You're kind, generous, sweet, funny and I would rather spend every single hour of every single day with you than someone like Samantha. Yes, you've been going through a rough patch lately. But we'll get through it, together, by letting your friends help you – not by pushing them away. Jules and Badger love you too. Badger was beside himself when you left earlier.'

I didn't want to hear it. I grabbed my bag and walked out of the church.

'Damn it Suzie, running away is not the answer.'

But I kept on walking, and when he shouted again the traffic noises outside swallowed it up.

Proposer's Blog

Day 5: The Love Actually Proposal. Location: Outside Suzie's house

Suzie's not actually talking to me. I'm an insensitive arse. She is going through the worst time in her life at the moment and I should have been there for her. I should have been more diplomatic. I should have let her cry on my shoulder instead of forcing my ideas and opinions on her.

As she won't open the door or answer the phone, there was no choice but to do today's proposal through the medium of cue cards, as in that famous scene from Love Actually with beautiful Keira Knightley and super sexy (or so Suzie tells me) Andrew Lincoln.

So with a bit of help from Ronan Keating, (a CD of 'You Say it Best When You Say Nothing at All' obviously, not the man himself, though that would have been awesome. Ronan Keating, if you're reading this and would like to help out a fellow romantic, give me a call) and three large white placards, I stood outside her house and proposed.

Placard 1. I'm sorry.

Placard 2. You're my best friend and I will stand by your side forever.

Placard 3. Marry me.

I'd like to say that she came out and ran straight into my arms, but of course that didn't happen. She watched from her window and then she walked away.

*

Damn. Shit. Fuck. Bugger. Arse.

I couldn't sleep. I was a selfish brat and to top it all my sulkiness had ruined another damned fine proposal.

Of course I wanted Jules to be happy. It was only the other day that I'd told her how good she looked, and how happy it made me to see her smiling again. Badger was responsible for that and how could I want to stop it? It might not last – it might be grief, pure and simple – but

Harry was right, if she had found some comfort in the months after Jack's death then that had to be a good thing.

I just wished it wasn't sexual comfort.

I thought about the times that Harry had held me in bed, held me tight as I cried myself to sleep. There had been many a time, even in my grief, that I'd wanted the hugging to be something more. It wasn't even entirely down to my inappropriate feelings for him that I'd wanted him to make love to me. I'd just wanted to feel my blood rushing through me, to feel his heat, his skin against mine, to feel alive, when my whole body seemed numb with grief. Could I really blame Jules for taking that extra step, the one I'd been too scared to take myself?

Because I needed Harry. After Jack's death, Harry had been the air I needed to breathe and I'd been too scared to do anything that might cause me to lose him. I'd seen many women come and go before Jack died, I'd watch Harry get bored and cast them aside before moving onto the next. I couldn't be that woman, who he slept with and wanted nothing more to do with after. I had only got through the last eight months because of Harry being doggedly by my side. The thought now of him not being there, of waking up in a different country and not seeing him every day, was unbearable.

And Jules had found the same comfort with Badger.

It might turn out to be something serious. Jules could end up with Badger for the rest of her life, get married to Badger, have more children with him. I shuddered at the thought. I loved Badger, he was a good bloke, but it didn't sit right that she was moving on so soon after Jack's death.

But then what was the alternative. I'd seen Jules in the months after Jack's death. She'd lost so much weight, her skin was grey, the bags under her eyes indicating a complete lack of any sleep – and the grief and pain in her eyes was something I couldn't bear to look at. It sliced through me every time she looked at me. I never wanted her to go back to that place.

Harry's words rang in my ears. 'You should grab happiness while you have the chance.' And he was right. Some of us were lucky to find love once in our lives. Who was I to deny Jules the chance to find it twice?

I hated that Harry was right. And the annoying thing was, I'd known he was right even in the church.

There was only one way this was going to be resolved.

I threw back the duvet, shoved my feet into my trainers and ran down the stairs and across the green. It was deserted again. It always surprised me that, despite how centrally we lived, our little green reflected a country village at this time of night.

I banged on Harry's door and rang the bell. His house was in complete darkness and I prayed that he was alone.

Eventually I saw movement in the glass door beyond.

As he came closer I realised he was naked apart from his shorts. Did the man walk round his house in a permanent state of nakedness?

He opened the door, his face screwed up against the street lights. I had clearly just woke him up.

'Please tell me that Badger isn't lying naked in your bed too.'

He blinked at me in confusion. 'He better bloody not be.'

'Samantha?'

'We broke up.'

I stalled over this.

'Any other hot beautiful ladies?'

He shook his head, trying to rub the sleep from his eyes. 'Nice pyjamas.'

I looked down at the pyjamas he had bought me. Maybe I should have changed before I came over. I shivered against the cold chill of the night. 'Look. I just wanted to say...'

To my surprise, he leaned forward and took my hand, pulling me into his house and shutting the door behind me.

'Are you going to shout at me again, because I'm really not awake enough for that? I'll most likely say something I'll regret.'

'I came to say I'm sorry.'

'Ah. You're sorry, I'm sorry...' he waved his hand in the air as if it all meant nothing. 'Come on.' Without another word he started walking back down the hall and up the stairs, pulling me along in his wake.

'Why are you not making a bigger deal out of this? Do you not want to hear my big apology?'

'No. I don't need to hear it. I'm going back to bed. Five minutes ago I was in the middle of the best dream I've ever had. If I hurry I can go back there.'

He climbed into bed and, as he was still holding my hand, I had to get into bed with him.

'But you were right. I'm a bitch.'

'I never said that.' He folded the duvet over me and closed his eyes as he sank back into his pillow.

'But everything you said. You were right. I should be happy that Jules has found love again. Jack would want that too. And tomorrow I'm going to go round and apologise to Jules and Badger. Do you not want to do some smug victory dance or at the very least say, "I told you so"?'

Harry reached out blindly and pulled me into his arms, so my head was lying on his chest.

'My best friend has just accepted her sister-in-law moving on with another man. I don't think there is anything to celebrate there. I can't even imagine the kind of strength it takes to find this out and then accept it a few hours later, I can't imagine how much it must hurt. So go to sleep, tomorrow I'll make you breakfast in bed and then we can go and apologise together.'

My heart swelled with love for him.

Within moments his breathing had turned heavy.

'Harry,' I whispered.

There was no answer.

'Harry, I'm trying really hard to fall out of love with you and this is not helping.'

There was still no answer.

His skin was like velvet, soft and warm to the touch. I closed my eyes and snuggled against him as I finally fell asleep.

CHAPTER SEVEN

Proposer's Blog

Day 6: The Alphabetti Proposal. Location: My kitchen.

Suzie ended up staying at mine last night, in my guest room of course. After a hard day for her yesterday and a hard one facing her today, I wanted to give her something to cheer her up. What better way to wake up than with a proposal breakfast in bed.

I luckily had a tin of Heinz Alphabetti Spaghetti in my cupboard. My nephew loves the stuff, so I always have some in for when he comes to stay. I figured I would do spaghetti on toast and spell out the proposal around the rim of the plate. I cooked the Alphabetti carefully, ensuring that I didn't break up any of the letters whilst stirring, then tipped the contents onto the plate whilst I was cooking the toast. Finding all the letters needed for the proposal was a lot harder than I thought. There was no Y – there were six Zs, six, but no Y. So I used a V and part of an L. There was only one R, so I had to use a P and the other part of the L. By the time the haphazard proposal was in place, the Alphabetti was cold and the toast was black, and the smoke had set off the smoke alarm, which roused Suzie from her sleep. I quickly cooked eggs instead, and fresh toast, and positioned the eggs like eyes *on the plate. I gave the plate a squirt of ketchup for the smiley mouth, perfected the arrangement of the proposal, and added the remains of the Alphabetti – which I warned Suzie not to eat as I had messed with it so much – as hair. The breakfast in bed part was ruined as Suzie came down to make sure I was still alive as the house was filled with smoke, so we ended up having breakfast in the kitchen instead.*

The reaction. I haven't seen Suzie smile like that for a long time. It seems everyone has an inner child and Suzie's likes Alphabetti.

I sat in the car outside Jules's place with Harry sitting next to me.

'Are you ready for this?'

I nodded.

'I don't want you to do anything you don't want to do. I feel like I've pushed you into this.'

'No, I want to do this. I'm not delighted, of course I'm not. But you can't control who you fall in love with.' If it was that easy, I wouldn't have spent the last two years in love with my best friend. I sighed. 'I want her to be happy again and if Badger can help with that then I'm ok with it.'

I got out of the car before I could change my mind and strode up the path.

When Jules opened the door, I tried to find some words to apologise, to make things good between us, but I had nothing. I was still hurting over this.

Tears welled in her eyes and I found myself stepping forward to hug her. I held her tight as she sobbed against me, and I soaked her jumper with my own tears.

I felt Harry shuffle us forward so we were no longer standing on the front door step, then he closed the door behind us.

'Badger!' Harry called. 'Put the kettle on, I think we'll all need a cup of tea in a minute.'

*

I tucked into a slice of Jules's delicious banana cake as I watched Badger lying on the floor, playing with Bella. It was clear for everyone to see how much he adored this little girl that wasn't his.

Harry was outside in the garden, taking some of our calls.

Jules and I had cried and apologised and cried some more whilst Harry and Badger had loudly and diplomatically talked about football. It would be a while before things were back to normal between us, but we were getting there.

'So you spent the night with Harry last night,' Jules said as she wiped the table.

I swallowed a big lump of cake. 'How do you know that?'

'We're following the blog too. It sounds like a lot of fun. But my point being that Harry doesn't have a guest room. Badger told me he doesn't.'

'He does. Just not one with a bed in it.'

'So…' she smiled as she sat down opposite me with her tea in her hand.

'So I slept in his bed. It doesn't mean anything. We've done it before.'

'Of course it means something, you're in love with him.'

'In love with who?' Harry asked as he came through the back door.

Jules paled.

'Tiny Tim,' I blurted out in panic at the same time Jules said, 'Ryan Gosling,' and slapped her hand down on Ryan's photo in the magazine she had been reading.

Harry looked between us. 'Which is it?'

'Well, we were talking about Tiny Tim before and Jules said he reminded her of Ryan Gosling and I said I loved him and Jules thought I was talking about Tiny Tim, but I wasn't.'

Jules stared at me, open mouthed, as I prattled on with my excuse. Way to play it cool.

Harry seemed to buy this, or in the least was willing to humour me. He joined me at the table, stealing a large crumb from my plate, as he slid the magazine towards him.

'So Ryan Gosling eh? What is it about him?'

I stared at Harry and dragged my eyes down to look at Ryan's photo. As beautiful as Ryan was, he was no match for Harry. Now I had to find something I liked about a man that had barely even registered on my radar. No man had, not since Harry had walked into my life.

'The white shirt,' I said, triumphantly, glad I had found something. 'There's something very sexy about a man that wears a white shirt. Ryan wears it particularly well.'

Jules' incredulous look deepened. Then she quickly recovered herself as Harry looked up. 'Have you ever been in love, Harry?'

I stared at Jules behind Harry's back. Why was she asking when she knew all about his past and his determination to protect himself?

He looked away as he cut himself a slice of the cake, though I suspected it was so he had something to do with his hands, rather than actually wanting any cake. 'Once. A year or so ago. It didn't work out.'

I stared at him. He'd fallen in love. After everything he'd said about not believing in it, he'd let himself fall in love anyway and whoever she was had let him down. There had been so many women for Harry, moving from one to the next before any emotional attachments could be made on either side. But somehow, amongst the many was one he had fallen for. A year or so ago? So someone he was seeing when I knew him. I racked my brain for faces and names of conquests past.

A thought occurred to me. 'There hasn't been anyone for you for nearly a year. Apart from Samantha. Was it the girl you were seeing before the big gap? Amelia. Did she break your heart?'

'No.' He laughed. 'Things were never that serious with Amelia.'

'But why have you not been with anyone for so long?'

He shrugged. 'Just haven't found anyone that took my fancy.'

'That didn't stop you before, anything with a pulse took your fancy.'

'It was just... I've been busy. A girlfriend would have just got in the way.'

I was confused. He was clearly embarrassed about this and I didn't understand why.

'So Harry.' Jules interrupted, clearly trying to change the subject. 'Did you catch that documentary on the pyramids?'

Harry was a big history buff, something he shared in common with Jules. But I was not to be put off.

'But you've not been busy. You've been with me at work, and most nights you were round my house or I was round yours.'

He looked at me and the penny suddenly clunked into place. He literally had dropped everything for me, to be with me in my moment of need, including any potential girlfriends.

I was so confused. Was all of that really just down to pity? Or something more... But Samantha was right, if he wanted to be with me, he would be.

Badger walked into the kitchen carrying Bella, slicing through the silent tension like a knife through butter.

'Want some juice, Bella?' Badger said, plonking her on my lap, which was a welcome distraction.

'Joows,' said Bella, her hands reaching out for the cup that Badger was quickly filling.

Seeing that Badger was on the case, Bella relaxed into me, sucking her thumb as she played unconsciously with my hair.

Badger stopped to look at the paper on the table. As he leaned over he touched Jules's shoulder which made her smile. It made me smile too, but I was distracted as Bella wriggled around impatiently on my lap.

'Dada,' she said to Badger, reaching out her hands for her juice.

My heart jolted like a punch to the chest and Badger paled.

'I've been showing her photos of Jack and trying to get her to say it. Now she says it to me too. To be fair, everything is Dada at the moment – the ducks, the ice cream van, the butterflies – she just points and says Dada,' Badger gabbled in a wild panic.

'Its fine, Badger, don't worry.' I swallowed a huge lump in my throat.

'I'll tell her all about her Daddy, when she's older, show her the photos, tell her about all the mischief we got up to. Jack won't be forgotten.' Badger was so serious. I looked down, brushing away imaginary crumbs from my lap. I looked at my watch, wanting to be out of there.

As always, Harry came to my rescue. 'Well, we better go, I've got that meeting with the magazine shortly and I've got some emails I need to send.'

I got up quickly, planted a kiss on Bella's soft cheeks and passed her back to Badger. I gave Jules a quick hug and hurriedly said my goodbyes and was out on the street a moment later. We rounded the trees at the end of their garden, sheltering us from the view of the house.

I put my hands to my knees and let out a gust of breath as if I'd been running or holding my breath for a really long time.

Harry stroked my back soothingly.

'Did I do ok?'

'You did brilliantly.'

I looked up at him to see if he was being honest or just being kind.

'No seriously. It takes a shit load of courage to do what you did today.'

'I want her to be happy again, I do, but it still bloody hurts.'

'I know, there would be something wrong with you if it didn't.'

I exhaled again. 'The "Dada" moment was a step too far.'

'Yes, I gathered that.'

I smiled as I straightened. 'You know me so well.'

'I know you need ice cream right about now.'

'Yes please.'

'Fortunately for you I know the perfect place.'

*

There were lots of Italian ice cream places in town, with thick, delicious ice creams and an array of different toppings. I wondered which one Harry was going to take me to. The one on Leicester Square was wonderful. I fancied a sundae, maybe with chopped bananas and chocolate sauce over the top. Mmmm…

So I was surprised when we parked up and walked down towards Tower Bridge. The place was teeming with tourists, but sitting on the side of the road, with quite a long queue considering how cold it was, was a battered pink and white ice cream van.

I finished another call, the fifth since we had left Jules's house. I didn't know why we were so busy all of a sudden, but I certainly wasn't complaining.

I stared at the van in confusion as we joined the back of the queue.

'Don't look like that, you ice cream snob.' Harry nudged me as he saw my face.

'There was no look.'

'Oh there was. It looked like this.'

Harry sucked in his cheeks and scowled like he was sucking on a bitter lemon.

I laughed. 'I like a ninety-nine as much as the next person.'

'Well you're going to be disappointed, Roberto doesn't do ninety-nines. But he does do the best ice creams for miles around.'

We shuffled up the queue, but I remained unconvinced.

I took another call whilst we waited, this one wanted candy floss and fairground rides in his back garden. Now that was sweet. I promised to email him back as soon as I could check the prices of the things he wanted.

Then we were next in the queue.

'Banana ok?' Harry asked. 'Or the chocolate orange is to die for.'

'Banana's fine.'

Roberto was not the Italian looking man I was expecting. There was no curly Mario moustache or dark eyes. I sort of expected him to be wearing a red and white stripy apron and have a big chef's hat, I'm not sure why. I was even more disappointed when instead of greeting Harry in Italian, he grunted to us in a thick Yorkshire accent as he swapped money for two pots of ice cream. Harry's was so dark it looked almost black.

We went and sat on benches overlooking the Thames to watch the boats that always seemed to go up and down it, no matter what time of day it was.

I dug into my ice cream and took a big mouthful.

'Oh my God.' I closed my eyes as the tastes exploded on my tongue. 'This is amazing.'

Harry grinned. 'I told you so.'

'It tastes so bananery.'

'Well it is banana ice cream.'

'Yes but banana flavoured things taste like powdered banana. Most banana things have never even seen a banana in their whole lives. This actually has banana bits in it.'

'Here, try mine.'

Harry scooped up a large lump of the black ice cream and fed it to me. The dark chocolate was complemented perfectly by the coffee and walnut.

'We need to come back here again and try the other flavours.'

'He only does ten with the occasional special, no toppings, no sauce, but he makes an absolute fortune.'

'I bet he does. And what a pitch too, with the tourists visiting the Tower and the bridge.'

I curled my legs up to my chest as I carried on eating.

I wanted to talk to him about what he had said before, that he had taken a year off from women so he could be there for me when I needed him most.

As I licked the last of the ice cream from my spoon, I reached down and held his hand, entwining my fingers with his. Although he gently squeezed my hand, he barely seemed to notice as he busily typed an email on his phone.

Suddenly he leapt up as if he had been burnt. My hand fell from his and back onto the bench.

'Crap, I better go, I have that meeting with Silver Linings, the magazine that wants to feature my blog. You ok to get back on your own?'

I nodded.

Harry passed me his half eaten pot of ice cream, kissed me fleetingly on the cheek and took off at a run, smashing into a tall, beautiful redhead as he went. She toppled and nearly hit the floor but Harry's reflexes were fast and he caught her, pulling her back to her feet with ease and gentleness.

I couldn't hear what was said as they stood there talking, Harry's hands still on her arms, but as she twirled her hair round her finger and threw her head back laughing, it was obvious he was working his charm again. Sure enough, within thirty seconds of them meeting, the redhead was handing over her number.

Samantha's words rung in my head. If he wanted to be with me, he would be. Watching him so effortlessly charm this woman without any reticence cemented that in my brain. He just didn't see me that way, never had, never would.

Harry threw me two big inane thumbs up as the girl fumbled in her bag and I threw two sarcastic ones back. As the swap was made, Harry kissed her on the cheek, just as he'd done to me seconds before, and ran off again.

The redhead and I watched him go and then we locked eyes as he disappeared from view. Her face was a picture of smug happiness. I'm not sure what mine was, but obviously not anything good as she recoiled slightly from me as she walked away.

*

I was standing naked in my bedroom when the front door crashed open. After Harry's departure hours before, I'd treated myself to a bit of retail therapy – buying a wildly inappropriate dress and ridiculously high heeled shoes. I'd just been trying them on, realised the underwear I was wearing was not suitable and had just taken them off to replace them with something else when Harry's feet thundered up the stairs.

'Suzie!' Harry roared.

I launched myself across the bed and slammed the door just as he reached the top.

'Where are you?'

'Bedroom. I'm naked. Hang on a sec.'

To my great surprise, Harry burst in, with his hand clamped over his eyes.

'Harry!'

'This can't wait.'

'Yes it bloody well can.'

Harry turned and grabbed my robe from the back of the door. With his eyes tightly closed he offered it out and I quickly pulled it on.

'Ok, what the hell was so urgent?'

Harry opened one eye and then, seeing I was safely covered up, he opened both. He reached out and grabbed my arms, his smile so big, his eyes so wide, I wasn't sure if he'd taken some hallucinogenic drug.

'Suzie, shit, I don't know where to start.'

Oh please don't let this be another woman story. Seeing him with that redhead this morning was bad enough.

'The beginning.' I wrapped my hands around his arms as he didn't seem likely to let me go any time soon.

'The video of my cow proposal has over two million hits on YouTube.'

I stared at him whilst the weight of those words sunk in.

'Holy shit!' I whispered.

'That's just the start. We now have close to thirty thousand followers on the blog.'

That at least explained the increase in calls today.

'You need to sit down for the next bit.' He pushed me down gently onto the bed, with his hands on my shoulders. Then he changed his mind. 'No, stand up. I think.' He pulled me to my feet.

'Just tell me.'

'I had a chat with the magazine people today.'

The bottom dropped out of my world. 'You're leaving, aren't you? The magazine wants you to go and work for them instead.'

He stopped with his excitement for a moment and kissed my forehead so sweetly that my heart leapt into my mouth.

'No. It's not that. They've offered us a deal. You won't believe this. I can't believe it myself. I can't believe that I actually managed to talk them into it.'

'Harry, for the love of God, what?'

'They asked me where I foresaw this proposal thing going and I told them I wanted to show you the world – I wanted to take you to every tiny little pocket of it and propose to you in the most beautiful, most barren, most extreme places. They were keen, very keen, I could see that. Suddenly I found myself telling them that I had a meeting with The Daily Mail later this afternoon, that they were interested in making it a daily article. I don't know why I said it, but it worked. The next thing they did was offer me this.'

He pulled out a crumpled piece of paper from his pocket and passed it to me. I read it, and read it again. The words danced in front of my eyes.

I looked at Harry. 'Is this what I think it is?'

He swallowed. 'Two round-the-world tickets. We leave on Friday.'

I sat down heavily on the bed as I read the words again.

'This is a joke.'

'No joke. They want exclusivity. I'm allowed to blog one more time on our website to tell our followers where to catch me next, after that I'll be writing for Silver Linings. They will feature my daily blog on their website and the best bits will be featured in their weekly magazine. We can post pictures and stuff as well. I made a deal too, that every blog will have links back to our website and our contact details et cetera, so you'll gain good exposure for your company out of this too.'

'Our company.'

He waved it away.

'Harry we can't leave, our company is just starting to take off. We've worked so hard to get where we are. We need to be here to help our clients.'

'You need a holiday, and it's just three months – ninety days. We can handle emails on our mobiles, take our laptops with us. I've had a word with Jules and, as she's at home with Bella, she was happy to take all our calls and then she can email over the main details to us. We can go through it with her before we go and Badger says he'd be happy to help too.'

I stared at him and read the contract again.

'Suzie, you have to say yes.'

'Then yes.'

Harry whooped like a big kid, yanked me to my feet and swung me round so fast I could barely breathe. I laughed and giggled against him. Around the world. Apart from a couple of family driving holidays to Spain and France, I'd never been out of Britain. I'd never even been on a plane.

The phone rang in the office but for once I ignored it.

'Harry, wait, wait, stop swinging me round, you're making me dizzy.'

Harry slowed and stopped, holding me steady as I wobbled a bit.

'Where are we going first? Do you have a plan? What do I need to pack?'

'I need to thrash a lot of this out with Sunlounger, the holiday company that the magazine are working with to run this feature. I have a meeting with them tomorrow. There will be a rough plan but also room for improvisation too. We're going to Australia - '

My heart roared in my chest. 'Harry I've always wanted to go there. It's so beautiful.'

He grinned. 'I know. I was quite insistent that was on our list. We fly to the Galapagos Islands first.'

'But this is all so expensive.'

'I would love to take credit for that, but Silver Linings and Sunlounger are paying for everything. A lot of it will be freebies or heavily discounted from the hotels and flight companies, knowing that they will get good coverage in the magazine.'

'But why?'

'Two million reasons why. Two million people and counting have watched our cow proposal, that's potentially two million people that will go and buy Silver Linings to follow our story.'

None of this made any sense.

'Harry, are we seriously doing this?'

He nodded

I squealed and launched myself at him, throwing my arms round his neck.

'Now that was the reaction I was hoping for,' he said, holding me tight against him.

CHAPTER EIGHT

Proposer's Blog

Day 7: The Blue Plaque Proposal. Location: Hyde Park.

I love history – the interesting snippets, the gossip, the intrigue, the filth and the glamour. Who was sleeping with who. Delving into the past is like reading a copy of Hello, there was so much backstabbing, treason, murder and sordid affairs. Suzie loves it too – she insists she doesn't, but with every little bit of history I tell her, her eyes light up like a kid in a sweet shop.

London is filled with so much history. I love how you can be walking the streets alongside men and women in their power suits, amongst red buses, black cabs and high rise office buildings, and suddenly you round a corner and – beyond the vision of the office workers who walk past it every day – there's this tiny corner of the city wall built nearly two thousand years before.

The blue plaques are great for this, just wander around London and you might unexpectedly come across the place where Samuel Pepys lived, where he wrote those famous diaries hundreds of years before.

I was with Suzie the other day when we stumbled across one for Ian Fleming. She's a huge James Bond fan, read all the books many times. She got very excited to have found where he lived.

This gave me an idea.

So, after work, I gave her a map with some of the more interesting blue plaques marked on it. Suzie lapped it up. We strolled through the streets with Suzie almost yelling with excitement as we found Charles Dickens, Florence Nightingale and Winston Churchill. The funny ones are good too, Sherlock Holmes in Baker Street and my favourite, and now Suzie's favourite too, simply reads: 'Jacob von Hogflume 1864-1909 Inventor of time travel. Lived here in 2189.

So after our little treasure hunt, we 'found' ourselves in Hyde Park, one of our favourite places. As we walked through the naked trees, amongst the snowdrops and crocuses that indicate the start of new life, we found a bench we regularly sit on and on it was a new blue plaque that Suzie had never noticed before. It read:

'It was here, on this bench, on February 17th, that Harry proposed to Suzie.'

I love seeing Suzie smile, it's one of my all-time favourite things in the world.

This is my last blog on this page. Next time you visit here, you'll be automatically redirected to my new blog page at Silver Linings magazine. You will still be notified as normal of new updates. As most of you will be aware, from our news page, our One Hundred Proposals is about to go international. We fly to the Galapagos Islands in three days.

Proposer's Blog

Day 9: The Underwear Proposal. Location: Suzie's Bedroom

We leave for the Galapagos Islands tomorrow, and then we'll spend ninety days travelling around the world. There is so much to see and not enough time to see it in. But we have to pack for every eventuality too.

We packed together as the amount Suzie wanted to take would fit in five suitcases rather than one – so I decided to help limit the intake.

I came up with a strict rule. I said one of everything. I thought that was fair.

One pair of jeans, one smart top, one pair of smart trousers, one pair of combats, one pair of hiking trainers, one pair of black flat sparkly sandals – they'll go with everything – one dress, one pair of shorts, one vest, one T-shirt, one long sleeved T-shirt, one hoodie, one cardigan, one hat, one scarf, one pair of gloves, one swimming costume, one bikini – because apparently a bikini doesn't count as a swimming costume, as it's so tiny I let that one slide. Every time I turned my back, she sneaked things into the corners of the case, or hid them underneath already allowed clothes. She thought I didn't know. I turned my back a lot.

Suddenly she remembered her underwear. Finally, my big moment.

I presented her with a box of little shorts with my face and the words 'Marry Me' printed on them. She didn't stop laughing for ten minutes.

Then she said that, as nice as they were, she would probably take her own underwear. When I asked her why, she laughed and said if she was with another man and if it ever came down to sex, seeing my face whilst undressing her would probably put the other man off. I told her that was all the more reason for taking them.

Then we had a big row.

She accused me of having double standards and asked why it was ok for me to screw around with a different woman every night but not for her. I did point out that she wasn't gay so she probably wouldn't be screwing around with a different woman every night anyway.

She said I'd probably have a woman in every port and she'd be left sitting in the hotel like a Billy No Mates.

I'm sure the topic of other men and women doesn't come up with other would-be proposers.

An excellent start to our holiday.

*

I stared across the aisle of the plane at Harry, sitting two rows in front of me, as he flirted with the air hostess. The cabin was busy with people getting ready for departure but she seemed to only have time for him.

I had been so excited about this trip, but my excitement had quickly dwindled over the week. In between all our planning and preparations, Harry had been out with Kate, the redhead, three times. The sex, apparently, was amazing. Of course I was jealous, but I think the worry of what he would be like on our holiday was also starting to set in. I think the final straw had been when Harry had written into our round-the-world plan, arrangements to meet with an old girlfriend, Chloe, who he had remained friends with and now lived in New York.

I suppose I couldn't expect Harry to remain celibate over the three months around the world, he'd already done that for almost a year after Jack had died, but I didn't want to be sitting in a foreign country alone. Hooking up with my own man was almost out of the question. I was hopeless when it came to flirting or approaching men. And on the rare occasions men approached me, I became a bumbling mess that quickly put them off.

Maybe I would try a little practice flirting now. If Harry could do it, I could do it too. I turned to the bloke next to me and I was disappointed to see a short, bald man in his late fifties, sweating profusely from every orifice and mopping his brow with a pink satin handkerchief. I glanced down to see he was holding hands with the man next to him, a man dressed entirely in black with a dragon earring.

I looked around for someone else who I could flirt with, but happy couples were everywhere. Honeymoon couples, middle-aged couples, even elderly couples who had probably spent their entire lives together.

I was alone.

The plane started to move and I gripped the arms of the chair so hard my knuckles turned white.

That was another thing I was upset about. This was my first time on a plane and amongst the manic preparations over the last few days I had discovered I was a nervous flyer. Nervous was an understatement. My stomach was rolling, my heart racing. In my nightmares I had seen our plane explode, crash into the sea, crash into another plane, and even get abducted by aliens. I wanted Harry to hold my hand and distract me but instead he was over there staring at the air hostess like she was the only woman in the world.

I hadn't told Harry about my fear of flights. I didn't want him to know that I was petrified. This flight was thirteen hours to Miami, then another two hours or so to Guayaquil airport in Ecuador, followed by a another two hour trip on a tiny little plane to Baltra Island. It was going to be a long day.

I looked over at Harry again. The air hostess was showing him how to use the seatbelt, as if he didn't know.

The plane rocked a bit as it bumped over the runway, but it was enough to make all those nightmares come flooding back.

Jules had recommended that I take sleeping tablets. Apparently I'd wake up the other side of the world, completely refreshed and none the wiser about the thirteen elapsed hours.

I swallowed two tablets and closed my eyes as I waited for the effects. There were announcements, people chatting, the noise of the engines. It all became white noise.

I heard the roar of the engines, the pitch of the plane as it took off, my ears popped and we levelled out. We were now approximately thirty thousand feet in the air. I'd researched it over the last few days. That was a long way to go when plummeting to the ground.

But I was thankful that the sleeping tablets already seemed to be taking effect. My last thought as I drifted into oblivion was of burning fire balls of molten metal crashing into the sea like meteorites.

*

I woke as the plane jolted underneath me. My eyes shot open with panic but buildings whizzed past the small aeroplane windows outside and I realised we had landed. My head felt so heavy and my eyes were already drooping, taking me back into the dark abyss again. My next realisation was that I was lying on the chest of the bald man next to me, a small patch of dribble soaking his shirt. My hand was resting on his crotch.

I quickly struggled to get up but the bald man stopped me with his arm round my shoulders.

'Take it easy,' said the bald man in a voice that sounded just like Harry. 'Give yourself a chance to wake up.'

I peered up at the bald man and to my surprise found Harry staring down at me.

'You're not the bald man.'

I felt like I was drunk.

'Not the last time I checked, no.'

'But…' I looked around me in confusion. The man with the dragon earring had also gone, replaced by another younger man in a suit.

'We swapped seats,' Harry explained.

'Oh.'

I relaxed into him before I remembered I was still angry at him, but with his hand in my hair, stroking me, it hardly seemed important any more.

'Are we in Miami?'

'Yes.'

I tried to surreptitiously wipe away some of the dribble from Harry's shirt when I noticed a huge skull and crossbones ring on my wedding finger. I looked up at him in confusion.

'What?' he asked.

I waggled my finger, as much as I could with the heavy weight of the ring on it.

'Oh yes, that. We got engaged.'

'Whilst I was asleep?'

'Yes. It was quite a big proposal, very elaborate. I'm sorry you missed it.'

'And I said yes?'

'Well no, obviously. But the bald man next to you nodded your head for you which everyone in the plane took to be a yes.'

'Everyone on the plane?'

'Yes, it was quite the show. I did record it on my phone. I'll show you later.'

I looked down at the ring and smiled. I liked the idea of being engaged to Harry a lot, even though it was a fake engagement.

'I know the ring isn't exactly to your taste, it was donated to us.' Harry indicated the seat where the man with the dragon earring had sat.

'I love it.' I said, honestly. Any symbol of our engagement, no matter how hideous, was fine by me.

I returned my attention to the dribble and Harry watched me try to wipe it off. I blushed. 'I dribbled on your shirt.'

'I noticed. It's ok.'

I closed my eyes and leaned into him, sleepily.

'I love you, Harry.'

I felt him tense under me straight away. Crap, crap, crap.

I looked up at him, his eyes were wide with horror or shock.

'Not like that. Never like that,' I said.

He continued to stare at me.

Thankfully then the seatbelt light went off and everyone around us scrabbled to their feet, reaching into overhead lockers and fighting their way down the aisle so they could be first off the plane. I lumbered to my feet as well, my legs not performing as I wanted them to.

I managed to get a few people between me and Harry as I walked up the aisle, trying to calm down my blushing cheeks. I felt so sleepy. What happened to waking feeling refreshed? I felt like I could sleep for a hundred years. I got to the end of the aeroplane tunnel and as everyone veered left to collect their baggage and go through passport control, I found a little bench to the right, out of view of the other debarking passengers.

I sat down and rubbed my face, willing myself to wake up so I didn't stagger through passport control looking like I was on drugs.

'I told you not to take those sleeping tablets,' Harry said, appearing from nowhere and passing me a bottle of water. 'How many did you take?'

'Just two.'

'Jesus.' He knelt in front of me. 'You're only supposed to take one. No wonder you were out for so long.' He peered into my eyes with concern.

'I'm fine.' I batted away his hand as he felt my forehead.

'Can you walk?'

'Of course I can.' I stood up and my legs wobbled treacherously.

'That doesn't look at all suspicious, does it, for the American authorities?' Harry sighed, swinging his rucksack on his back, followed by my own. 'Here.' He scooped me up as if I weighed nothing and walked purposefully down towards passport control.

'And this doesn't?'

'We're married, honeymooners, play along, look at me as if you really do love me.'

I could do that.

I wrapped my arms round his neck and nuzzled into his neck. He smelt so good.

'Here we go Mrs Forbes,' Harry whispered in my ear, his hot breath on my skin making my gut clench with desire.

'Good evening sir, would you mind putting your girlfriend down for a moment.'

'My wife,' Harry said, without batting an eye. 'We're on honeymoon, and I promised to carry her over the threshold of every country we enter.'

I glanced at the passport officer. He didn't seem amused.

Harry slid me down, but held me pressed tight against him.

The man looked at us, looked at our passports and back at us again.

'Married you say?'

I nodded, happily. Oh God. What if he asked us questions about our wedding? Would he be suspicious about the lack of wedding rings? Wouldn't we have a marriage certificate with us? Did we need one? What if he discovered we were lying? Would we be thrown in jail for fraud?

The man smiled at us and passed us back our passports. 'Welcome to America.'

I let out a huge sigh of relief which drew the man's attention to me again. Harry ushered me on, his hand clamped firmly round my shoulders.

'Oh, sir,' the man called after us and my heart started thumping loudly again. We turned back, both smiling rigidly. 'Congratulations.'

'Thank you.' Harry turned me away before I sagged to my knees and confessed the lie and we were in the safety of the main airport moments later.

Proposer's Blog

Day 10: The mile high proposal. Location: Thirty thousand feet over the Atlantic

So we've just landed in Miami, we have a half hour wait before we fly south to Ecuador and then in a much smaller plane west to the Galapagos Islands. So a quick update of my latest proposal.

I'd arranged with one of the air hostesses to use the intercom to propose to Suzie. I started off by playing

'*Marry You*' *by Bruno Mars and singing along to the lyrics. Nothing could have prepared me for the reaction I got.*

First the air crew joined in as backing singers, helping me out with the chorus and clapping their hands in the air in time with the music.

When the chorus came round a second time the whole cabin joined in. It was one of the most uplifting experiences of my life, I literally had goose bumps as I walked up the aisle to propose to Suzie.

Unfortunately she slept through the whole thing.

Buoyed up by the support of the crowd, I proposed anyway and with a little help from the man next to her, nodding her head for her, she said yes.

I won't get too excited though. A forced yes is hardly the yes I was looking for.

Though when she eventually did wake up and saw, from the donated skull and crossbones ring on her finger, that she was engaged, she did take it all in her stride.

Watch the video clip of my proposal here.

The next few hours passed in a blur of airports, two more plane rides, more passport control, baggage carousels and a taxi ride. I was so tired it was ridiculous. I wasn't sure if it was still the effects of the sleeping tablets or the general fatigue of travelling.

It was dark and I guessed from the quietness of our surroundings that it was late at night or early hours in the morning.

Through my sleep hazed eyes I was aware of the harbour, filled with lots of white boats bobbing gently on the water. I registered that our boat was called The Star before Harry ushered me inside. A man dressed all in white showed us to our cabin. It was small but brightly lit, with cream walls and the comfiest looking bed. A large window filled one wall and outside stars peppered the night sky. I crashed out on the bed and sank into the pillows, watching the water ripple in the moonlight.

'I can't believe we're here, in the Galapagos Islands. It seems so unreal,' I said, my eyelids drooping.

'I can't believe that we have arrived in one of the most beautiful places in the world and all you want to do is sleep.'

I yawned, hearing the fondness in his voice. 'It's been a long day. I got engaged, I got married.'

'And now for our honeymoon.'

I opened one eye and saw Harry pull off his shirt. Bloody hell. The man should never wear clothes. I loved his arms, so strong and safe. When he took his jeans off I couldn't resist lifting my head off the bed to watch. Mmm... the tight little shorts, his great, muscular thighs.

I looked up and realised he was watching me.

He stalked towards me like a panther and knelt on the bed by my feet. I giggled at the predatory look in his eyes as if he wanted to do dark and evil things to me. 'Are you ready?'

I closed my eyes, sleepily. 'Sure, I'm insatiable, I could go all night.'

I felt his hands either side of my head and I looked up into his face as he leaned over me.

'Really, because you look exhausted.'

I closed my eyes again. Sleep was there. If I relaxed it would take me within seconds. 'You start. Just give me five minutes to sleep and I'll be right there.'

Harry huffed dramatically. 'That's what every husband wants on their wedding night, to find out that he's so good in bed that his bride falls asleep during the act.'

'If you want, I'll throw a few cursory oohs and ahhs your way, make you feel better.'

'That would be great.'

'Ohhh Harry. That feels so good.'

'I haven't started yet.'

I felt his weight disappear off the bed and I peered round to see him taking my shoes and socks off.

'Let me know when things get going then.'

'I would hope that you would know.'

I smiled. 'You know, just in case I miss it.'

He flashed me a dark look and I closed my eyes again, this time I knew I wouldn't be opening them again, not least for several hours.

I felt my breathing going heavy and just as I felt myself fall asleep, I heard Harry speak again.

'Trust me Suzie, you would know.'

*

I sat up in bed and watched the iridescent blue waves glide past. The sun sparkled off the water and there was a heat coming from outside that we hadn't felt in Britain for many, many months.

I quickly ate the breakfast that Harry had left on a tray by my bed. I was starving – and the eggs, toast, croissants and jam filled the gap perfectly.

There was a note on the tray telling me to get changed, and I guessed from the bright pink wetsuit hanging on the back of the door that I was supposed to get changed into that.

I dressed quickly, hating how clingy the wetsuit was around the stomach and how loose it was around the crotch, reminding me of a baggy nappy.

I raced up the stairs and out onto the deck. In my sleep-induced state the night before I hadn't appreciated the beauty of the little yacht. Little blue sofas, sun loungers, and double beds dotted the sun deck, which was lined with AstroTurf to give it a garden feel.

Voices at the back of the boat drew my attention and I went down some steps to get to the launch deck. A dozen people were milling about, in various stages of getting ready for snorkelling and scuba diving.

My heart leapt with joy. I had done a lot of scuba diving a few years before – there were some brilliant wrecks around the British coast and I had seen many of them, at varying depths. British diving required warm clothes, a thermal undersuit and a drysuit over the top so I was padded out like the Michelin man. Diving here would be so much freer and the visibility, I expected, would be outstanding. I had never dived in warm waters before, though I'd had wetsuit training in a local pool. I was hoping to see something a bit more exciting than a few plasters and hair ties today.

I noticed Harry chatting to one of the crew. He looked magnificent in his wetsuit, the black neoprene clinging to his body like a second skin. It was unzipped slightly at the chest, and I could see his smooth skin glistening in the sunlight.

I said hello to a few of the other passengers as I approached him. He continued to talk but slung his arm round my shoulder, including me in the conversation.

He introduced our dive leader, Elias, who was beautiful – with warm caramel skin and dazzling green eyes, flecked with gold. His wetsuit was tied at the waist, revealing a wonderfully toned, brown chest. He was obviously smaller than Harry, everyone was, but he was clearly very strong – years hauling around heavy diving equipment had done things for his body that working out in the gym simply couldn't achieve. When Elias took my hand to shake it, I felt a spark of pure lust slice through me. His eyes darkened as he continued to hold my hand. He had felt it too.

Though any thoughts I might have had of me and Elias finding our own little island paradise somewhere to get to know each other better, if those sorts of things actually happened in real life, were quickly quelled, when Harry introduced me to Elias as his girlfriend.

Elias dropped my hand like he had been burnt.

'My apologies, I was told you were friends,' Elias said, with a glorious Hispanic accent.

I was confused too. There had been incidences over the last few days where we had lied about our relationship status, to Frank to get the hot air balloon ride at such short notice and the American authorities the day before, but I wasn't sure what gain we would get from lying here.

Harry pulled me tighter against him, claiming me as his own. The vibes telling Elias to back off were so strong, I was surprised he didn't pee up my leg to mark his territory. Well if Harry wanted to prove we were together, I could do that. Feeling brazen and silly, I ran my hand down Harry's back and squeezed his bum hard. Harry jolted in shock and stared down at me incredulously. I raised an eyebrow, daring him to protest. Elias smoothly changed the subject, telling us about the dive instead. He talked to Harry, hardly even glancing at me again.

It seemed the dive route we were going to go on was the site of some old volcanic activity, that had left the sea bed textured with walls, ridges and trenches which were now home to a huge array of sea life.

I was itching to get started.

Elias left to help the other passengers and I looked around the bay we were in. We were too far out to appreciate the true beauty of the Galapagos Islands, I hoped that would come later. The boat glided through the tranquil indigo waters, barely causing a ripple. Out in the distance, green hills undulated in rolling peaks, forming a loose circle around us.

Harry turned me into him with his hands on my shoulders, giving me his full attention. I loved it when he looked at me like that, as if I was the only woman in the world. I ignored the voice in my head that told me he had stared at many women like that. He arched his eyebrow at me.

'What?' I tried to supress the smirk.

'I was just surprised by the bum squeeze.'

I shrugged. 'I was surprised by the upgrade in our relationship status.'

Harry seemed completely unabashed as he lowered his mouth to whisper in my ear, turning my legs to jelly as his hot breath moved over my neck.

'People are more inclined to help with proposals when they believe they are real.'

It was a fair point but I was still annoyed that the only man that had looked at me in the last two years had just been scared away.

'And nothing to do with the fact that Elias is some kind of god?'

I blushed as Elias scooted round Harry at that moment to grab a mask for one of the other passengers.

Harry glossed over my embarrassing outburst.

'How did you sleep?'

'Went out like a light.'

'After the great sex we had, of course.'

I smiled at him sweetly. 'It might have been great for you darling, but it certainly didn't rock my world.'

I saw Elias wince as he walked away, though nothing seemed to bring Harry down, not even a slur on his manhood. He smiled. 'I'll try better tonight then, my love.'

Before I could come up with a smart answer, the boat juddered to a stop and Harry instinctively held me to stop me toppling over.

Activity around us suddenly intensified as people finished their preparations.

I quickly kitted up, clumsily pulling on an air tank and weight belt, finding a mask that fitted and struggling to put the fins on my feet. Harry seemed to kit up with an ease and elegance I simply didn't possess.

I tested the regulator in my mouth to make sure the air was turned on and flowing. It was. Clearly not happy with my own ability to test my regulator, Harry took it and put it in his mouth, breathing deeply as he watched me. There was something incredibly intimate about seeing him with his mouth wrapped around the same piece of equipment that had been in my mouth seconds before.

'Happy?' I said, being forced to lean into him as he pulled the regulator towards him.

He passed it back to me and nodded.

There were six of us going on the dive, the others were just snorkelling. We were going in pairs, Harry and I watching out for each other whilst Elias would flit between the six of us, guiding us to the best places.

With one giant step I jumped in, Harry right behind me. The water was cool but not cold. The others jumped in too. Once we were ready we sank beneath the waves.

The water had crystal clear visibility, allowing us to see seemingly for miles in every direction. Coral reefs and rocks peppered the sandy bed about ten metres below us, but the water was alive, teeming with fishes of every size and colour.

Something big and silver flashed past my field of vision and I turned in that direction to see two sea lions twisting and gambolling through the water. I watched them playing until something nudged my elbow. I turned to see Harry patiently waiting for me. The other divers had already moved off, following Elias to a larger section of the reef.

Harry stayed at my side as we slowly moved through the water after the other divers. Fish swam in between us, unperturbed by our presence, but every time I tried to touch them they moved just beyond my reach.

We reached a wall of reef, the colours of the plant life, the coral and the fishes that swam around it were amazing. I had kind of expected it all to be blue – but reds, greens, golds, oranges, whites and silvers shimmered and twinkled through the water. Harry pointed to something over my shoulder and I turned to see a great ray flying through the water towards us, his great wings flapping like a giant bird. As he reached the top of the reef, hundreds of tiny fish swam out to eat the algae and parasites off his skin; this was what was known as a cleaning station and was one of the things that Elias had said we would probably see.

Harry nudged me again and I watched him descend to the sea bed. Knowing there would be more sea life in the shadows of the wall, I let the air out of my stab jacket and followed him, being careful not to kick up any sand as I neared the bottom.

I could see the other divers getting further away, but Harry was looking at something in a small crevice at the bottom of the reef. He glanced round for me and took my hand, pulling me closer to him. There hiding in the shadows was a tiny seahorse, its fins fluttering wildly as it moved in the water. My heart filled to see it. I wanted to touch it, but it looked so tiny and fragile I was afraid that doing so would break it.

Realising that we had it trapped and it was probably panicking wildly, I nudged Harry to move on, which he did and we left the little horse behind.

Out beyond the wall, the sandy sea bed stretched out into the deep blue but I could see large shadows moving out there and one was coming closer. I waited to see if it was another ray or sea lion but as it appeared from the gloom I screamed with joy through my regulator. A hammerhead shark was swimming towards us. It was the most magnificent sight as his tail propelled him silently through the water. I couldn't believe it. Of all the animals Elias had said we might encounter, the hammerhead was the one I had been most keen to see.

Harry was suddenly in front of me, protecting me as if the hammerhead was actually a great white. There was no threat here, and Elias had told us that, but Harry it seemed wasn't taking any chances.

I peered round my over protective bodyguard as the hammerhead swam over us and, with a last flick of the tail, disappeared from view.

From the amount of bubbles Harry was emitting from his regulator I knew he was breathing heavily. He turned to look at me and I gave him two big thumbs up to show him how excited I was about our visitor. When he didn't look convinced I did calming down gestures with my hands, hoping he would breathe a little slower. He moved on, following the wall but keeping his body between mine and the open sea at all times. I glanced surreptitiously at Harry's air gauge as we swam – he still had well over a hundred bar left, at this depth that would give us plenty of time.

I saw Elias up ahead, his bright green fins almost glowing in the water. He was waiting for us, making sure we were all right. I gave him the 'ok' symbol and he pointed towards something on or in the wall. Harry nodded and we followed Elias in that direction. Brightly coloured stalks of seaweed swirled gently in the water, as if caught in a breeze, fish continued to dart around us, escorting us on our swim. As we rounded a corner of the wall, I could see two of the other divers taking photos of a large turtle as it pushed its way through the water. Its eyes watched us warily as it swam away from the wall and disappeared into the blue gloom.

Of all the diving I had done, this had to be one of the best – there was so much life and colour. It couldn't possibly get any better.

Harry nudged me again and I looked around to see what other creature we had stumbled upon.

As he moved to one side, I smiled round my regulator. Propped up on the reef was a whiteboard with the words 'Marry Me' written in shells. I turned round to look for Harry, only to see him on one knee down on the sea bed.

I floated down to land in front of him and I was very aware of the divers who had been taking photos of the turtle now taking photos of us.

I quickly took my regulator out and kissed him on the cheek. I saw him smile too.

*

I sat on the sunbed under the shade of the roof canopy as the boat bobbed on the water, furiously replying to as many emails as I possibly could. In the one day I'd been away from work due to travelling, there had been fifty-six different enquiries. But despite the sudden surge in my workload, I was blissfully happy. I couldn't remember the last time I had felt this happy. I was on a plush yacht bobbing on the crystal blue waters of the Galapagos Islands. I was on holiday with my best friend and I had just been proposed to surrounded by hammerheads, turtles, rays and seahorses. My face was aching from smiling so much. Nothing could ruin my mood. Nothing.

I gritted my teeth as a stupid girly giggle broke into my reverie. No – absolutely nothing was going to bring me down today, so I was just going to studiously ignore the only tiny blip in my nirvana. Another giggle and a deep laugh from Harry and I peered over the top of the laptop to see him chatting to some blonde Barbie on the next sunbed. He had actually been talking to her for the last hour. He was now sitting next to her on her sunbed as she showed him some photos on her phone. They were sitting so close that every part of their body from the knee to the shoulder was touching. As I watched, she laughed again, nudging his knee playfully.

I closed the laptop and walked inside, Harry watched me go but I didn't look back. The bar was cooler inside and the crew were just putting the finishing touches to a buffet of cold meats, roasted vegetables, rice, pasta, and fresh fruit. I took a plate, loaded it up and found a sofa to sit down on.

As my mouth was filled with chicken, a shadow loomed over me. I sighed, really not wanting to speak to Harry at the moment. But when I looked up I was surprised to see Elias standing over me.

I quickly swallowed my food.

'Do you mind if I join you, Suzie?'

I liked the way my name sounded on his lips. There was an extra oo in my name so it sounded like Sooozie. And with his accent, it was sexy.

I indicated that he should sit down.

He looked at me with those deep green eyes and it felt like he could read my every thought and feeling. I wondered what he would make of my sudden inappropriate thoughts about him.

'I do not mean to speak out of turn, but I do not like your fiancé.'

'Harry? Why?' This surprised me, everyone loved Harry – especially the women – and he made friends so easily, being warm, charming and attentive to anyone he spoke to.

'He is out there talking to another woman while you are here alone. I see the way he looks at her too. Many men look like that, but normally with a couple who have just got engaged, the man reserves that look for his fiancée, not some woman he's just met.'

'Oh.' I couldn't lie to this gentle man, I couldn't have him thinking badly of Harry – although I didn't like him talking to Barbie either, he wasn't actually doing anything wrong. 'Elias, we're not engaged. We're not even together.' I dug around in my bag and handed him our business card. 'We create proposals for couples. That's our business. We're doing this big promotion at the moment trying to find the ultimate proposal. What happened today was just another on the list.'

Elias looked at me again and I felt like I had disappointed him in some way.

'I'm sorry we lied to you, it wasn't done maliciously. Harry just finds it easier to say to people that we're boyfriend and girlfriend, otherwise it just seems weird when he keeps proposing to me.'

'You sleep in his bed.'

'Yes, but we're friends. Nothing has ever happened between us, nor will it.'

He watched me. His eyes were startling and I found my gaze drifting to his lips – they were full and pink and I wanted to touch them, first with my fingers and then my own lips.

What was wrong with me? Had it really been that long without sex that I was willing to throw myself at the first man that smiled at me?

I was in love with Harry and just because being with him, or more to the point, not being with him, on a daily basis was sexually frustrating didn't mean that I should jump into bed with any pretty man. Though Elias was more than just pretty, he was stunning. He was still looking at me and I felt beautiful in his eyes.

'I think I like Harry even less now.'

'Why?'

'Because he lies in bed with his beautiful friend and doesn't make love to her but then sleeps around with these vacuous creatures that mean nothing to him. He is shallow, yes? He doesn't appreciate the truest beauty, the wonder of friendship in all its forms.'

My mouth was dry and I rolled my tongue around inside my teeth to attract some moisture. I tried to find the words to defend the slur on Harry's character, while at the same time being ridiculously flattered that Elias had just called me beautiful.

'I bet women throw themselves at you all the time. Women go on holiday to beautiful places like this, see someone like you, and they fancy a bit of a holiday romance. I would imagine you've slept with a lot of women over the years. I can't blame you or him. I think if beautiful men were constantly throwing themselves at me it would be very hard to say no. Especially as there's always the hope that one day, one man would be my happy ever after. I think it's hard to find love if you're not looking for it.'

'Is that what Harry is doing, looking for the one?'

'I hope so. My brother was the same, slept with lots of different women and one day there was Jules, there was no one for him after that.'

'And you? You also sleep with lots of men?'

I laughed. 'No, I can count on one hand the amount of men I've slept with.' Wow that was embarrassing, why did I say that? But there was something about this man that commanded honesty. 'I don't get the opportunities that I'm sure you and Harry do.'

'Then I think all the English men are fools if they are not appreciating your worth.' He brushed a hair fondly off my face. Oh my. 'And as for the opportunities that you say are offered to me, yes there have been a few women that have, as you say "thrown themselves" at me, but just because they are thrown doesn't mean that I catch them.'

I smiled.

'I was married to my wife for ten years. She died three years ago, there has been no one for me since.'

'Oh, Elias I'm so sorry. I know what it is like to lose someone you love.'

He smiled at me, sadly. 'I could tell. The grief in your eyes, it never really goes away. Your brother?'

I gasped. 'How did you know?'

'The grief is different when you lose a lifelong friend than to losing a lover. It taints you differently, you carry the scars in a different way, though the pain you are feeling is still the same. It never really goes away, it just becomes easier to deal with.'

I stared at this man, willing myself to not suddenly burst into tears and cry on his shoulder. He knew, he understood.

'I'm sorry, it was not my wish to make you sad. Maybe I misjudge Harry, if he has a friend as special as you, he must be pretty special too.' He leaned forward and kissed me on the forehead. 'I should go, I have jobs to attend to.' He stood and took my hand, clasped between both of his. 'Sometimes you wait for your dreams to come true, but sometimes the dream is just a fantasy, when in the real world there are things or people who could make you happier than any of your wildest dreams ever could. You should not wait any more, young Suzie.'

He kissed my hand, his eyes searing into mine, and then he turned and walked away.

I stared down at my plate of food, no longer hungry.

CHAPTER NINE

The afternoon was spent island hopping to see a plethora of wildlife. Normally people would spend a week or more travelling around the islands – we had to do it all in one day, tomorrow we were flying north to Mexico so one of the guides had volunteered to take us on a whistle stop tour of the islands to see, as he put it, 'the best bits'. We went to Punta Espinoza and saw blue footed boobies, iguanas and amazingly penguins. I had always thought penguins were only found in cold locations, but here they were on the beach of this tropical paradise. Then we zoomed across to Puerto Ayora to see the giant tortoises lumbering slowly through the trees. Our little speed boat traversed the incredible coastlines and coves, our guide trying to give us as much information and as much beauty as he possibly could in the limited time allowed. As the sun set into the sea, leaving scarlet ribbons on the water, we finished our trip visiting Cormorant Point to see the flamingos. Their bright pink plumage, reflecting off the water as they gracefully waded through the shallows, was a startling sight to see.

It was just starting to get dark as we made our way back to The Star, our yacht. I sat staring out at the waves as they darkened in the early night sky. Harry, who had been taking hundreds of photos, finally sat down by my side, pulling me in close to him with his arm round my waist.

I turned to look at him.

'Are you happy?'

I nodded and leaned against him. 'Very. I feel like I've been tense for so long and now I can finally relax'

'Good, I've seen you smiling so much today, I really like it.'

We drew closer to the yacht and I could see Barbie leaning over the rail waving at Harry, her boobs almost falling out of her little top. Harry waved back.

'And if you stopped flirting with everything that has a pulse, my life would be perfect.'

Harry pulled back away from me. 'What's that supposed to mean?'

Can open. Worms all over the place.

'Well you're on holiday with me, and you go off and talk to other women.' It sounded so petty, even to my ears.

'So I'm not allowed to talk to other women?' He was pissed, all humour and warmth had completely vanished.

'It's what else you want to be doing to them that bothers me.'

'Why does it bother you? Are you jealous?'

I stood up. 'No, of course not.' The boat bumped against the back of the yacht and Harry instinctively caught my arm to stop me toppling over. I shrugged my arm free of his hold. 'I just think… its shallow, sleeping with a different woman every night.'

He stood up and towered over me. 'You think I'm shallow?'

'No, I don't. I think you're wonderful. I think what you are doing is shallow, there's a big difference. These women obviously don't mean anything to you and I think you should pick one woman, one that makes you happy, one that you actually care for and stick with her rather than sampling all the delights the buffet has to offer.'

'Someone like you?'

I stepped aboard the yacht. 'No, clearly not, you don't have those kinds of feelings for me do you?'

He looked down, rubbing his hand over his head and although he didn't say it, the answer was clear in his eyes.

It was like a punch to the gut to see the denial etched so vividly on his face as he tried to find the words to say it.

I swallowed the lump in my throat, biting my lip to try to supress the tears that were threatening to come.

'Of course you don't.' My voice broke and I cursed my treacherous body for betraying me. 'I mean you're you and I'm...' I gestured to his beautiful body and then mine. There was no comparison. He stepped closer to me but I stepped away. 'I'm merely saying that if you're here with me, then you should be here with me, not pick me up when you get bored of your other playthings. That's not jealousy talking, it's just good manners.'

'I have spent the last year being there for you, dropping everything for you, all of this was for you.' He gestured wildly to the yacht and the islands. 'What more do you want?'

I turned away but he grabbed my arm and pulled me back.

'Hey!' Elias was suddenly between us, seemingly appearing from nowhere. 'Take your hands off the lady right now.'

Harry was clearly bigger and stronger than Elias and if it came down to a fight it would be over very quickly – and certainly not in Elias's favour. Harry duly dropped my arm anyway.

'Suzie listen...' Harry was forcing himself to calm down, as Elias stood in front of me.

'No, you listen, if I'm really that much of a burden, then please, go have fun with Barbie tonight. I don't want you in my room, being somewhere you'd rather not be. Then tomorrow you can contact Silver Linings and call off this stupid charade and go and work for that big company who offered you all that money. I'd hate to be in your way.'

I quickly ran off before Harry saw my tears, bursting through the door of the dining room, much to the surprise of the other guests who were all busy eating. I ran out the other side and up onto the top deck, which was now deserted.

I sighed, heavily, closing my eyes in embarrassment at my sudden outburst.

The truth was, as his friend, it didn't bother me in the slightest him going after these other women. Whenever Peri and I used to go on holiday together, I used to laugh at how she would be with a different man every night where I would quite happily go back to my hotel room alone and devour the pages of the latest book. The only reason it upset me with Harry was because I *was* jealous. I wanted him, I wanted him to want me too. And the horrible truth was, he didn't. He would never be mine.

*

It was nearly midnight when I found myself wandering round to the back of the boat, near the launch deck. We were anchored in the middle of Darwin Bay and the still inky waters were lapping gently against the side of the boat. I hadn't seen Harry all evening, he was clearly giving me some space. I was glad for it, because in reality how did I explain my little outburst? Either that or he was with Barbie, not giving me a second thought.

'Sooozie, are you ok?'

I turned and smiled at Elias.

'I'm fine.'

'The man is an idiot.' He came to stand next to me.

'It's fine, really. It's me being sad and pathetic. He's done so much for me, especially since Jack died. I can't blame him for wanting to have some fun away from me. I'm not exactly much fun to be around at the moment.'

'You are not sad and pathetic Suzie, you are the most beautiful woman in the world.'

He ran his finger down my arm, causing my whole body to erupt in goose bumps.

'Come for a swim with me.'

He pulled his top off, his chest and arms glistening in the moonlight.

'Now?'

He pulled his shorts off, revealing a pair of tight black boxer shorts.

'Life is for the living. You should know that as well as I. There is nothing more liberating than swimming naked.'

'Swimming naked?' I squeaked.

Elias dived gracefully into the black waters and surfaced a few metres away from the boat. A second later his shorts came flying out of the water to land on the edge of the deck.

I swallowed and looked around. There wasn't a single person in sight, everyone else tucked up in their beds for the night, ready for the next adventure tomorrow. Harry was probably tucked up in Barbie's bed.

And that was the clincher.

I pulled my top off and my shorts, though I wasn't quite brave enough to go completely naked, and then I dived into the sea next to Elias.

The water was cooler now the sun had gone in, but Elias had been right, it was liberating. I laughed out loud.

Elias swam closer. 'You have a wonderful laugh Suzie. You will enjoy it all the more if you were completely free though. It is an exhilarating feeling, to be at one with the sea.'

Feeling shy, even though he couldn't see me, I peeled off my bra and tossed it up on to the deck. Elias arched an eyebrow at me and, not wanting to be prudish, I wriggled out of my pants too.

'Perfect,' he whispered, swimming closer.

He moved his hands to my waist and I wrapped my arms round his neck. The way he was looking at me now it was very obvious what his intentions were for tonight. But to be desired by someone so beautiful, so sweet, was incredibly flattering. Harry didn't want me but Elias did.

He kissed me, his tongue in my mouth straight away, which was a bit of a shock. But once I got used to the rhythm and the urgency of his kiss, I found I was quite enjoying it. His hands roamed my body, grabbing my breasts as he moved me back through the water until I was pressed against the side of the boat.

'We have a connection Suzie, you felt it too, didn't you?'

He reached over my head onto the deck and rummaged in his shorts pocket, pulling out a condom. Oh. The shortest amount of foreplay ever. The little voice in the back of my head asked why he was walking around with a condom in his pocket, when he wasn't someone who slept around, but as he kissed me again, I suddenly didn't care. If Harry could sleep around, then I could too. The pain of rejection was lessened slightly when someone else wanted me so much. As he leaned against me, I could certainly feel how much he wanted me.

He pulled my legs around his hips and I closed my eyes and leaned back against the boat. Was it wrong that all I could think of was Harry?

*

Elias walked me back to my cabin, with his arm round my shoulders, keeping me warm against the chill of the night.

I leaned into him, kissing him on the cheek. 'Thank you.'

'For what?'

'Tonight, for being lovely.'

He smiled at me. 'You are lovely. It was a pleasure meeting you.'

I let myself into the bedroom and was surprised to see Harry sitting on the bed waiting for me. I couldn't read his face at all.

'Did you have fun?' His voice was cool and clipped.

I shut the door behind me. 'What do you mean?'

'With Elias. I came looking for you, I was worried. I see I didn't need to be. I saw you with him.'

Anger erupted through me again.

'And? You've probably been with Barbie all night, so don't you dare preach to me.'

'I've been here, waiting for you ever since you flounced off, and I think I have every right to preach to you as the whole point of your little outburst was you didn't want me to leave you alone on holiday, you didn't want me to be sleeping around with women that meant nothing to me – and then you go off with some man you've just met?'

'How did that make you feel?'

'Angry over your double standards.'

I rubbed my face, feeling suddenly very tired. 'Why are you being so arsey about this? You kept telling me that I should get back on the horse.'

'Not with the first bloke that flashes you a smile.'

'Why not, it works for you, but they normally flash you their tits as well.'

He stood and started pacing the room, breathing heavily through his nose. He whirled to face me. 'Fine then, we can both screw as many different men and women as we want on this holiday, we can do our own thing and meet up once a day for these stupid proposals.'

'Great, that sounds perfect.'

'Good.'

'Good.'

We stared at each other. It was ridiculous and we both knew it.

'Well we'd better get some sleep, we have to be up in five hours,' Harry snapped.

'Fine.'

'Fine.'

I got changed into my pyjamas and when I turned back Harry was already in bed, facing away from me. I slid in beside him and clicked off the light. Of course I didn't sleep a wink and neither, I don't think, did he.

*

The plane touched down in Cancun, Mexico and my stomach rolled. It hadn't been a smooth ride, we had hit every patch of turbulence possible. The windows had rattled, wind whistled through the toilet door, which I had been sitting next to. It was as if the plane had been made from paper. The toilet door banged open now, sending a waft of chemicals and toilet smells all over me. My stomach heaved again.

Harry and I had not spoken at all since we'd gotten up this morning. We moved around our cabin preparing for our departure as if we were strangers.

We'd endured in silence a boat ride back to Baltra Island, a taxi, a plane ride to Ecuador and then another plane here to Cancun. It only really occurred to me now, if we were to see the world in ninety days, most of our time would be spent travelling. We were halfway through the third day of our holidays and we'd only just touched down in our second destination.

I was exhausted. Lack of sleep, so much travelling and then the horrific journey – I felt rough.

The taxi trip to the hotel was awful, an hour's journey as the taxi driver swerved round corners, screeched to a halt at traffic lights, spoke on the phone and shouted and swore a lot to anyone or everyone who was listening.

Harry sat in stony silence next to me, staring out of the window.

We arrived at the hotel and I noticed the reception area was huge and white. White marble floors gleamed as they stretched down to white sandy beaches and turquoise waters. White curtains billowed in the windows, even the reception desk was white. It was so bright, it hurt my head.

Harry checked us in but I heard him ask if there was any chance of having separate rooms. They were fully booked due to a wedding and I found myself sighing with relief. We needed to sort this out, not add fuel to the fire.

The lift took us up twenty floors so quickly my ears popped and I felt my stomach roll again. What was wrong with me today? I felt so tired, so weak.

The white theme continued in our hotel room, which had the largest double bed I had ever seen in my entire life. I pushed open the balcony doors, letting the warm breeze wash over me. It did nothing for my lethargy and nausea. There was one word to describe what I could see. Paradise. Miles of white beaches stretched out as far as the eye could see. Turquoise waters danced with sunlight as if jewels were buried beneath the waves. Stalks of palm trees peppered the sands beneath me like oversized green daisies.

'I need to go out.'

He speaks. I turned around to face him, but he wasn't looking at me.

'You need to be at the far end of the beach near the jetty at two o'clock. It's just coming up for one-fifteen now. It should take you about ten, fifteen minutes from here.'

I sat down on the bed – my stomach was churning and I thought I was going to pass out at any second. I just needed to sleep off the horrible journey, that was all. Then I'd be fine.

'Can we do this later?' I said.

'No. It's booked for two.'

'Can you do this one without me, I really don't feel well.'

'Can I do it without you? Can I propose to you without you?'

I saw his fists clench at his side. I knew he would never hurt me but he was clearly still upset and I had just poked at the angry bear with a sharp stick.

'If you can't even be bothered to turn up for the proposals then we might as well go home now. The aeroplane proposal that you slept through I can let slide…'

'That was the sleeping tablets, that wasn't really my fault and it was a lovely proposal, I saw it. I've said I'm sorry about missing it, I'm not going to keep apologising.'

'If you don't turn up this afternoon then I'm catching the next flight back home. You can do whatever the hell you want but with no funding from Silver Linings or Sunlounger once the blog is pulled, I expect you'll have to come home too.'

He was right, I was being incredibly ungrateful. I sighed. 'I'll be there.'

Harry walked out the room and slammed the door behind him.

I lay down on the bed, but keeping my eyes open so I didn't accidentally fall asleep. Though there was no chance of that, my stomach was rolling and cramping. I took a few deep breaths to quell the sickness but it did nothing.

Suddenly I ran to the bathroom and threw up everything I had ever eaten in my entire life – it was as if my stomach was being squeezed like a tube of toothpaste. I was pretty sure that I had just thrown up a liver or even a kidney.

After my stomach was seemingly empty, I lay down on the bathroom floor, pressing my head into the cool tiles. I had to get up, I wasn't going to let Harry down. My stomach rolled again. I'd get up in a minute.

*

I heard the bedroom door slam – Harry had no doubt returned because he had forgotten something, or to shout at me again. If there was going to be more shouting I wanted to at least be standing for it. I couldn't move, I couldn't even open my eyes. Harry was talking to me, shouting at me, but I couldn't understand anything he was saying, almost like I was underwater. I felt his arm round my shoulders as he lifted me and the next thing I knew I was lying on the bed.

A wet towel was wiped gently across my face. 'Come on baby, open your eyes and look at me,' Harry urged.

I did as I was told, staring up into his face and he smiled with relief.

I saw the clock over his shoulder and my heart jolted with sudden fear. 'What time is it?'

'It's half two.'

'No! No, no, no, no.' I struggled to sit up but he pushed me back down. 'I'm so sorry, I was sick. Oh God, no! I didn't mean to miss it, I'm sorry.'

I shivered and Harry pulled a blanket over me.

'Are you mad?'

'Oh I was spitting feathers. I was going to come back here and declare world war three. Strangely, seeing my best friend unconscious in a pool of her own vomit kind of made any anger go away. It puts it all into perspective a little bit.'

'I'm so sorry.'

'Don't be. I didn't realise you were sick, I just thought you were tired and being grumpy with me again.'

'I'm sorry for being grumpy with you too.'

He smiled. 'I'm sorry too. I was an arse and it was completely uncalled for.'

'No it was definitely called for. You've been amazing, all of this,' I gestured feebly, 'it's wonderful. If you want to sleep with a different woman every night you go ahead.'

'Ok enough of the apologies, how are you feeling?'

I reflected on how I felt. 'My stomach hurts. I don't feel sick. Not at the moment.'

'Good. I've called a doctor. It's probably just a sickness bug, but better get you checked out just to be on the safe side.'

'How long have you been back?'

'Five minutes maybe. I couldn't wake you at all. I was panicking.' He was still in panic mode now, I could tell that. 'I was going to get you in the shower to see if I could rouse you and clean you up a bit, but then thought I'd better ring a doctor instead. He suggested that I just try to bring you round first. Would you like a shower now, it might make you feel better?'

I did feel sticky and I smelt bad; the thought of the doctor examining me when I smelt like this was not a pleasant one. I nodded.

'I'll help you.'

'What?'

I was very awake all of a sudden.

'Suzie, you're as white as... Ryan Gosling's shirt.'

I smiled at this. As if he remembered the inane ramblings I had uttered the week before.

I sat up carefully and swung my legs off the bed. Harry was right – I was wobbly – but I managed to make it into the bathroom without any help.

He switched the shower on and we stood staring at each other. We were about to crash straight across the boundaries of friendship by showering with each other and we both knew that.

'So, I'll erm...' I gestured that I should get in.

'Well you should probably take your clothes off first.'

I plucked at my T-shirt and then slid it up over my head. I didn't dare look at him as he pulled his own T-shirt off.

Ok this was no different than beach wear – me in my underwear, him in his shorts. I certainly wasn't going to take anything else off.

I stepped in the shower and he got in behind me. I would just have to ignore him, ignore his heat, ignore the sudden desire to kiss him. God, he was standing so close.

Desperately trying to ignore his proximity, I stepped directly under the water, soaking my hair. The shower was having the desired effect. It was cooling me down, clearing my brain of the fog. But suddenly his hands were in my hair, his fingers running through from root to tip. He leaned round me to get the shampoo and I heard him squeeze it out into his hand and then he was massaging it into my head, softly flexing his fingers into my scalp.

I closed my eyes, every nerve ending alert, zinging with his touch. He was thorough, ensuring the shampoo was rubbed into every strand of hair. He gently tilted my head back, so he could wash the shampoo out, his hands running through my hair again.

Once the shampoo was out of my hair, he swept my hair off my neck and over my shoulder. He reached round me again, and opening one eye I saw him take some shower gel.

My breath quickened at the thought of him being as thorough with my body as he had been with my hair.

He started rubbing my neck, moving his hot hands to my shoulders and then to my back. But it became very evident that he wasn't washing me, he was massaging me. He ran his hands down my spine, and then back up to my shoulder blades, his fingers pressing firmly into my skin, applying the exact amount of pressure in some areas and being gentle on other parts.

I realised, when my lungs started to scream in protest, that I had been holding my breath, and as I let out the air, a noise escaped from my throat that was guttural, filled with desire. I prayed he hadn't noticed.

'Turn around,' he mumbled into my ear, his hot breath sending delicious shivers through my body.

I did as I was told, wobbling a bit as I did. I watched his eyes. He was trying really hard not to look at me, finding the floor strangely fascinating. He squirted more soap into his hands and he ran them down my arms. As he reached my hands he linked fingers with me, pulled my arms up and rested them on his shoulders.

'Lean on me if you need to.'

Taking advantage of my friend's good nature, I slid my hands round his neck and his eyes immediately flicked up to meet mine, searing into mine.

He let out a slow, long breath as his hands moved tentatively to my waist and he shuffled slightly closer.

A loud knocking on the hotel room door echoed through the bathroom.

Harry swallowed. 'That will be the doctor.'

I nodded, unable to say anything. If the doctor was going to listen to my heart right now, it would sound like hard rain on a tin roof.

'You look a lot better, actually.'

What did that mean? Was he going to turn the doctor away? 'I feel a lot better.'

He nodded and I saw his eyes glance down to my lips just for a second before the knocking sounded again.

He turned the shower off and stepped out of my arms. The moment, if indeed there ever had been one, was gone.

He pulled a fluffy towel off the rail and wrapped me in it.

'I'll get you some dry clothes and then the doctor can take a look at you.'

I nodded, and the next moment Harry was gone. I heard him talk to the doctor and he briefly returned to the bathroom with a pile of dry clothes and then he left me alone.

What had happened then? Had he been about to kiss me? No, he was just helping me to take a shower. But the way he had looked at me, like a lion about to devour his prey…

I got dressed quickly and walked out into the bedroom. The doctor examined me, felt round my stomach, asked me loads of questions and declared that it was probably just a bug – but I was to drink plenty of fluids, get some rest for the next day or so and that if it got any worse to call him again.

As soon as he left, the atmosphere changed in the room. It lay heavy between us. I sat on the bed watching Harry mess around with his camera, his phone, his clothes, as he deliberately didn't look at me.

I wanted to ask him whether what I felt in the shower was completely one-sided. These emotions that were flying about, surely he felt them too.

I had to do something to clear the air, even if I was only clearing it for myself.

'What was the proposal?'

He smiled, and I wasn't sure if it was out of relief that the tension had been broken, or just because he was keen to show me his latest proposal. He grabbed his camera and plonked himself next to me on the bed, leaning into me so we were touching knee to shoulder, just like he'd done with Barbie back on the boat. I didn't know whether to be delighted by this intimacy or not. Did he see me the same as the girl he had been flirting with on the boat, a friend? Something more? Why was I reading into everything, why couldn't I just accept things for how they were? I had the best friend anyone could ever hope for and I should be happy with that, not try to push for more.

He flicked on his camera.

'A proposal by land, sea and air,' Harry said.

I watched the video and smiled as first someone rode a bike trailing a banner with the words 'Marry Me' along the beach front. Then the camera turned to catch a banana boat, trailing the same banner and finally the camera tilted upwards as a tiny propeller plane, obviously used for promoting bars and clubs, dragged the now familiar words in its wake. Then the camera went black.

The fact that there was no commentary or no huge smile from Harry recorded on film was testament to how angry he was when he had filmed it.

'It's lovely. I'm so sorry I missed it.'

He kissed me on the forehead and I knew he didn't need to hear it. He shuffled back and lay down with me, his arm round my shoulder as my head fell onto his chest.

'Listen, about yesterday…'

'It doesn't matter,' he said.

'I didn't sleep with Elias.'

Though if I had that was the least of my crimes. I'm sure he was more bothered about me getting angry over him simply talking to another woman.

He was silent for a moment. 'Suzie I saw you, not that it matters of course, we're both free agents.'

'I know. But I'm not that woman who would sleep with a complete stranger. Sometimes I wish I was, but I'm not. I don't know what you saw, you might have seen me and Elias getting naked and jumping in the sea and kissing, and you might have seen him getting a condom out of his shorts – but if you'd hung around a bit longer you also would have seen me telling him I couldn't do it. I'm never going to see him again and it just didn't feel right. I kept thinking of you…'

'Of me?'

I bit my lip, wishing I had some kind of filter on my brain that would stop inappropriate words coming out of my mouth. I was glad that he couldn't see my face. 'Just… that it was hypocritical, as you said, to go off with someone I'd just met when I'd shouted at you for the same thing. I'm on holiday with you so…' I shrugged, hoping he would agree.

'I'm glad.'

I looked up at him. 'You are?'

'Just that the man was a creep.'

I sat up. 'Harry!'

He closed his fingers over my lips so I couldn't talk. 'The "my wife died and I've never been with another woman since" story. It's a crock of shit. He trots that story out to every woman that stays on the boat. Works like a charm. The other crew were telling me. I'm glad you didn't fall for it too.'

I scowled because I nearly did fall for it. Elias had seemed so nice. It was only because of somehow feeling disloyal to Harry that I hadn't slept with him.

He sat up. 'I want you to be with someone special, someone who knows how fantastic you are, someone who would go to the ends of the earth for you.'

'Someone who would love me despite the cow print onesie?'

'No, someone who would love you because of it.'

I smiled.

'I don't think you should sleep with anyone until you find that person, someone who loves you and would worship you in bed. In fact, don't sleep with anyone until you're married, that makes more sense.'

I laughed. 'Harry, I haven't slept with anyone for two years, not since Alex. I can't wait another two years or more until I have sex.'

Good lord. Had the sickness addled my brain? I literally had no filter on my mouth at all.

'Greasy kebab boy was your last lay?' Harry seemed delighted by this. 'What about Tiny Tim? You said the sex was amazing, even the sideways sex.'

I was never going to get away from Tiny Tim, and the lies surrounding him were going to keep coming back and tripping me up.

'Ok, ok, I lied about me and Tim having sex. We went out on a few dates. He wanted to, he kept pushing me for sex but I just wasn't ready.'

I looked away and stared at my reflection in the mirror incredulously. Now I sounded frigid. Or that I had some serious issues. This is why lying was bad, I was rubbish at it.

'Did something happen with Alex?' Harry's hand was on my arm. 'Did he hurt you? Is that why you haven't been with anyone else since?'

I groaned inwardly. I was actually making it worse.

'No, Alex was lovely. Very dull, but lovely. I don't think he would know how to hurt me. No, I'm just rubbish with men, Harry – if they show the slightest flicker of interest I run away embarrassed.'

'But you went out with Tiny Tim, why didn't you...?' I could feel him trying to understand.

How could I explain that there had been no one for me for two years because I had fallen head over heels for him, because no one else ever came close? And how could I explain why I hadn't had sex with my imaginary boyfriend?

'It was just, he was very full on. Kept on telling me how he'd like to tie me up and well... Fifty Shades my arse.'

'Your arse?'

'Not specifically my arse.'

'But you loved Fifty Shades, you read the trilogy twice.'

'Yes. I did.' I had to remember that Harry had loved that kinky stuff with Sexy Samantha and although I'd never thought about being tied up during sex before, having Harry tie me up and do wicked things to me would be very pleasurable indeed. 'That kind of sex takes time and trust. I don't want to have sex with someone for the first time and they whip out a gimp mask and genital clamps.'

Harry visibly paled and quickly crossed his legs, protecting his manhood. 'Genital clamps?'

I nodded.

'What were you doing with this guy? He sounds like a right freak.'

'He seemed nice at first.'

'All the freaks do.' He shuddered. 'That's decided then. Definitely no sex with anyone until your wedding night. I'm not having you go out with any more freaks.'

'Harry…'

'Listen. The right guy for you is just around the corner. I promise.' He took my hand and trailed his fingers lightly across my palm. Goose bumps exploded treacherously over my body, though he didn't seem to notice. 'I can see your future. This line here is your love line. Before the year is out, you will be married to the most marvellous man. He will treat you like a queen and carry you everywhere.'

I shifted closer so I could humour him and look at my palm too. Nothing to do with being closer to him. He smelt amazing, his sweet, spicy, earthy scent.

'What's he like?'

'Tall, dark and handsome.' He looked closer. 'And magnificent in bed. No kinky stuff at all.'

'I don't mind a bit of kink. With the right man.'

His eyes flicked up to mine again. 'Just wait, Suzie, you'll find him soon enough, I'm sure of it.'

I sighed and nodded, just hoping this mystery man would arrive sooner rather than later.

Harry dropped my hand and I sensed the subject was over. 'Fancy going down the beach for a bit? Fresh air might do you some good.'

I nodded and he was off the bed and away from me a second later.

I just had to fall out of love with him first.

CHAPTER TEN

I lay on the bed staring at the sky as it turned from blue to candyfloss pink. Cancun was a typical beach paradise with the white sands and turquoise waters – but the cherry on the cake was the four poster beds, with duvets, soft pillows and white chiffon curtains billowing gently in the breeze. We had spent the entire afternoon lying here in sumptuous comfort as lovely bar men brought us drinks and snacks at our every whim. The beach was quiet at this time of year, and with the curtains surrounding us, it helped to close us off from the outside world – making it feel like we were the only ones here.

I had dozed on and off all afternoon, in the heat of the day, recovering from my bout of sickness earlier. Every time I woke, Harry was lying by my side, either reading or answering emails or staring out at the sea or even one time staring at me.

I rolled over now, hugging a pillow as I watched the waves. Harry was out in the sea and I found myself biting the pillow as I watched him swim. Large muscled arms sliced through the waves, droplets of water dripping off his powerful back. He really was a walking cliché – big, beautiful, and rich.

He stood up and started walking towards me, his huge thighs sloshing through the waves. I bit harder on the pillow and I felt sure it would pop in a minute and I'd be left explaining why I was surrounded by a cloud of feathers.

As the last of the sun glistened on his wet body and I imagined drying him off with a towel, or even better my tongue, he stumbled head first into the water. I sat up to see if he was ok, but the laugh was already bubbling up in my throat. He stood back up, clearly embarrassed and to my delight he had seaweed stuck to his head. I snorted and laughed so hard, he clearly heard me from twenty feet away. He stopped and looked in my direction, a scowl marring his beautiful features, though this did nothing to stop my laughter.

He walked into the shallows and it was then I noticed a girl waiting for him – she was about my age, stick thin, long brown hair cascading down her back in beautiful curls. The white bikini she was wearing left very little to the imagination.

'Are you ok? That was quite the tumble you took there.' she asked.

Harry approached her, clearly not knowing that the seaweed was still stuck to his head. I couldn't help but laugh even more as he flashed her his most charming smile.

'Yes, I'm fine, thank you for asking.'

I noticed that he had seaweed sticking out from the bottom of his shorts too, like he had very dodgy, long green pubic hair. My laughter doubled in volume.

Harry flashed me another look and the girl scowled in my direction too. 'Some people are so rude, laughing at other people's misfortunes, you could have been hurt.' Her hand was on his arm.

'Yes exactly, so rude,' agreed Harry. 'Excuse me.'

He left the girl and came back to the bed. I caught the look in his eyes and I quickly scooted away from him, but he grabbed my ankles and dragged me back across the bed towards him.

'No, Harry, please, I wasn't laughing at you, I'm sorry,' I squealed through my laughter.

He plucked the seaweed off his head, and as he pinned me down he dragged it across my belly – leaving trails of cold water across my skin. I shouted and squealed, trying to get away from him. He picked the other strand from his thigh, then leaned over me and draped it over my face.

'Harry, no, that's disgusting,' I squealed, trying to wriggle away from him.

Through the curtains I saw the girl watching us wistfully as she turned and walked away. I couldn't help the uncharitable thought from forming in my head, though I had the good grace not to say it.

Jog on, he's mine.

*

'Fancy going to watch the wedding?' Harry asked, his words vibrating through my head as I was propped up against his stomach reading my book. The sun had almost gone in now and in the fading light I was finding it hard to make out the words.

I rolled over to face him and he pointed down the beach. Not far away, people were gathering on golden chairs and candles and flowers lined the aisle up to a flowered archway.

'We can't just gate-crash a wedding.'

'I'm not suggesting we pitch up and sit on one of the chairs, I'm saying we could just, you know, walk past very slowly.'

I looked again and watched as the bride came down through the gardens of our hotel, surrounded by her bridesmaids dressed in the same azure colour as the sea. I nodded keenly. We quickly grabbed our things and then sauntered nonchalantly up the beach.

The bride looked beautiful in a silvery dress that glittered in the candlelight as she approached the back of the aisle. Soft harp music was being played and the guests stood to welcome her down the aisle towards her groom.

The way he looked at her sent shivers down my spine, this was a man in love. He reached out to take her hand and pulled her against his side just like Harry had done to me a hundred times.

We watched the ceremony in silence and I couldn't take my eyes off them.

As the registrar announced them man and wife and they kissed, Harry put his arm around me and I leaned into him.

'Do you see yourself getting married?' I asked.

'Maybe.'

I looked up at him, in surprise. 'But you don't believe in love.'

'I'm coming round to it. Being with you makes me think it's possible.'

'Being with me?' I squeaked.

'I mean all the proposals, the couples we've helped. You were right. Seeing all these newly engaged couples, seeing how happy they are – love can be a good thing, with the right person. And don't forget I fell in love didn't I? Despite my best efforts not to, it happened anyway.'

'You don't seem the "settling down with one woman" sort.'

'I know I have a bit of a reputation when it comes to women. But when I find that woman, the one I want to spend the rest of my life with, I'm going to grab onto her and not let her go.'

My heart soared with happiness for Harry, even if we never got together, he was slowly breaking his barriers down – and opening up his heart to the possibility of love was a great turning point for him. And I had helped with that.

'Won't you get bored, sex with the same woman for the rest of your life?'

He smiled. 'No, not one bit. I cannot imagine anything better actually – making love to the woman I love, every day, every night.'

'But these women you're with, you never really give them a chance, one of these could be your one.'

'Trust me, they're not.'

'How do you know?'

'Because not one of them has made me feel like… like I did when I was in love. I'm looking for that.'

'This woman, that you were in love with, was it Chloe, the one we're meeting in New York?'

'No.'

I had more questions but I was suddenly distracted by the newly wedded husband scooping his bride up into his arms and running out into the sea.

'No! The dress,' I squealed so loud that some of the congregation looked round at me. But the bride didn't seem bothered. As they both sank into the waves, she wrapped her arms round her husband's neck and kissed him like her life depended on it.

Proposer's Blog

Day 13: The Sunrise Proposal. Location. The Mayan Temples at Tulum.

As you know from yesterday's blog, Suzie wasn't very well yesterday and although she seemed a lot better last night, I was still a bit reluctant to drag her out of bed so early this morning, but I'm so glad I did.

Suzie wasn't exactly impressed when I left her in the pitch black, alone on the beach, to set up the proposal – though I was rewarded on my return by her throwing herself into my arms and clinging to me like ivy. My dear would-be proposers, if you want a definitive reaction, I suggest you scare the crap out of your girlfriends first. I could barely prise myself out of her arms as she mumbled into my chest something about noises and heavy breathing.

The temples at Tulum stand on the cliffs, facing out towards the sea. The walled city was originally called Zama, City of the Dawn because it faces the sunrise. So I thought, what better place to watch the sunrise than from the top of the El Castillo, the tallest building in this ancient Mayan city.

Of course you can't just walk into historical ruins that are thousands of years old. So my plan was clearly not going to happen. Note to self, must do more research.

There are steps from the beach leading up to the Castillo but there was a wall preventing us from going any further. It didn't look like my proposal was going to happen at all and the clock was against us.

To my shame, and completely through my encouragement alone, we hopped over a small rope fence and scrambled precariously along the cliff edge. With our backs to the Castillo, this ancient ruin, we watched the sun rise over the Caribbean Sea, as the Mayans would have done hundreds of years before. Within minutes, the sea ranged through black, inky blue, turquoise, pink and scarlet, the sun sending garlands of colour across the waves. It was incredible and right there, we were the only people in the world to watch it from that position, touching the past as the future rushed towards us in all its golden splendour.

I pulled Suzie to her feet and pointed down onto the empty beach – there in six foot high letters, written in the sand, was my proposal. 'Marry Me' with a big heart underneath. In the heart was a picnic blanket and breakfast laid out ready for us to eat.

I told Suzie that there were chocolate covered strawberries and... That's as far as I got before I turned round and saw her scrambling across the cliff, running down the stairs and across the beach towards the picnic blanket.

Quite a success I feel.

After my wonderful proposal we had gone back and checked out of our luxury hotel, travelled down the coast and checked into a cabana – a beautiful beachside thatched cabin. We could literally step out of the cabin, down the steps and we were on the beach, the warm shallows of the Caribbean merely ten metres away. We were told that in the morning, when the tide was in, the water would come right up to the bottom of the steps.

The cabana was basic; a bed, a bathroom, that was it. It didn't even have any electricity. I loved its rustic charm. There was a sheltered veranda area with a table and chairs, two hammocks and at the bottom of the stairs we had our own barbeque, which Harry swore he was going to cook freshly caught fish on later. I wasn't sure if Harry intended to catch the fish himself, though it wouldn't surprise me. Everything the man turned his hand to he was good at.

I scowled at him lying happily in his hammock. Even now, where other mere mortals had failed, it had taken him mere seconds to climb easily into his hammock.

I stared back at my nemesis darkly. I would not be beaten. If Harry could do it, I could do it too.

I approached the hammock like you would approach a wild animal. It swung gently in the breeze, taunting me. I heard Harry turn a laugh into a cough as he tapped away on the laptop, answering emails as he swayed in his hammock.

I turned around, and sat carefully into the middle of the hammock but as I lifted one foot off the ground, the hammock tilted and deposited me on the floor. Harry shuddered with suppressed laughter.

I stood up. No piece of string was going to get the better of me.

I straddled the hammock, one leg either side of it, and lowered my bottom into the material. So far so good. I lifted my legs slowly into the hammock and it rocked precariously. I froze, waiting for it to be still, and when it was I lowered myself down into the hammock, my back, my shoulders, my neck… But suddenly, without provocation, it flipped over, causing me to land face down on the decking again.

Harry's laughter went up an octave.

'What do you suggest then, smart alec?'

'Show it who's boss. You're being too namby pamby with it. Just get in, like you're getting into bed.'

I stood up again. I put my hands out, holding the hammock flat, rolled in and rolled straight out the other side.

I lay on the decking, staring up at the thatched fronds rustling gently in the breeze.

'Right, enough. You're going to be black and blue by the time you've finished. Share the hammock with me. I'm already in the right position, you just have to join me.'

'And tip us both out? That's ok, I'll just sit in one of these chairs.'

'No seriously. I'm a big guy, my weight will help to balance us out. Come on.' He patted the hammock temptingly.

'If we tip out, don't blame me.'

'I promise.'

I shuffled closer and Harry hooked an arm round one of the front pillars of the veranda. I slowly sat down in the hammock and to my surprise it barely moved at all. I carefully relaxed into it and as Harry let go of the pillar, the hammock swung out gently and then was still.

'See. It's fine.'

I ignored his smugness and indicated his laptop. 'Anything important?'

We had both been studiously replying to emails since we left, but since I'd got sick the day before, Harry had insisted I take a few days off from it.

'Nothing I can't handle.'

He was reading an email now and as I leaned back on my arms, I heard him laugh.

'What?' It was probably from Badger.

'Oh, nothing, an email from Chloe. She's looking forward to seeing us.'

I felt myself tense. If I could, I'd avoid New York altogether, but I'd always wanted to go there – I couldn't miss this chance just because one of Harry's exes was there too.

I lifted my head to look at the email, but he quickly closed it down and opened up a work one. He clearly didn't want me to see it.

'Are you looking forward to seeing her too?'

'Yes, God yes, I can't wait to see her, she's one of my best friends.'

I bit my lip and closed my eyes against the sudden pain in my chest. I was his best friend.

'You'll like her, she's lovely.'

I doubted that.

'What's she like?'

'Blonde, cute as hell.'

I changed the subject. 'Where are we going tomorrow?'

'We fly to California tomorrow, we're spending one night in the Disneyland resort, then we fly to San Francisco, Vegas and then on to New York.'

'Great, can't wait.' I tried to hide the dryness in my voice. 'Are we just spending one night in these places?'

'One night at Disney and San Francisco, two or three nights in Vegas, there's loads to see – and maybe a week in New York.'

'A week?' I sat up so quickly the hammock rocked precariously. Harry grabbed the laptop and then pulled me back down to stop the rocking. A whole week with Chloe.

'New York is one of my favourite places in the whole world.'

'Because of Chloe?'

'No. I'm looking forward to seeing her but it's New York I'm desperate to go back to. It's just the most incredible place.'

I smiled at his enthusiasm. 'Tell me about it.'

'It just has an amazing atmosphere, it feels so safe. You can wander the streets at two in the morning without fear of being attacked. And that's a stupid thing to say, I know, you could get mugged in this city as well as you could in any, but there is something about this place that just makes me feel content. The people are brilliant, all walks of life. They're so friendly, even the kids that you would cross over the other side of the street to avoid in England – in New York they are lovely, respectful wholesome kids, even if they do wander round with their jeans hanging off their bums. And the food is just heaven. So many good places to eat, so many different foods, different nationalities. I put on a stone the last time I was there and I was only there a month. They say it's the city that never sleeps and it really is, you can buy a pair of trainers from a sports shop at one in the morning. The place just hums with this energy, this maelstrom of life.'

I loved him when he got so passionate about things like this. He was like this about his love of history too, it was hard not to get caught up in his enthusiasm. Then my heart sank.

'You were going to move there, weren't you? You had a job out there.'

The shine from his eyes faded slightly. 'It just wasn't meant to be.'

'You cancelled it because of Jack, didn't you?'

He looked at me for a moment in confusion. 'No, that was absolutely not the reason I cancelled it. There was all that office politics stuff that I didn't want to get involved in.'

'You didn't cancel it because of me?' It sounded so arrogant, even to my ears. 'To be there for me?'

He studied me for a moment. 'In truth. I fell in love and I couldn't bear to be parted from her.'

I felt my mouth fall open at this. He had cancelled all his big plans, his dreams, for *her* – the woman he had fallen in love with. How disappointed he must have been when it never worked out between them.

'I'm sorry that she didn't know how fantastic you are. You're a beautiful person Harry, and she must have been blind and completely stupid not to realise that.'

He smiled. 'She's neither of those things. But I could never find it in me to hate her because she didn't return my feelings. I loved her too much for that.'

'But you must regret not going now.'

He grinned. 'Not one bit. Things have a way of working out exactly how you want. My life is pretty damned fine the way it is. I've got you, my best friend, a great job and I'm lying in a hammock next to the Caribbean Sea. It couldn't get any more perfect.'

It was at that moment the laptop rang with the familiar Skype ring tone. I prayed it wasn't Chloe, I could just pretend she didn't exist for a few more days.

Harry propped the laptop up on his knees and answered it. To my surprise, Bella sat in the screen alone.

'Bella,' I crooned. She clapped her hands when she heard my voice but I don't think she was really taking in the fact that I was on the screen too. 'Bella, can you wave?' I called, wondering how the hell she had managed to call me on her own. Jules had probably given her the iPad to play with and she had pressed the wrong button. Bella blew bubbles through her mouth.

'Oozie,' she giggled and my heart soared.

'Did she just say my name?'

Harry nodded, grinning inanely next to me.

Just then the screen tilted and Badger and Jules came into view as they cuddled in behind Bella. They looked like a happy, loving family and my stomach lurched because of it. Off camera, Harry squeezed my hand.

'We thought we'd let Bella say a few words first, especially now she's learnt to say your name,' said Jules, kissing Bella's soft head, fondly. 'Say Suzie.'

'Oozie,' Bella said, clapping her hands together again.

'How's it all going?' Badger asked, one arm round Jules's shoulders, the other holding Bella in place on his lap. I looked at Bella, her beautiful dark eyes and dark hair, she had changed so much and we had only been gone a few days. Would she forget what I looked like by the time I came back, would she have forgotten me altogether? Did she have any memory of her dad at all?

'Good thanks,' Harry said, realising that I was having trouble getting past this sweet family scene to be able to find the words to talk to them. His fingers entwined with mine and he stroked the back of my hand with his thumb. 'We're having a lot of fun.'

Bella turned round and cuddled into the side of Badger's neck, sucking her thumb. I saw Jules watch her daughter being completely at ease with Badger and smile with love for him. It still made me feel a bit uncomfortable and I didn't know how long it would take for me to be completely ok with it.

'Hey listen, we've taught her a few more words too,' Badger was saying and he moved Bella from his neck back onto his lap. 'What's your name?'

'Bella,' Bella said, obviously enormously proud of her achievement.

'Who's this?' Badger said, pointing to Jules.

'Mama'

'What's my name?' Badger asked.

'Badger,' Bella said triumphantly, and Harry laughed.

I smiled and a look passed between me and Badger and I knew he had seen the look of gratitude from me. Badger not Dada. It was a small but important distinction and Badger knew that.

Proposer's Blog

Day 14: Space Mountain Proposal. Location: Disneyland, California.

Disneyland is fantastic, one of the places I never went to when I travelled America many years ago.

I was a cool twenty year old though, of course I didn't want to go somewhere populated by Disney characters and little kids. How I missed out. I think I'd like to live here.

We're staying in the fairy tale suite, which is really like something out of a Disney film, a room fit for a princess. A beautiful four poster bed, ornate carved woodwork, satins and silks in rich colours, a chaise longue, embroidered coverings, old fashioned lamps, the most amazing bathroom that even has old Greek columns around the bath.

We'd done all the touristy things, buying Mickey Mouse ears, having our photos taken with the characters and been on a load of rides and as day turned to night we watched the character parades and the beautiful fireworks over Cinderella's castle.

Then, as most people left the park, the hard core amongst us stayed on to make the most of the rides.

We went on Space Mountain, and my God, Suzie has a pair of lungs on her – she screamed so loud, I feared deafness.

The Americans love the English and they love the idea of a romantic proposal even more, so the people in our car were more than happy to help.

As we plummeted down the big drop, almost in complete darkness, our photo was taken as part of the official ride memorabilia. It was only as we went to view our photo when we left the ride that Suzie saw the proposal. Each of the people in our car had held up cards spelling out the letters for my proposal. 'Marry' down the left side of the car, 'Me' down the right side of the car, with Suzie sitting at the front screaming her head off. Brilliant. One of my favourites so far, as she had no idea it was coming. I love surprising her.

Proposer's Blog

Day 15: Land Yachting Proposal. Location: San Francisco Bay

We're going to a baseball game tonight, ('Let's go Giants' clap, clap, clapclapclap) so Suzie was convinced I would propose to her at half time, if baseball matches have a half time. But I had a different plan up my sleeve.

I'm keen for Suzie to do and see the things everyone does in these cities, but I want her to experience the hidden parts too. Tomorrow, before our afternoon flight to Vegas, we are taking a boat up the coast to Alamere Falls. How impressive it will be to see the water from Alamere Creek cascade straight into the Pacific Ocean.

But this morning, as soon as we had checked into our hotel, we did all the touristy things. We rode a cable car up and down the steep hills (to the uninitiated, these are trams – to me cable cars are the things that take you up mountains – the hills in San Francisco are steep but not that steep), we went to see the Golden Gate Bridge, we ate a clam chowder soup out of a bread bowl in Fisherman's Wharf, laughed at the sea lions fighting over the floating decks at the end of Pier 39 and caught a taxi to drive down Lombard street, the 'Crookedest Street in the World'.

This afternoon we took to the beaches that line the bay and in the shadow of the San Francisco Bay Bridge, we went land yachting. Suzie was so excited when she saw the yachts, little three-wheeled carts with wind sails attached.

Our instructor, Kenny, gave us lessons, involving moving the sail to catch the wind using levers we operated with our hands and feet. We spent two hours playing up and down the beach, getting it mostly wrong. I have never seen Suzie laugh so hard, as time and time again her sail, or rather her lack of skill, left her stranded in the middle of the beach. She kept on using her hands to wheel herself across the sand until the wind caught her sail and she was off. But eventually we both started to get the hang of it and by the end of our session she was better than me.

Then came the moment of the big race. Me versus Suzie. Kenny gave the signal and we took off down the beach. I'd like to say it was a high speed race, with twists, turns and death-defying manoeuvres but due to our lack of skill we were moderately fast at best. With a few cheating moves from Suzie she inched ahead and as we approached the finish line, it looked likely that she would win, but suddenly there was a last minute entry and Kenny with his years of experience overtook us easily, sailing past us with the words 'Marry Me' emblazoned on his sail. Suzie was so distracted by this that I managed to use this to my advantage and pip her into second place. She was so surprised and so pleased by the high speed race proposal that she didn't even mind.

Proposer's Blog

Day 17: The Pirate Proposal. Location: Siren's Cove, Treasure Island, Vegas.

After my tacky Elvis proposal yesterday I wanted something a bit classier today. We left the MGM hotel this morning and we're staying in the Paris hotel tonight.

It's one of my favourite hotels on the strip. I love the little streets and tiny cafés that populate the hotel just like the real streets of Paris. I love the cloud painted ceilings, tinged with soft pink lighting, making it look like it's dusk at any time of day. The Eiffel Tower is a great addition, with stunning views over Vegas.

Suzie was convinced I would propose to her at the top but, as I said at the beginning of this quest, not one of my proposals would include the Eiffel Tower, even if this one is not the real one.

We went to The Venetian today, with its grand archways, bridges and beautiful colour changing ceiling and of course the Gondola rides. Suzie was again waiting for me to propose on the Gondola but I didn't want the cliché.

After catching the stunning, dramatic Cirque du Soleil show last night, I wanted something a bit different for tonight's show – so we went to see the Tournament of Kings at Excalibur Hotel. A jousting show in an underground arena with horse riding, Merlin, magic, dancing maidens, death-defying stunts, an evil king and eating food with your fingers. Suzie loved it.

The beauty of Vegas really shines out at night, with all the hotels lit up to try and entice you in off the street. We walked along the strip, a bit cooler now the sun had gone in, eating peanut M&Ms and appreciating the atmosphere.

Treasure Island Hotel is the opposite end of the strip to Excalibur but we were in no rush. Well I wasn't, I knew that after the Treasure Island show they would have to do a quick turnaround for our arrival.

Our contact at the hotel, Simon, had taken a bit of a shine to me and was already waiting for us in the foyer when we turned up. This was one person that Suzie didn't mind me flirting with. He led us up through the hotel, down gleaming corridors and then we were outside and in front of us was a huge pirate ship. The Song, the Sirens' ship in Treasure Island Hotel, is part of a huge, pirate themed swashbuckling free show, with explosions and people diving into the waters from great heights – but also it's a place where people can get married.

Normally, weddings take place during the day – but when I mentioned that we would be featuring the hotel in our magazine blog, Simon pulled out all the stops. Plus a harmless bit of flirting didn't go amiss.

As we stepped out onto this grand pirate ship, flowers covered the decks and the stage lights lit up the ship and water making it look magical and ethereal. Up on one of the higher decks, two pirates were sword fighting, our own private show, which we were about to become a part of.

The pirates ran down the spiral staircase towards us. One pirate grabbed Suzie, seized a nearby rope and swung with her in his arms off the boat onto some nearby rocks. I must say, Suzie played the damsel in distress very well, screaming loudly, though the fear that she would be dropped into the water was probably a real one.

Then it was my turn. I took the sword from the remaining pirate, tucked it into my belt, grabbed another rope and swung after them. The pirate was waiting and we fought, as prearranged only hitting each other's swords. Sparks rang from the metal as Suzie looked on in shock.

Finally I defeated the pirate, pushed him into the water, grabbed Suzie and swung back onto the boat.

'Quick,' said the remaining pirate. 'We must make ready to leave, grab that rope there and hoist the sail.'

It was quite obvious we weren't going anywhere – as spectacular as the boat was, the cove we were in was barely bigger than the boat itself. But Suzie, bless her, played along. She grabbed a rope and hoisted a sail. As it fluttered and billowed in the wind, the words 'Suzie, Marry Me' appeared in foot high letters.

Despite the lateness of the night, there was a small crowd gathered on the other side of the cove and they cheered when they saw this proposal.

When Suzie looked around for me, I was down on one knee holding the skull and crossbones ring in my hand.

She didn't say yes, but she did take the ring and put it on her finger which I took to be a very good sign.

Playing to the crowd, I grabbed her, threw her over my shoulder and carried her off into the hotel with shouts and cheers ringing in our ears and Suzie's laughter vibrating through my body.

CHAPTER ELEVEN

The thing with Harry's proposals is you never knew what to expect or when to expect it. Our flight to New York wasn't until tonight, so Harry had promised me an easy day. He'd said we could sit by the pool this morning, answer some emails, make some calls. I had plans to have a bit of lie in, Skype Jules by the pool and then maybe have a last wander around a few of the hotels we'd yet to see. I didn't expect to be woken at some ungodly hour and, with only time for a quick shower, to then be bundled into a jeep. I now found myself bumping along a desert road with nothing but dirt and a few bushes as far as the eye could see. If I didn't know Harry better, I'd be afraid he was going to kill me and dump my body where no one would ever find it again. There was nothing out here, so quite why we were driving through the wilderness at this time in the morning I didn't know.

Ok, truth be told, I wasn't grumpy about the early start, or the never-ending desert, but the forthcoming visit to New York and how many times Chloe's name had cropped up in the last few days. Tonight I was going to meet her and Harry already had plans to go out with her – alone. There was a pain in my chest and it refused to go away.

Harry was chatting to our driver, whilst I scowled at the wilderness. Our driver, Thomas, was what I could only describe as a cowboy, with his black Stetson, boots and handlebar moustache. Though there was absolutely nothing camp about this man. He was in his sixties, and had that air about him that suggested he'd been there and seen it all.

The landscape started to change. Rock formations started to pepper my view and mountains were on the horizon as the roads started to become steeper.

As we rounded a corner, just for a brief moment before we disappeared round some bushes, I saw it. An image I had seen on many websites, posters, films and magazines.

'We're going to the Grand Canyon?' I squealed, interrupting Harry and Thomas talking.

Harry turned to look at me, a huge grin on his face. 'Yes, but it gets better than that. A lot better.'

We arrived shortly after at the visitors' centre, and Thomas went in to sort out our permits and tickets for lunch. I was itching to get out and see it all. I could see the tops of the canyon as it stretched out for miles, seemingly in every direction, but I wanted to peer over the edge and see all of its beauty.

I realised Harry was watching me and not looking at the scenery at all.

I scooted closer to him and he put his arm round my shoulders.

'This is incredible, thank you.'

He smiled and pulled me into him. 'I'm looking forward to seeing it myself.'

'Have you not been here before, when you last travelled around America?'

He shook his head.

'Then why aren't you looking out there, absorbing every inch instead of looking at me?'

'Because watching you get so excited is incredibly endearing.'

My heart leapt a little, especially at the way he was looking at me so fondly. I opened my mouth to speak but Thomas opened the door with a handful of paper.

'These are your tickets, the green ones are for lunch, these are for the coach up to Eagle Point and then onto where you'll eat for lunch and these are for...' He smiled and nodded towards the edge of canyon.

I turned and followed his gaze to a sleek burgundy helicopter. My eyes widened.

'Noooooo!'

Harry grinned and as he got out of the car, he offered me his hand and I greedily took it.

'We're going in the helicopter?'

Harry nodded, pulling me along the path towards it as my legs suddenly seemed unable to work on their own. It wasn't possible to be more excited than I was right then.

We quickly climbed on board and the pilot, Eric, introduced himself to us and told us how to fasten our harnesses.

I fumbled round in my bag, desperate to get my camera out and record the whole thing, and when I looked around we were already about ten metres off the ground. It had been so smooth that I hadn't even noticed that we'd taken off.

I quickly grinned at Harry, grabbing his hand and then the ground beneath us fell away and a mile below us I could see the green of the Colorado River.

I let out an involuntary scream, mainly of joy and excitement, but a tiny part fear at being over such a huge drop.

The helicopter dropped into the canyon, the steep reddish brown rocks towering over us as we soared over the river. We were so close to the canyon walls, I felt like I could just reach out and run my fingers along the sides. The rocks had a reddish gold colouring but on closer inspection were a multitude of different colours and different rock types, revealing millions of years of history in its rich veneer. Layers of red, brown, grey, white, yellow, pink and black zoomed past us as the helicopter hugged the undulations of the canyon cliffs.

I was still screaming at every twist and turn of the helicopter and I heard Harry laughing next to me. We swooped down, nearing the river, the sun glinting off the ripples in the green water, hinting at the promise of gold on the river bed.

My face was aching from smiling so much as we hovered over a spot where we were clearly going to land. I could see a boat waiting for us, ready to take us on the next part of our journey on the Colorado River.

With the tiniest bump we landed and after thanking Eric profusely, we made our way over the rocks to the boat, where we were introduced to a very excitable Chinese man called Sam.

He was super excited about taking us down the river but he seemed very excited about something else.

The helicopter roared into life again and Sam waved at the pilot, encouraging us to do the same. The helicopter took off and hovered over us for a second and I laughed as on its underbelly in big letters were the now familiar words, 'Suzie, Marry Me.'

Harry slung his arm round me and I wrapped my arm round his waist as I watched the helicopter get smaller and smaller as it disappeared over the edge of the canyon.

It took every muscle, every fibre of my being to physically stop myself from screaming yes at the top of my lungs.

*

I peered out of the airplane window at the dark sky and the twinkling lights of New York below us. I tried to pick out landmarks but it was too dark and we were coming in to land too quickly. I felt like I was having some kind of split personality moment, with half of my body thrumming with excitement at seeing everything that New York had to offer and the other half wishing that the plane could keep flying to Quebec and we never had to land in New York at all. Chloe's name had come up in conversation a grand total of seventy-eight times since we had taken off from Las Vegas. I'd actually counted them. And with each mention of her name we were getting ever closer to the troll that was going to steal my man away from me. Harry could barely contain his excitement at seeing her again.

He leaned over me now to peer out the window and I felt a little piece of me die at the huge grin on his face.

'You look tired,' he said.

I forced a smile on my face. 'I'm fine.'

'Me and Chloe are going to head out for drinks when we get in.'

Seventy-nine times. I wondered if he was going to go for the full hundred.

'You're welcome to come along, though it might be an idea to get some sleep so you're ready to explore tomorrow, there's loads to see. There'll be a lot of walking.'

I glanced out the window again at the lights that were rushing up to meet us. That was code for 'I'd prefer it if you didn't come out with us' if ever I'd heard it.

The tannoy pinged to get our attention. 'This is your captain speaking…'

I willed him to say we couldn't land in New York because of leaves on the runway and we had to divert to Quebec or even better the North Pole. I felt the thud of the plane's wheels as we touched down and sighed with disappointment. The captain was still talking. 'Welcome to La Guardia airport, the local time is twenty-three ten – ten minutes past eleven. There's quite a bit of rain out there folks, so wrap up warm. We hope you enjoy your stay.'

I was deliberately slow in getting my things ready to leave the plane – ensuring we were one of the last to disembark. I dragged my feet through baggage collection, stopping to go to the toilet and to do up my shoe laces, but inevitably we were soon in arrivals.

'Harry!' screamed a girly voice nearby. 'Harry James Forbes, look at you.'

A little blonde tornado threw herself into Harry's arms, leaping up and wrapping her legs round him as she hugged him tightly. He laughed and hugged her back. James? His middle name was James? Why didn't I know this? It was a small gesture of familiarity but it was another thing that added to the pain in my chest.

Her hair was short at the back and fell in a long fringe across her face. As I stood awkwardly waiting for our introduction, I could see that Harry's description of 'cute as hell' was vastly understated. She was beautiful – any idiot could see that. And that same idiot could clearly see how completely and utterly besotted Harry was with her.

*

The annoying thing was that Chloe was lovely – she'd hugged me almost as eagerly as she had hugged Harry, and she'd linked arms with me as we'd walked out of the airport. She was as enthusiastic as a puppy, and although I tried to find her exuberance really irritating I couldn't manage it. She was very endearing, simple as that.

We caught a taxi into Manhattan, crossing over the spectacular Queensboro Bridge, and checked into a hotel on Fifth Avenue overlooking Central Park.

Chloe, to my dismay, was staying in the hotel with us – as she apparently lived outside of Manhattan and had booked the hotel so she could spend some time with us, or mainly Harry. To make matters worse, her hotel room was next to ours.

Harry must have spent a grand total of thirty seconds in our room, as he changed into a clean shirt.

'You sure you don't want to come?' Harry asked as he inched towards the door, clearly hoping I wouldn't.

I had spent the last hour with Chloe fawning all over Harry, which was enough for a lifetime. My only saving grace in all of this was that Harry would most likely spend the next few days with her away from me and I wouldn't have to see it – and on Tuesday, just three days from now, we would be flying to Quebec together, hundreds of miles away from New York and Chloe.

'I'm fine, I'm going to go straight to bed, get some rest.'

Harry nodded and was gone a moment later.

I plonked myself down on the bed and heard their laughter recede down the corridor. Just three little days. I could do that. And if I was to suffer for past life crimes, New York was a spectacular place to do it.

I fired up the laptop to reply to a few emails and do a bit of research into the wilds of Alaska, the location of a mountain climbing and hiking proposal one of our clients wanted to do. Research would keep me distracted for a while. Only this time it didn't. Harry and Chloe were stuck in my head.

If Harry and Chloe were really just friends, and nothing was ever going to happen between them, then she was no threat at all. And if Chloe was The One, the one that Harry could trust and spend his life with, then that was only a good thing. He had been hurt somehow in the past and this was stopping him from moving on. I wanted him to move on with me, but if he couldn't do that I had to be happy that he could move on at all, find love, live a happy ever after.

Harry had been my rock, been there through good times and bad, I wanted happiness for him so much. I suddenly wanted to do something for him, something wonderful just like he had done for me with the proposals.

I looked up from my laptop with a sudden idea. He was as excited about coming to New York as he was about seeing Chloe, he loved the place. I thought back to that conversation that I'd had with Jules about his dream job, the one that he'd turned down probably because of Jack. What if I could get him a job here? An idea started to form in my brain. What if we moved out here together? This would be a good thing for me too, moving away from all the Jack memories, starting out somewhere new and fresh. I could run the.PerfectProposal.com anywhere in the world. Yes, there would be work permits and visas to sort out but the look on Harry's face when he found out he had a job here would be worth all the hassle.

I had a friend who lived in New York – well he was a good friend of Jack's but we had stayed in touch a bit since Jack died. I probably couldn't get Harry a job, but I could most likely get him an interview. Harry was hugely talented with computers and websites, he would be very easy to sell.

I quickly fired off an email. It was late at night but my friend would at least get the email first thing the next day.

I switched the laptop off and lay down, closing my eyes, smiling to myself. I had made the first step to help both of us move on.

*

I was woken in what must have been the early hours of the morning by the bedroom door slamming shut in the next room. I could hear Harry and Chloe laughing and talking, though it was impossible to make out what they were saying. I listened to them for a while. She made him laugh. A lot. But it was getting late now and in a minute he would come back to me, to spend the night with me as he had done from the beginning of this trip. I mean all his stuff was in here, of course he was going to sleep here. The talking tapered off and then it went very quiet. As much as I strained my ears, I could hear nothing. What were they doing? A sinking, sickening feeling prickled in my stomach. No, no, no, no. Harry had assured me that nothing would happen between them. They were friends, nothing more than that. Yes there was a history between them but that was in the past.

I grabbed a glass off the bedside table, finished the water in it and put it to the wall, pressing my ear to the bottom. Nothing. Wait. They were on the bed, I could hear it creaking. Ok. Maybe they were just sitting down on it, having a chat. There was silence and I didn't know if that was a good thing or a bad thing. I waited to see if there were any further noises but there was nothing. So that was it. He was either in there making love to her or cuddling up to her whilst they slept. Either option was not great.

I lay back down. I had no claim over him, he wasn't mine. Nothing had ever happened between us and nor would it, so I had no right to be upset by this latest development. I would be happy for him. He was my best friend and I would be happy that he was happy.

But the pain in my chest with the fear of losing him refused to go away.

*

I walked through Central Park, eating a pretzel bigger than my head as I steadfastly ignored my phone ringing in my bag.

I had slipped out very early this morning, desperate not to see them clinging to each other over breakfast. It hurt, a lot more than it should. I'd had Harry to myself for so long that I now felt bereft that he was with someone else. As ridiculous as it was, I actually missed him.

But New York was in my top five places in the world I wanted to visit, so I wasn't going to let it get me down.

The phone rang off and immediately rang again. I fished it out of my bag and stared at Harry's name flashing on the screen. I guessed I should answer it. He would be worried and at the very least I should arrange to meet him for the proposal. Besides, I had to retain an air of indifference.

I quickly answered it and tried to sound cheery.

'Hi.'

'Where are you?'

'Out. Enjoying the sights.' There, that sounded bright and breezy.

'Why didn't you wait? I wanted to take you round myself.'

'Well I figured you'd want to catch up with Chloe, I didn't think you'd want to babysit me around all the places you've been to before. It would be boring for you. I'm sure you two can find something to do with your time.' I couldn't help the sarcasm from entering my voice with that last comment.

There was a silence as he digested what I'd said.

'You're pissed off with me.'

'No I'm not.'

'Did you hear us when we came in last night, did we wake you?'

'No. I slept like a log. Look, I'm about to go in a museum so have fun with Chloe, I'll be fine on my own. Just text me to let me know when and where I need to be for the proposal.'

'Right.' He sounded disappointed.

I sighed. 'Don't be mad, I just feel like I'm in the way.'

'But you're not, of course you're not.'

'I'll see you later.'

I rang off before he could argue.

*

New York was everything I expected it to be and more. The place hummed with constant activity, so that it buzzed through my skin. My eyes swivelled in every direction trying to take it all in. Yellow cabs whizzed past, horns blared and people didn't stop moving as they walked briskly down the sidewalks with their steaming cups of macchiato, mobile phones and iPods. Gleaming skyscrapers towered over every road coupled with huge department stores and great eating places. I had already pigged out on two different pieces of pie and a cheesecake from Lindy's. The beautiful, gothic St Patrick's cathedral with its huge steeples looked out of place in the shadows of so many skyscrapers, but somehow it was fitting to have it there. I had taken so many photos my camera was starting to protest with the lack of memory. I'd even taken photos of the steam billowing out of the grates in the pavement. Photos of Times Square, the Flatiron Building, the Empire State Building from the top and the bottom. I had spent a good hour playing with all the toys in FAO Schwarz and another hour in dazed rapture in Tiffany's.

I'd had the most wonderful day. There were so many different ways here that Harry could propose to me and I was dying to see what he would do. New York had also given me so much inspiration for creating my own unique proposals here. It was the perfect place in so many ways. I had been out all day, my feet were aching though my brain was still buzzing with excitement. Day had long since turned to night and New York was taking on a new atmosphere. Street lights and neon signs indicated that the city wasn't going to sleep for a long time yet. I checked my phone again but it stared blankly back at me. I hadn't heard from Harry all day, probably too busy with Chloe to give me any thought.

I wanted to see Times Square lit up at night, so – clutching my now battered map – I made my way through the streets, enjoying the vibrant bustle of people rushing past.

I was halfway there when my phone beeped with a text. I dived in my bag, eager for any contact from Harry.

It didn't say a lot. *'Central Park, on the corner of 5th Avenue and West 59th Street. Nine o'clock.'*

I stared at it. No 'I hope you've had a good day,' or 'I missed you,' or 'How are you?' Just a curt instruction. Was he mad? He had no right to be, not when I was the one that had been ditched. To my annoyance, I now had to double back to get to Central Park. I would have to leave Times Square for tomorrow night.

The night had turned chilly now and little foggy clouds of breath preceded me as I hurried along the streets. The sun had been shining when I'd left the hotel this morning and as I was in such a rush to leave I hadn't thought to bring my coat, something I regretted now. I wondered if I had time to run back to the hotel to grab it before I met him but a quick squint at my watch told me I didn't.

I saw the vast expanse of green stretching out in front of me as I moved up Fifth Avenue, but though Harry towered head and shoulders over everyone else, as I scanned the crowds there was no sign of him.

I approached the corner and found myself bitterly disappointed to see Chloe hurrying towards me.

She looked radiant in the cold, her blonde hair gleaming in the streetlights, her cheeks glowing rosy pink, whereas I was pretty sure the only thing I had that was pink was my nose.

She enveloped me in a tight hug and I couldn't help but hug her back, her enthusiasm was infectious. She was small and delicate and smelt of vanilla.

'Have you had a good day?' She linked arms with me and we started walking into the park.

'Yes, it's been lovely. New York is such an amazing place, I can see why you moved here.'

'I've been here three years now, and I never get tired of it. I think Harry would love to live here too.'

I smiled to myself at my little smug secret.

We were silent for a moment as we walked along. I wondered if she was waiting for me to ask about her day. I really didn't want to hear what she'd been up to with Harry in case it involved some passionate embrace. I was better off not knowing. I quickly cast around for something to say.

'Harry says you work in TV and film, you're a make-up artist?'

'No, not really, not lipstick and stuff. Cuts, bruises, demons, vampires, elves, prosthetic noses, prosthetic lips, third eyes, one eye, car crash victims, murder victims, monsters, aliens, that sort of thing. Anything that's a bit disgusting is down to me.'

'Oh, cool.' It was cool, so much more interesting than what I did.

'So you and Harry?'

Urgh. I should have seen this coming. I made some non-committal noise.

'Harry said you were friends, I know he adores you, I mean to go to all this trouble for you, it shows he really cares…'

'He doesn't see me that way.'

'Do you see him that way?'

'No,' I answered quickly, probably too quickly.

'So not tempted by any of his proposals?'

I laughed. 'Can you imagine his reaction if I said yes?'

Chloe giggled. 'You totally should say yes, just to see what his reaction is.'

I smiled at the challenge. 'It would start with his eyes widening in horror and end with a Harry-shaped hole through the trees.'

Chloe laughed. 'Well try it, I dare you. Here we are.'

I had been so intent on the conversation I hadn't paid attention to where we were walking. In front of us was a black, open topped horse and carriage and a man dressed in a long green coat with gold buttons and a top hat.

'Miss McKenzie?' the man said. I nodded. 'I'm George, I'll be your driver for this evening.'

I looked at Chloe. 'We're going for a ride in a horse and carriage?'

She smiled at me. 'You are.'

A lance of pure joy sliced through me.

'Miss McKenzie,' George said. 'Mr Forbes was keen for me to introduce you to my horse.' He offered me his arm and with a bemused look at Chloe I swapped her arm for his as he walked me to his great steed. He was a big black beast that towered over me. I stroked his nose and he leaned into my hand, staring down at me with soft brown eyes, just like Harry's.

'This is Harry,' George said and I laughed.

'Hello Harry,' I said, softly, stroking his velvety nose, 'you are beautiful.'

'Well Miss McKenzie, we better get a move on, there's lots to see.' George escorted me back to the carriage and Chloe handed me a heavy bag.

'Put these on when you get there, but no peeking until you do.'

I nodded numbly and climbed in.

The carriage started moving and Chloe waved me off. 'Don't forget the dare.'

I smiled and then sat back in the carriage, watching the trees glide gracefully past with the soft clop of Harry's hooves. Old Victorian style lanterns sent little puddles of light across our path, reminding me of the green at home.

Up ahead the path curled into darkness. Despite the noise of the city, we were secluded here.

I caught sight of something pink hanging from the trees ahead and as we passed under it, George stood up and plucked it from the branches and then leaned back to pass it to me.

'I believe that's for you.'

I took the small envelope, there was something thick inside. I tore at the paper and a small crystal moon fell out into my palm. I stared at it in confusion, there was no note, nothing by way of explanation. It was beautiful, so intricately carved. I held it tight in my palm. As we made our way along the path, I lifted the envelope up to my nose. It smelt of him.

George found two more envelopes hanging from the trees on our journey, containing a crystal star and a crystal sun.

Bright lights shone up ahead through the trees and I craned my neck to see what it was.

'We're nearly there Miss, you might want to put on what's in that bag.'

I grabbed the bag with barely concealed excitement and opened it to see two ice skates inside. I grinned and quickly yanked off my trainers and laced up the boots, throwing my trainers back inside the bag.

'Whoa!' George said to Harry the horse, as we came to a slow stop. I finished lacing up the boots and looked up to see the ice skating rink, almost deserted apart from a straggle of people.

George helped me down from the carriage and I gave him a wave as I hobbled down to the side of the rink. It sparkled in the lights that were surrounding it, but my eyes were drawn to a pink glow of light on the far side of the rink. Harry was standing underneath it, waiting. Waiting for me.

I was perturbed slightly to see Chloe also on the ice, but for now she was skating away from him. She'd obviously taken a more direct route than our long amble through the trees.

I tentatively climbed on the ice and, once I found my balance, I skated over to him.

'Hi,' he said, and I saw his eyes scan down me. 'Aren't you cold?'

'A bit, it's fine, I should have brought my coat.'

Before I'd even finished my sentence he took off his big long coat and wrapped it round me, helping me to put my arms through the sleeves and buttoning it up. I smiled at him, all anger vanishing. He took my hands in his big paws and blew on my fingers, the warm breath made my stomach clench with desire.

'I missed you today,' I said.

He kissed my forehead briefly, though he didn't say it back. Instead he let out an ear piercing whistle. Behind him, beyond the barrier, I heard a big machine start up and I frowned in confusion as white stuff was projected into the air. But as it came down in soft flakes around us, I realised the noise was coming from a snow machine. I watched the flakes swirling above us, silhouetted against the night sky, and found myself grinning inanely as they peppered my face with tiny icy crystals. It was amazing.

I turned back to look at Harry, who was watching me intently.

'I got your gifts.' I held out the little crystal charms.

'I gave you the sun, the moon and the stars, now I'd like to give you my heart.'

He got down on one knee and held out his hand to reveal a pink crystal heart charm. I picked it up and held it, touching its smooth surfaces with my finger, it was cool to the touch.

'Marry me, Suzie.'

I looked back at Harry and reached out to hold his face in my hand. 'What would you do if I said yes?'

My heart was thudding now, what was I saying? His eyes widened a little bit and then he laughed. 'I'd find a church or registrar that could marry us tonight and we'd be husband and wife by midnight.'

He was grinning at me and there was nothing in his eyes that suggested he was taking this seriously.

'Well, is it a yes?'

Just then Chloe skated near us, obviously curiosity getting the better of her and wondering if I was carrying out the dare. But just as I was about to answer yes, Chloe did a startling jump and span in the air twice before landing gracefully and skating past.

Harry laughed and clapped. 'Well done Chloe, that was amazing.' He watched her go with admiration and my hand dropped from his face as he stood up.

'And join you and Chloe for a threesome, I don't think so.' I stepped back. 'Thanks for this, it was beautiful. I'll leave you two to it. I'll see you tomorrow.'

I turned but he caught my arm and pulled me back. I wobbled a bit on my skates at the sudden movement and he wrapped his arm round me and pulled me against him, supporting me with his weight.

'What's wrong?'

'Did you sleep with her?' Oh God, there really was no filter on my brain at all.

I waited for him to get angry. I had no right to ask him that question or mind about the answer.

His eyes were dark as he stared at me. He wrapped his other arm round me, shifting me closer. 'No. Well yes, but not in the way you're thinking. I didn't want to wake you so I slept in her bed but just in the same way that we sleep together. Nothing happened. We're friends, nothing more.'

I didn't know if that was actually worse. I thought the intimacy, the close friendship we shared was unique to us, a special bond that only we had, but it seemed he had that friendship with Chloe too. Maybe he was touchy feely with all his female friends and it wasn't special at all.

He reached his hand up and brushed a few snowflakes from my cheek. His touch made my stomach clench with desire. 'Why are you getting weird over this? I've been out with lots of women since we first met and you've never got like this before. But first that blonde in the Galapagos Islands and now Chloe. If I didn't know better I'd say you were jealous. Are the proposals having an effect on you? Are you suddenly falling in love with me?' He laughed, dismissing his assessment.

I pushed my way back out of his embrace and he let me.

'It's just a big joke to you isn't it, all this? You don't get it, do you?'

Oh God, no, I had to stop talking.

'It's not a joke.' All sign of humour had vanished from his eyes. 'Not one bit. And no, I don't get why you are so upset over something that means absolutely nothing to me.'

My heart jolted. Sleeping with Chloe meant nothing to him, but he'd said that it was the same as sleeping with me, so that meant nothing to him either.

Something was digging hard into my hand and I looked down to see the tiny crystal heart. I pushed it into his hand.

'Save this for someone who does mean something to you then.'

I turned and skated away.

'Suzie wait,' Harry called.

I skated off the rink, dumped my boots and his coat on a nearby chair, quickly tugged on my trainers and walked towards the hotel, refusing to look back.

*

I was on the Staten Island ferry when my phone beeped with a text message the next day. Harry hadn't come back to our hotel room the night before.

I decided to wait until the ferry had passed by the Statue of Liberty, the whole point of this journey, before I fished the phone out of my bag. She was a lot smaller in real life than the films and photos led me to believe – but she was still an iconic, powerful image. She had a steely resolve in her eyes as she looked out to sea.

It was early morning and the weak winter sunshine was casting a candyfloss glow over the waves.

As the statue grew small in the distance, I grabbed my phone and opened up the text.

'Be at the Top of the Rock, 70th floor, the outdoor observation deck in the Rockefeller Centre at twelve noon. Face Central Park, use the binoculars. I won't be there so you'll need to keep your eyes open.'

He wouldn't be there? He had the audacity to moan at me when I wanted to miss the proposal in Mexico and now he was too busy to attend this one himself.

I noticed I had an email waiting for me as well. I opened it up and saw it was from Mark, Jack's friend that lived in New York. I scanned through it. To my surprise, Mark already knew about Harry – he'd worked with him briefly a few years before he'd moved out to New York. I could tell that Mark was practically salivating over the prospect of Harry coming to work with him, saying that he would be just what the company needed.

Mark wanted Harry to come for an interview in two days. I bit my lip, we were supposed to be flying to Quebec tomorrow, but we could easily change it.

I still wanted to do something nice for Harry. I felt guilty about my sudden outburst the day before, especially after everything Harry had done for me. Although that guilt had waned slightly when he hadn't returned to our room the night before. This was a way to give something back, maybe to somehow indicate my feelings for him without putting my heart on the line.

I sent Harry a text saying we needed to talk and if he wasn't going to be at the proposal, could we meet for drinks tonight. He didn't reply.

*

I arrived a little earlier than I was meant to be there, so I had time to enjoy the view before the proposal. In some ways the view was better than the one from the Empire State Building as it was closer to the other skyscrapers and therefore it didn't seem like we were looking down on a load of roofs, plus the almost unobstructed view of Central Park was unrivalled and beautiful.

Just before twelve, I positioned myself facing Central Park and wondered what it was I was going to see. I had bought a small pair of binoculars from one of the touristy shops on the way so I wasn't going to use lots of quarters and hog one of the public binoculars on the observation deck.

I waited and waited and saw nothing. I scanned the park, the sky, the streets below and still saw nothing. Five minutes passed. Ten minutes passed, still nothing.

It was bad enough that Harry wasn't going to be here, but for him to have forgotten altogether was unforgiveable.

Next to me a man got down on one knee with one red rose and asked his girlfriend to marry him, she squealed with joy and threw herself into his arms. At least someone was getting proposed to today.

Then suddenly I saw it. In the big black skyscraper near the park, a big M appeared in one of the windows. An A appeared in the window below it. Below that was an R. Slowly, slowly, each letter of the words 'Marry Me' was revealed across seven floors, eight if you included the empty floor between Marry and Me.

It was huge, and even without the binoculars it was easy to see. I smiled as I quickly fired off a few shots with the camera. Harry's originality was hard to top. The newly engaged woman next to me saw it too and threw the rose back at her boyfriend.

'Why didn't you do something like that, you give me a stinking rose whilst someone else gets a proposal spread across an entire skyscraper? Cheapskate,' she squawked in a shrill American accent.

The boyfriend floundered and I smoothly stepped in. 'Sorry Miss, I'm from The Perfect Proposal dot com,' I handed her my business card. 'Your boyfriend arranged this for you – unfortunately our proposal was a little late so your boyfriend did your proposal first. You have my apologies but the logistics of this sort of thing are quite hard to organise.'

The girl turned to her boyfriend. 'You did this for me?'

The boyfriend looked at me then nodded, clearly wondering how much this was going to cost him.

She threw herself into his arms again and kissed him all over. He mouthed thank you to me over her shoulder.

'Congratulations,' I said, though I doubted the girl even heard me.

I turned away, smiling, and that's when I saw him. Jack.

CHAPTER TWELVE

I couldn't move, I couldn't breathe, I could only gaze at the man that was clearly my brother. I stared at him. Every bone in my body was screaming at me, telling me this wasn't Jack, that it couldn't possibly be as I slowly stepped towards him. I had watched him die, I had held his hand as he took his last breath, I had been to his funeral – yet here he was, standing just three metres away from me, with his arm wrapped round another woman.

Had he faked his death purely to be with this woman? How could he leave Jules and Bella? But suddenly it didn't matter. I could be angry with him later, now I just wanted to touch him, to hold him and smell him once more.

I took another step towards him and he spotted me staring at him. There was no recognition whatsoever, not even a glimmer in his eyes. This should have been enough to stop me, to doubt this insanity, but my hand was already outstretched to touch him.

'You all right love?' he said to me. He was English, though he was more northern than Jack.

I felt tears brimming my eyes. It wasn't him. I knew it wasn't but my hand was still outstretched to touch his heart, a tiny glimmer of hope.

'Gareth, who is this?'

The man shrugged, looking a bit scared now by my endless staring.

Suddenly, a hand grabbed my outstretched one and pulled me away into Harry's hard chest, enveloping me into a protective hug.

'It's not him, baby.'

'I know,' I said, as my tears soaked his shirt, a huge wave of disappointment washing over me.

He pulled me down onto a bench next to him, clamping his arm round my shoulder. I was still crying but now Harry was here, my tears were quickly fading.

'I'm such an idiot,' I muttered, wiping my eyes. 'I just wanted it to be him so badly, I started to believe it was.'

I looked over at the man now, he was still eyeing us warily. With the fresh perspective, I could clearly see it wasn't Jack. He was thinner in the face, at least an inch taller and lacked the tiny mole on his cheek that had often earned him the highly original nickname of Moley from his friends.

'Are you kidding?' said Harry. 'The man is Jack's doppelganger, they could be twins. I had to stop myself from leaping into his arms and giving him a big hug too.'

I laughed weakly. 'I wish you had, then I wouldn't have looked such a weirdo.'

'For you baby, anything.'

Harry stood up and grabbed the poor man into a big hug, nuzzling into his neck like a cat. The man was clearly stunned and I laughed.

Harry released the man with a friendly pat around the cheek and came back to sit next to me, scooping me onto his lap as he sat down. I leaned into him as he stroked my back.

I looked up at him and touched his cheek. 'Where would I be without you?'

He smiled and kissed me sweetly on the nose.

We sat staring at each other for a few seconds, the tension from the day before returning.

'What did you want to talk to me about?'

'Oh. I have a surprise for you. I may have gotten you a job.'

He stared at me, his eyes unblinking. 'I have a job.'

'This is better, it's working for one of the big computer firms here, "Euphoria". You'll be able to put some of your amazing skills to better use than just working on web design all day. And you get to move here, you love it here, you wanted to move here before, I know you did. Now you can…'

I trailed off at the expression on his face. He was furious.

'If I wanted a job here I would have got a job here. You had no right to interfere in my life like that.'

How had I got this wrong? I thought that's what he wanted. He hadn't stopped talking about New York for days before we came.

'I was trying to do something nice…'

'You were trying to get rid of me.'

'No, that wasn't it at all.'

'I've served my purpose, haven't I? I held you after your brother died, stood by you through the worst moments of your life, and now that's behind you and you're looking to the future – one that doesn't involve me.'

'No, you don't understand…'

He shifted me off his lap and walked to the exit. I stared after him for a moment then got up and ran after him, but I was too late. I saw the lift doors close between us and he was gone.

*

I had waited for ages in our hotel room, but Harry hadn't come back. I had phoned and texted him but he hadn't answered. In the end, hunger called me down to the restaurant.

As I walked in, I saw Harry with Chloe. He looked absolutely devastated. Blood turned to ice in my veins. This wasn't to do with the job. This was something far worse. The worst case scenarios ran through my mind. Something had happened to Badger. Or his sister or nephew? I ran towards him, ignoring that Chloe was holding his hand and trying to comfort him.

'What is it, what's happened?'

Harry stared at me, but his eyes were cold. 'Nothing for you to worry about.' He downed the rest of his drink in one. 'I'm going to bed, Chloe are you coming?'

'In a moment,' Chloe said, gesturing to her unfinished drink.

Harry stood, towering over me. His eyes softened as he looked down at me. He reached out a hand towards my face then changed his mind and walked away.

I slid into his empty chair opposite Chloe. 'What's happened?'

She watched me carefully as she swirled her drink. All her enthusiasm and giddiness had now gone. 'Do you know anything about his past?'

'No. Do you?'

She nodded.

My heart sank. 'He won't tell me anything.'

I rubbed the pain in my chest. I was gutted that he could share that part of his life with Chloe but not with me.

'I thought something terrible had just happened.'

Chloe sat staring at me. 'You care about him?'

'Yes, a great deal. He's my best friend.'

'You're in love with him?'

I was not ready for such a direct attack and had no words with which to defend myself. Literally no words at all.

She rubbed her eyes and sighed. 'What were you thinking when you got him this job?'

I felt like a naughty child sitting in front of the headmistress. 'I wanted to do something nice for him. He talks about New York with such love, I thought… I wanted to make him happy.'

'And he seems miserable at home, does he?'

Harry, the Harry before all this aggro that I had foisted on him with my jealousy and terrible ideas, was a happy man – always walking round with a smile, always finding the humour in everything. I had never seen him sad or angry or stressed, he was the happiest person I knew. I thought back to what he said in Mexico, that life was perfect. Had I really ruined all that for him? I didn't understand how this could be a bad thing and how what happened in his past could affect it.

I stood up. 'I have to talk to him.'

'He doesn't want to talk to you right now.'

I looked at her. Was it her that was driving this wedge between us? Did she have designs on him herself?

'Do *you* love him?'

She stared at me for a moment. 'No, I don't love him like that, but I love him like a brother and I won't see him hurt.'

'I don't want to hurt him either, but I need to talk to him. I made this mess, so I can clear it up.'

She sighed. 'I'll get another drink in then. But if I go up to the room and find him in a worse state than he is now, you and I are going to have words.'

I nodded and hurried back upstairs.

To my surprise, Harry was waiting for me outside my room.

'Harry… Look…'

'I need my stuff.'

'What?'

'You're flying to Quebec tomorrow, I'm staying here for this interview. I need my stuff.'

'Now hang on a minute…' I realised I was shouting as an elderly couple walked past, the woman shaking her head with disapproval.

I shoved the key card in the door and gestured for Harry to come in and then closed the door behind him.

'I was going to change the flights, thought we could stay here a few more days and then go to Quebec together, but if this whole job thing is upsetting you that much then I'll cancel it.'

Harry shook his head and grabbed a few of his things and stuffed them into his suitcase.

'Why are you being such an ass over this?' I marvelled at my attempt to make things right. I was shouting at him and calling him an ass.

He rounded on me. 'Why am I being an ass? You've messed up my perfectly perfect little life with this bombshell.'

'How is your life perfect? You cancelled your dream job in your favourite place in the whole world to be with a woman that doesn't love you. You earn pittance in a job that completely wastes all your talent and experience, you move from one woman to the next, never letting yourself fall in love because you might get hurt.'

He looked wounded. I was making it worse, a lot worse.

I deliberately softened my voice. 'Tell me why you're so upset by this?'

He shook his head.

'Tell me what happened when you were a child.'

'No.' He zipped up his suitcase.

'You have to give me something here, something, anything to show that our friendship means as much to you as it does to me. You have been there for me every single day since Jack was diagnosed. Let me be there for you.'

He shook his head stubbornly, not even tempted for one second to share his life with me.

Pain lurched inside my heart. 'Do you have any idea how that makes me feel? Chloe, Badger, even Jules knows what happened to you and I know nothing. I'm supposed to be your best friend, you said you trusted me completely but you won't trust me with this. That hurts me so much.'

He stared at me. 'It's in the past.'

'Not if it's stopping you moving on, not when you have such a reaction to me trying to do something nice for you.'

'Let's look at your reaction to me doing something nice for you. I'm doing all these perfect proposals, taking you around the world and yesterday you flip out over it. Somehow, I've upset you too. Want to tell me about that?'

I stared at him and he stared back.

I deftly changed the subject. 'This woman you fell in love with, did she know about your past, did you tell her?'

'No, it doesn't affect her.'

'It does, why can't you see that? No woman is going to give themselves to you completely, give you their whole heart unless you can trust them with who you are. Your past is a huge part of that. What did she say to you when you told her you were in love with her?'

For the first time his anger gave way to embarrassment. 'I never told her.'

I felt my mouth fall open, and my heart bled for him. I took a step towards him. 'How do you know she didn't feel the same way?'

'She never said…'

'Oh Harry, no woman is going to walk down the aisle with you and spend the rest of their life with you unless you tell them you love them. You can show them with nice gestures and your actions, I mean you're full of them, you're the kindest, most generous person I know, but the woman needs to hear the words.'

'I'd tell her, if she told me first.'

'When there's absolutely no risk of you being rejected, when the woman has already made her feelings known?' Something in his face said I had hit the nail right on the head. 'It doesn't work like that. I know this is the twenty-first century, women are equal partners in a relationship, but we still want to know that our men will fight for us, be brave enough to declare their feelings. We want to know that the love our man feels for us is an all-consuming, shout-it-from-the-rooftops kind of love, not just an "I love you too" kind.'

He rubbed his hand over his hair, refusing to look at me as he stared at the ground.

'You're a beautiful person, inside and out. Why do you feel you have so little to offer someone? Why are you so scared of rejection?'

His head whipped up and I knew this was totally the wrong thing to say. 'I'm not scared of rejection. I've never let anyone get close enough to hurt me. Apart from you.' I opened my mouth to protest but Harry wasn't finished. 'Maybe time apart will be a good thing. It will give you time to think about what you really want from me.'

I swallowed the huge burning ball of pain in my throat. I couldn't bear the thought of being away from him. I searched for the words, anything I could say to make this right, but I had nothing.

He picked up his suitcase and walked out.

*

I sat on the plane, staring at New York City as it disappeared beneath the clouds. The lump in my throat was so big I could hardly breathe.

I was alone. Though it wasn't that that bothered me. Somewhere, underneath the grief, I was quite excited about seeing Canada on my own, discovering its delights and hidden secrets with fresh eyes rather than accompanying someone who had seen it all before. But losing Harry, being apart from Harry for the first time properly in over two years, was like a knife to the chest.

Pathetic as it was, I missed him already.

'Hi,' said an American voice next to me. I tore my eyes from the tiny skyscrapers to look round at the tall dark haired lady that was standing over me. She had ice blue eyes that stared unblinking at my face.

I cleared my throat of the lump that was lodged there. 'Hi.'

'Mind if I sit here?' She gestured to the empty seat. 'I have a snorer next to me, and he's just snuggled up to my shoulder and started dribbling. It might only be an hour and a half flight to Quebec but in my mind that's an hour and a half too many to put up with snoring and dribbling.'

I smiled and nodded. She threw herself down next to me.

'I'm Francine, by the way.' She stuck out her hand and I groaned inwardly that I wouldn't be allowed to wallow in my own self-pity for the next few hours, Francine was obviously a talker.

'Suzie.' I shook her hand, it was a surprisingly firm handshake.

'Why the long face?'

Wow. Cut to the chase straight away.

'Did you break up with your boyfriend?'

'Something like that.'

'Know what that feels like. I'm trying to give myself some space from my boyfriend for a few days. He's driving me mad and it's great to get away to give yourself a bit of perspective. Do I really want to be with this man for the rest of my life? If I miss him, then I guess the answer is yes. If I enjoy myself more alone than when I'm with him, then it's time he packed his bags and left.'

She shrugged so casually. She clearly didn't need a man to complete her, whereas Harry was the other half of my heart.

I stared at her, willing myself to be as strong as she was.

This time away from Harry would be a good thing. It meant I could finally get over him. I couldn't do that when I was with him every day and he was always doing lovely and sweet things for me.

'What's the problem with you and your man?' I asked, keen to get some perspective.

'He wants to marry me.' She shrugged again.

'And you don't want to?'

'Urgh, I don't know. One man for the rest of my life. One! Waking up every day to see the same ugly face in bed with you, being screwed in the same mundane way. Having Mexican for dinner every Thursday, pizza every Friday, I can't bear the thought.'

I thought about this. What it would be like to spend twenty-four hours a day with Harry, to wake up with him, with his arms wrapped tightly round me as I had done several times since Jack had died, to work with him, to go out and socialise with him. There was absolutely nothing bad about this thought. I could do that every day, all day for the rest of my life. We had practically been married for the last few months anyway. Harry even had clothes and a toothbrush at my house, it was only in the last month or two before we had flown out here that he had started spending more time away from me and not sleeping in my house every night. The only thing our marriage lacked was the sex and intimacy. If we had that, would I eventually get bored of him? What if the only thing keeping me interested now was the lack of it, the need for it?

You hear about this sort of thing all the time; couples that were madly in love slowly getting bored with each other, to the point where one of them or even both start plotting ways to kill the other one. A friend of mine, who had been one of those goofy doe-eyed brides, who even called her husband something sickening like Snookums, told me her husband constantly left his socks strewn about the place and it got to the point that she wanted to force feed him every single one of his socks until he choked to death. Snookums told me, after the divorce, that he had often fantasised about shoving her in the washing machine and switching the dial to fast spin and watching through the glass door as she span so fast her brain exploded. How could couples who were so in love end up like that? But the divorce rate was so high, especially in Britain. Maybe you were never meant to spend the rest of your life with just one person.

I couldn't believe that though. Not when my whole working, waking life was built around bringing couples together. Some people were destined to be together and when you found your soul mate, surely waking up every day to that person would be a joy not a chore.

'Why don't you talk to him? Tell him you want to spice things up a bit, have pizzas on Mondays some weeks instead of Fridays, try different sex positions, go out to new places, try new things.'

The eternal optimist in me wanted to see everyone happy, even if I couldn't find that happiness myself.

She stared at me. 'Oh, you're one of those aren't you?'

'One of what?'

'The happy, clappy, glass is always brimming over types. Bet you live in a rose-tinted world where everyone gets a happy ever after.'

I took offence to this. I was about to protest when she interrupted me.

'What happened between you and your boyfriend?'

'He… doesn't love me.'

'You see – happy endings don't happen; they cheat on you, you cheat on them, or at the very least you want to punch their stupid little faces in.'

I looked out the window. New York was nowhere to be seen now. I had always believed that if Harry finally did fall in love with me, we would have the perfect happy ending, but maybe Francine was right. Maybe this was for the best.

*

SECRET BLOG.

My dear would-be proposers and fellow romantics. I'm starting this secret blog because I want you all to know the real reason behind the One Hundred Proposals. You guys have been incredibly supportive of my quest to find the perfect proposal and many of you have physically helped out with the organisation and logistics of some of the more complicated ones, so I wanted to let you in on a little secret. What I say here is highly confidential and I would appreciate it if it can stay between us. It's a big ask, with over five hundred thousand followers of this blog, I know I may be shooting myself in the foot here by declaring my secrets, but I didn't want to string you guys along any further.

When I started this venture, many of you believed it was a publicity stunt to promote our company and I'm not going to lie, our little business is thriving because of it. Some of you thought it was just me trying to do something nice for Suzie after her brother died and partly it was.

But the main reason is… I love her. I love her with every single fibre of my being, she is the first thing I think of in the mornings and the last thing I think of at night. I love spending time with her, holding her, making her laugh or when she makes me laugh. She is my favourite person in the world and I could spend every single waking and sleeping hour in her company and never tire of it.

I think I've been in love with her since the first moment we met, although I didn't want to admit it at the time.

I've seen no sign from her that she has any feelings for me at all but I started this One Hundred Proposals thing because I wanted her to fall in love with me too. I'm hoping one of them will be big enough or meaningful enough that one day she will eventually say yes.

Recently, cracks have started to show. With the Ice Skating Proposal the other day, I thought I was finally going to get the answer I wanted. But I didn't.

The next day she texts me saying we need to talk. I thought this was it, she was going to fall into my arms and tell me how much she loved me. I have never felt so excited or happy. How wrong could I be?

She had secretly arranged for me to get a job in New York, thousands of miles away from the woman I love.

My disappointment that the conversation wasn't the one I wanted quickly turned to anger that she was pushing me away, three thousand five hundred miles away to be exact. The rejection that I have feared all my life had happened again, this time from the only person I've ever loved and trusted.

We had a big heart to heart last night, well probably more of an argument, and in my stubborn pride, I've sent her to Quebec alone.

I've woken up this morning realising what a terrible mistake this is but I was too late, she had already gone.

I know now what I must do. I have to tell her I love her, I have to be honest and find it in me to tell her what's in my heart. Even if that means I may lose her. This secret blog is the first step to this. If I can find the courage to share my feelings with you, then hopefully I can find the courage to tell her too.

My friend Chloe thinks I need to give her some space to cool down and some time to miss me. Maybe being alone will be a good thing for her, it will help her independence but maybe, without me being there, she might find she has feelings for me too.

I'm giving her a week, then I'm catching her up.

CHAPTER THIRTEEN

Old Quebec City was like walking through a small French town, with the cobbled streets and seventeenth century buildings and so many outdoor cafés. People walking past and speaking fluent French cemented the European feel. The city had winding roads that led down towards the river, lined with little houses, restaurants, shops and great gothic churches. I felt like my eyes were constantly swivelling in my head trying to take it all in. The sun was just starting to set, leaving scarlet ribbons in the cloudy purple sky. There had been a recent snowfall and so, in the fading light, the city was bathed in a beautiful lilac glow. Lights twinkled in bars, hotels and restaurants invitingly.

Although it was dark now and getting late, the streets were still buzzing with people laughing, chatting and calling to each other. It felt safe here, whereas in many cities of the world I would never walk the streets alone after dark. The snow on the ground added a magical glow to the city – the warm yellow lights, tumbling out of the café and shop windows, reflected off the snow making it sparkle. As I crunched over the ice, I couldn't help but smile at the magical beauty of the place.

I felt alive. Although I missed Harry with a huge ache in my heart, I wanted to be able to get over him so much

– and being here alone, I finally felt like it was an actual possibility. There was another good reason to try and get over him now. It didn't seem he was capable of loving me like I loved him. Even if he ever fell in love with me and we actually got together, he would always hold himself back and I didn't know whether I could live with him only ever giving me part of his heart. I was an all or nothing type of girl and if he couldn't love me with a ferocity and passion then it was a love I didn't really want.

I could function on my own, I didn't need to turn to him for every little thing. I had got to my hotel safely from the airport and found somewhere to eat. Although I had got lost three times since leaving the hotel, I had found my way again. Over the last year I had turned to him time and time again. Maybe this time alone would finally give me some perspective. I could make it without him. I swallowed the pain in my heart at this thought. Yes it would hurt, it hurt like hell, but I wasn't just going to collapse into a sobbing heap and refuse to leave my house ever again.

'Miss, Miss.'

A hand tugged on my coat and I looked down to see a small boy of about nine or ten staring up at me. 'Miss, you come with me,' he said, in stilted English. He tugged my coat, pulling me towards a darkened alley and I dug my feet in and refused to move. The boy looked sweet and friendly but still, I wasn't a complete idiot. 'Miss please, you come with me. Monsieur Forbes, he sent me for you.'

'Harry?'

'*Oui*, yes. Monsieur Harry, he tell me to take you to the river.' He pulled on my coat again. 'This way is quickest, we must hurry.'

'You spoke to Harry?'

'*Oui.*'

Nobody here knew me or why I was here. Harry had no way of knowing where I was in the city, I hadn't spoken to him since the night before. He hadn't even come to say goodbye that morning, how could this boy know who I was?

'Please Miss, you come with me.'

I stood my ground and I saw the look of desperation on his face.

'Please Miss,' said the little boy, still tugging at my coat. 'Your proposal.'

I looked down at him. He couldn't possibly know about the proposal without talking to Harry. Harry had organised many wonderful proposals over the last few weeks, it wouldn't be completely implausible that he had help in this city whilst he wasn't here. I had naively assumed the proposals would stop now we were apart, but it seemed that Harry wished to continue torturing me by proxy. Maybe this was one that was already organised and Harry didn't want to waste it. I couldn't forget that although we were on holiday, it was a working holiday and Sunlounger and Silver Linings were paying for this. Regardless that our relationship was in tatters, they would still want to see the daily proposals.

I nodded, reluctantly, and the boy, clearly relieved, ran off down the lanes, checking over his shoulder to make sure I was following.

'Miss, this way,' the boy called, catching my attention as he ran down a side alley. I followed him and caught sight of the city lights sparkling and dancing on the St. Lawrence River below me. I pulled my coat tighter around me, feeling the cool wind blowing from the river. The boy was running flat out now but I could see his shadow illuminated against the moonlight as he ran straight out onto a pier. I hurried along in his wake.

A small covered boat was waiting, its engine idling in the still waters.

My feet thudded onto the wooden pier as I slowed down.

'Miss, Miss.' The boy gestured for me to get on board. There wasn't a single person in sight. This wasn't a public vessel, this was a privately hired boat.

'Miss McKenzie?' an American man shouted from the boat. 'Please, we need to hurry, your proposal is starting in five minutes.'

Comforted slightly that the man at least knew about the proposal too, I hurried down the pier and stepped aboard.

'Here.' The man passed me a cup of something hot and steamy. 'I'm Eddie, I'm afraid we don't have much time. You're very late. I was supposed to show you the sights before the proposal but the proposal is about to start and I'm afraid we'll miss it. Please take a seat. We may have to move quite quickly.'

I sat down, feeling thoroughly reprimanded. 'I didn't know I was supposed to be here.'

'No, apparently Harry has been trying to ring you, but your phone was off.'

Eddie moved the boat into gear and I was pushed back in my seat as the boat took off. Hot coffee sloshed over my hands and legs and I quickly dabbed at it with my coat to take the pain away.

Harry had tried to phone me? But my phone wasn't off.

I rummaged in my bag and grabbed my phone. Sure enough, the phone was powerless. The battery had either died or I had inadvertently turned it off when going through my bag. I quickly turned it back on but as the phone loaded up, suddenly there was a huge boom in the sky. I leapt back in shock, sloshing myself with more coffee. I looked up, and saw ribbons of silver and gold fizzing through the night sky. Fireworks. Down the river, another rocket took off – this time, as it exploded, arcs of blue lit up the river and the city beyond. I gasped and stood up. The city looked amazing, glowing lilac in the snow and now the fireworks, probably for some party or other, had just put the magical cherry on the cake.

My phone beeped several times in quick succession and I looked down momentarily at the text and answerphone messages that were filling my screen. Another bang distracted me from the phone, as patterns of scarlet and gold cascaded through the sky, reflecting off the inky waters. I felt incredibly privileged to get so close to this display when I blatantly hadn't paid to go and see it.

Rocket after rocket launched itself into the night sky, leaving trails of emerald, ruby, sapphire, silver and gold above us and as we moved quickly along the river, we came closer and closer. I could see the fireworks were being launched from a boat, about a hundred yards ahead of us now – we were slowing down and I could tell Eddie didn't want to get too close to them.

Suddenly we seemed to enter into the finale as lasers lit up the sky to accompany the quick succession of rainbow explosions.

The fireworks finally stopped and our boat inched closer to the one giving the display.

'They were for you, Miss McKenzie,' Eddie said.

'What?' My heart leapt as I gave him my full attention.

'Harry organised all this for you.'

'The fireworks?' My voice was very small.

Eddie nodded. 'And this.'

He gestured to the display boat behind him and suddenly there appeared to be a white fire on board the ship. I let out a little scream of fear – something had gone wrong – but as the flames spread, I could see letters forming in the flames and within seconds the words 'Marry Me' were scored in white fire, silhouetted dramatically against the night sky.

I don't know why this proposal affected me more than any of the others, maybe because Harry wasn't here so I was free to react however my body saw fit, or maybe after three weeks of successive empty proposals I had reached my limit, or maybe it was because after all this effort, Harry was still hundreds of miles away with no idea how I felt for him and no desire to reciprocate these feelings. Maybe it was a combination of all those things. But as the flames dwindled, I sat down and burst into tears.

*

Eddie hadn't said a word to me on the way back. He was probably unsure of what to make of this less than enthusiastic response to an incredible proposal. We passed beautiful bridges and wonderful buildings and churches but I barely saw any of it. The tears finally stopped and I picked up my phone to read the messages that Harry had sent me. They didn't say a lot, asking where I was, telling me where to be. Not one of them showed any sign that he had forgiven me. Except... I checked back through the messages again. Every one ended with a kiss. Was that normal for Harry? Was I now clinging to any glimmer of hope no matter how desperate? I scrolled through some of his older messages. Not one of them had a kiss.

I cursed myself for reading too much into something as meaningless as a text kiss. I sent kisses in all my texts and that never meant anything either. Harry was messing me up spectacularly.

I gave my thanks to Eddie as he tied the boat up against the pier and he helped me off.

As I walked back to the hotel I started composing a text:

'Harry, thank you for the proposal tonight, it was an incredible, beautiful gesture. You have gone to so much effort so far and I am so touched that you would go to all that trouble just for me…'

I stared at the words, wondering what I could say to make things right between us.

Suddenly the phone burst to life in my hand. Harry's name flashed on the screen. I quickly answered.

'Are you ok?' Harry's voice was urgent and filled with concern, something which very nearly brought me to tears again.

'Yes, I'm fine.'

'Eddie said the proposal upset you.'

'No… Just feeling a bit emotional.'

'Because I'm an ass.'

I stifled a giggle. 'Partly.'

There was silence for a moment.

'I'm sorry about last night,' he said.

'I'm sorry too, I would never do anything to hurt you, you mean too much to me for that.'

There was another long silence and I feared I had said too much but at some point during these painful proposals my true feelings were going to come out. It really wasn't a case of if but when.

'Maybe I should come out.'

'Maybe you should.'

I heard a whispered 'no' on the other end of the phone. A female voice.

'Maybe I'll come out in a few days,' Harry said.

Chloe was obviously standing next to him, telling him what he should do, preventing him from flying out to join me. I understood that she cared about him and she worried that I was bad for him, but we were meant to be together. Maybe we were always just going to be friends but we were supposed to be in each other's lives and I wasn't going to let her put a stop to that.

'Maybe you should get the last plane out of New York tonight,' I said, stubbornly.

He laughed but I got the sense that Chloe was shaking her head vehemently.

'I'll see you in a few days.'

I wasn't going to beg. I had enough pride left in me for that.

'Thank you for my proposal, it was beautiful.'

I heard Harry sigh softly. 'Goodnight Suzie.'

'Night.'

Then he was gone.

*

SECRET BLOG

So after a sort of reconciliation last night, I caught the last plane out of New York to go and join Suzie. My friend Chloe didn't agree with this, apparently leaving Suzie on her own for one day is not enough time to let her miss me. Although it was plenty enough time for me to miss her.

So I justified my sudden dash across the state line. Being here means it's a darn sight easier organising these proposals when I'm able to co-ordinate the logistics rather than trying to find people to rely on. And in addition to the tangled web I've woven for myself,

Sunlounger and Silver Linings have no idea that me and Suzie have separated so the Proposer's Blog posts will continue to be written like I'm actually there, so I sort of actually need to be. Chloe reluctantly agreed to this and we flew out together.

In truth I just want to be closer to Suzie. I have to tell her I love her. To prove it to her with these proposals is not enough. I just need to tell her now.

Though apparently I need to pick the right moment. I would be lost without Chloe – I think I would barge into Suzie's hotel room and just blurt out that I love her if Chloe wasn't here to stop me.

So Chloe and I came up with a compromise. I could organise and watch the proposals from a distance and Chloe would provide the disguises so Suzie wouldn't recognise me. That's Chloe's thing you see, stage make-up. If anybody can make me look not like me, it's my dear friend Chloe.

To be honest it all feels a bit creepy to me, like I'm stalking her. Suzie and I were better off when we were two friends travelling together, but I guess Chloe knows best. Let's face it, my track record with women or falling in love has been a disaster so far, so I trust her to point me in the right direction.

COMMENTS

Victoria Stone says: What's wrong with just grabbing her and telling her you love her? If that's what you want to do, then do it. Ignore what everyone else says. Follow your heart.

Kirsty MacLennan says: If I was Suzie and you burst into my hotel room to tell me you loved me, I'd be jumping into your arms before you'd even finished speaking and then taking you to bed.

Megan Wood says: You and Suzie are too cute, I love you guys sooo much. I just want you to get together and have lots of babies. Tell her you love her. Any time is the right time to hear those words.

Laura Lovelock says: Why is Chloe trying to stop you from telling her? I don't know her but it seems to me that she likes you too.

*

Proposer's Blog

Day 22: The Dog Sledding Proposal. Location: Valley of Jacques-Cartier (Vallée de la Jacques-Cartier)

We spent the day wandering around the Ice Hotel today. It is the most incredible place in the world. Any words that I write to describe it won't do it justice, but I will do my best. From the little rooms to the great big chambers, the seats, the walls, the furniture, even the drinking glasses – everything is made from ice. Great columns populate each room, each with its own unique carving or pattern. The walls are carved with pictures as well. A multi-coloured array of lights set the rooms aglow something akin to the Northern Lights. The wedding chapel is beautiful, with the lights flickering off the crystal walls. I think I'd like to get married there one day, with my bride wrapped up in a long white fur cloak. I wonder where Suzie would like to get married. I think she fell in love with the place as much as I did. It is truly a breathtaking work of art. Suzie, naughtily, even tried to break a leaf off one of the sculptures so she could take it home with her, which obviously would have melted if she had succeeded. I love the ice slide and as Suzie had several goes on it, I'm guessing she loved it too.

But my proposal didn't take place here – tonight I had arranged for Suzie to go dog sledding. A short trip out of Quebec City and we were in the wilderness of the Valley of Jacques-Cartier, a stunning glacial national park. With imposing mountains, towering fir trees and the river that curls through it, it is a spectacular taste of Canada and it looks even more incredible under a blanket of snow.

The people at the dog sledding place were very friendly and welcoming and after a brief lesson on how to steer and stop we were off. The night time rides were beautiful, as the dogs, barking and yapping, pulled us along torch lined paths. Suzie picked up the skills needed straight away, she was a complete natural, and with the biggest grin on her face she steered our team of dogs with ease. It was an exhilarating journey. It was as we were nearing our destination that she saw the proposal. Hanging from each tree along the path were the letters formed in fairy lights. As the path straightened up in front of her, the three foot high words 'Marry Me' stood proud against the snowy trees.

She was grinning hugely when the dogs finally stopped. A big improvement on the reaction from the night before.

Tonight we slept in a yurt – with our own fire filling the room with heat, and a bed of animal furs to keep us warm, there was nothing sexier than snuggling up in the warmth and going to sleep with my best friend.

I stared at the blog in confusion. I'd read it through twice and was still confused. I had just got back to the hotel in Quebec City after spending a delicious night in the yurt. I'd fired up my laptop and spent over an hour replying to all the emails that Harry hadn't had a chance to reply to. Then I had turned to the blog, having not looked at it for a few days, but this was very confusing. It read like he had been with me at these places instead of me being alone.

He clearly hadn't told Silver Linings that he wasn't coming with me to Canada. It probably wouldn't go down well, given how much money they were throwing at this project.

But how did he know so much about what I had done? Yes, I'd had multiple goes on the ice slide, laughing and screaming like one of the kids. And I'd tried to break a piece off one of the pieces of wall art, but the only person who had spotted me had been some huge Hells Angel biker bloke. Yes, I'd watched a wedding with a bride wrapped in a long white fur cloak and wished with all my heart that it had been me. I'd loved the dog sledding, it had been so much fun – and then to be proposed to along the fairy light trail was very romantic. But how had he seen my reaction?

And what was with the comment about there being nothing sexier than snuggling with his best friend under a blanket of animal furs? Sexier?

My eyes caught one of the comments at the bottom of the blog. I generally didn't read the comments from our followers any more. When we'd first started I'd diligently replied to every single one, but now there were hundreds of them, all of them saying the same thing, 'We love this,' or 'This is so cute,' or from the men, 'Just give her one already.' But this comment leapt out at me.

'I love these proposals, so romantic, and I'm loving the secret blog too. So exciting.'

I stared at it then grabbed my phone, composing a quick text to Harry.

'Thank you for my proposal. I loved it so much. Are you spying on me?'

The reply came back almost straight away.

'Of course. I have to make sure my proposals run smoothly. So no going off with strange men, my spies will tell me everything.'

I texted him back.

'What's the secret blog?'

This time the gap between the reply was longer, but eventually my phone pinged with a new message.

'I have no idea, I saw that comment and was going to ask you the same thing. I thought you had started a blog too. Some of the comments are very weird. Did you see the one about the giraffe the other day? I don't think some of our followers have all their marbles.'

My fingers hovered over the keys, not sure what to reply to that. I had the feeling there was something he wasn't telling me. Before I had the chance to reply, another text came through from him.

'Are you having fun on your own?'

I quickly replied. *'Yes, it's actually been a really good thing.'*

His reply was almost instantaneous. *'See, you don't need me.'*

What was that supposed to mean? Did he want me to need him? Did he want me not to need him so he wouldn't feel guilty?

I wrote a text and sent it before I could change my mind. *'I don't need you Harry, but I want you here with me. I miss you, so much it actually hurts.'*

There was no reply to that. I'd said too much and he didn't know how to respond.

I had to send some message to clarify it. As my fingers hovered over the keys, there came a knock on the door. I put the phone down and ran to answer it.

It was the proposal I saw first – Harry's grinning face emblazoned on a T-shirt with a speech bubble and the words 'Marry Me' coming out of his mouth. I laughed and then looked up to see who was wearing the T-shirt. I screamed and threw myself into his arms.

*

'It's a cracking view,' said Badger, as he tucked into a sandwich we'd ordered from room service, watching the sky turn from a pale pink to scarlet as the sun set over the city.

'I still can't believe you're here.'

'I was coming out anyway, give Harry a hand with some of the proposals. I didn't realise I'd be on my own whilst Harry's in New York.' He rolled his eyes. 'I can only stay for a few days but then Harry will be with you soon.'

'You didn't have to come out here for me. I was doing fine on my own.'

'I wanted to. Harry's an arse for leaving you like this.'

'I hurt him.'

Badger sighed heavily. 'Do you know anything about his past?'

'No. I wish people would stop asking me that question, unless of course you want to follow it up with, "Once upon a time…"'

'It was no fairy tale Suze. And I can't even tell you, it's just not fair for me to do that. But I will tell you that his parents were rubbish. They didn't physically abuse him but apart from that they were the worst parents in the history of all parents. They let him down spectacularly and he never really got over the pain of that. He vowed he would never trust anyone after that.' Badger rubbed a hand over his eyes, wearily. 'Just... sometimes he needs a bit of gentle handling.'

He turned back to look at the view and I guessed that was the end of the conversation. I stared at his back in confusion, then decided to change the subject. My head was starting to hurt with it all.

'How's Bella?'

He turned, his whole face lighting up, and I felt a flash of anger that he loved my niece so much and then a huge stab of guilt for thinking like that. I wanted to be happy for them, it just was going to take some time.

'She's beautiful – she's into everything, exploring, touching, grabbing. I just love her…'

He trailed off.

'It's ok. It is weird for me. I think it will always be weird that another man is raising my niece, that she will never know her real dad. But I'm glad that man is you and that you love her as much as you love Jules.'

Badger rubbed his neck, awkwardly. 'I am sorry, I never meant for it to happen…'

'Don't be. You've made Jules happy again and I can't possibly hate you for that.'

There was an awkward silence that hung in the air between us.

'Oh hell, Suzie, let's go out and get drunk.'

I smiled. 'I'll grab my coat.'

*

I finally slotted the key into the hotel room door and fell into my room. The lights of the city glowed from the streets below me and I stared at the view in childlike wonder for a moment. I heard Badger crash into something in his hotel room next door and giggled as I heard him swear. I don't know what we had drunk tonight. It started off with wine, but then the pitchers of liquid that arrived at our table started getting increasingly brown. I knew we had drunk a lot of it, five or six jugs had come to our table throughout the night, but I hadn't felt drunk at the time. It was only as we stepped out into the cold, winter air that the alcohol seemed to hit me. We were catching a plane to Toronto tomorrow but thankfully it was later in the afternoon.

I noticed my phone on the bed and grabbed at it, thinking I would try to take some photos of the startling views, but there was a text from Harry. I opened it and read his reply to the text I'd sent earlier.

'I miss you too Suzie. It doesn't seem right without you.'

I let out a giggle – everything seemed funny and wonderful tonight. I quickly found his number in my phone and called it. I noticed the clock on the wall said it was past two in the morning. For some reason, I found this even funnier.

When Harry answered, it was clear I'd just woken him up.

'Yep?' His voice was thick with sleep.

'Hi, it's me.'

'Hey. Are you ok?'

'I'm fine. Bloody brilliant in fact.'

I could sense the smile from him.

'Are you drunk? I hope Badger hasn't been getting you into trouble.'

'I may be a teeny, tiny bit drunk.' I held my finger and thumb together to show that it was only a tiny bit before I realised that Harry couldn't see them. 'What are you doing?'

'I *was* sleeping.'

'I love you Harry.'

Where the bloody hell did that come from? The words just fell out of my mouth without any warning. My drink-addled brain had let me down. A giggle that turned into a snort escaped my mouth too. I threw myself down on the bed and I laughed into my pillow.

'That's nice,' Harry said, dryly. 'But as lovely as your drunken proclamations are, I'm going back to sleep now.'

'You're angry with me.'

'No. I'm not. It's always nice to be told you're loved. But I would have preferred to hear it when you hadn't drunk six pitchers of Caribou.'

Caribou, that's what we'd had. Some kind of special whisky and wine Quebec drink. It was delicious, my lips tasted of maple syrup.

'It's true though.' My mouth was talking again. 'I do love you.'

'Get some sleep my love, if you still feel the same tomorrow, then give me a call.'

'I will.'

'Ok, I'll look forward to it. Goodnight.'

He hung up and I tossed the phone onto a nearby chair, and with a huge grin on my face I drifted off to sleep.

CHAPTER FOURTEEN

'No, no, no, no!' I sat up in bed, my head reeling. I hadn't phoned him, I couldn't have done. The sun was streaming through the window, almost unbearably bright as it reflected off the snow. It hurt my eyes but I had more pressing matters. I grabbed my phone quickly and groaned when I saw the last call made had been at two-fifteen that morning. To Harry.

I felt sick. I'd told him I loved him and now there was no going back.

He'd never said it back to me either. Admittedly, I had been steaming drunk at the time, but still, it would have been nice of him to reciprocate.

I didn't know whether to ring him and apologise or just ignore it completely. Sticking my head in the sand seemed like a much better option.

In fact, sleeping for the rest of the day seemed like a much better option – that Caribou was potent stuff.

There was a knock on the door and I staggered out of bed to answer it. I passed a mirror on my way to the door and was shocked to see my hair sticking out like a wild bush, and mascara smeared across my face. I prayed it wasn't Harry.

When I opened the door, the young bell boy recoiled in shock before he readjusted his face into a much more professional expression.

'Delivery from Mr Forbes.'

My heart leapt then sank. After last night's declaration, it wasn't likely to be good.

He brought the tray into the room, placed it on the table and left.

There was a thick envelope, a glass of orange juice and a black box, about the size of my hand.

I grabbed the envelope first. Inside there was a packet of painkillers and a note that simply said, 'Take these, love Harry x.'

Well at least he wasn't angry with me. I swallowed two down with the glass of orange juice and then turned my attention to the black box. Surely he hadn't bought me an engagement ring.

I opened it up slowly, not sure what I'd find. Inside was an iced leaf, or what appeared to be one. I picked it up and, although it was cool to the touch, it was evidently not made from ice. It was crystal – little tiny rainbows of light sparkled inside it. I held it up to the window and that's when I saw the proposal. Written in gold inside the ice leaf were the now familiar words, 'Marry Me.'

There was a note propped inside the box. 'This one won't melt.'

I smiled. It was beautiful, and a fitting memento of my time in Quebec and the ice hotel. That was the thing about Harry's proposals, whether they were on a grand scale with fireworks or tiny little thoughtful gestures like this, each one was perfect in every way.

I was hugging it to my chest when there was another knock on the door. Harry? This time I desperately wanted it to be him, regardless of what I looked like. I ran to answer it to find a rather green looking Badger, looking at me through bleary eyes.

'We're late.'

'What do you mean?'

'We have to be at the airport in half an hour.'

It took me a few seconds for the words to register, still hugging my leaf with a silly grin on my face, and then I finally caught up to what he'd just said.

'Crap.'

'My thoughts exactly.'

*

Proposer's Blog

Day 25: The Maid of the Mist Proposal. Location: Niagara Falls.

I know it's touristy and clichéd but you can't visit Toronto and not visit Niagara Falls – and you can't visit Niagara Falls without going on the Maid of the Mist, the boat that goes to the very bottom of the falls.

Suzie was as giddy as a kid at Christmas about going on this boat, I just wanted to hug her, she was so excited and I love seeing her like that.

My friend Badger was accompanying us as well and he hates boats. He looked greener today than he did yesterday on the plane when he was recovering from one too many Caribous the night before.

Can I just state for the record now – the Canadians, the Americans, I love them so much. This proposal would not have been possible had it not been for their help, but they do love a good proposal.

The ride along the river and past American Falls and Bridal Veil Falls is a great one, past tall trees and jagged cliffs, but Horseshoe Falls is obviously the most dramatic – being surrounded by that huge wall of water. It was as we were nearing the very base of the falls that the proposal took place. The boat inched nearer and nearer and Suzie, hanging over the rail, was reaching out to touch the spray.

Then cheers broke out behind her and as she turned she saw an array of multi-coloured umbrellas, protecting the tourists from the spray. One by one, the tourists holding the umbrellas turned round revealing a letter on each umbrella. 'Suzie Marry Me.'

I love surprising her, seeing her face light up is absolutely the best part of these proposals.

Until she says yes. Then I think that might just be the best part.

I stared at the words. What was he playing at? He wanted me to say yes? Then there were the comments underneath again. Three more mentions of this secret blog.

***Olivia Bloom** says: This is so cute, and I love being a part of the 'secret blog'. Can't wait to see what happens next.*

***Mia Hemsworth** says: How can she not know how you feel for her? Even without reading the secret blog it's pretty obvious.*

***T Hardy** says: Duh! The secret blog is supposed to be a secret, hence the name. Idiots like you are kind of spoiling it. I suggest you delete your comments straight away.*

To say I was confused would be an understatement.
Well if he could play games, then so could I.

I clicked on the add comment box and quickly added a comment of my own.

'Yes.'

The screen stayed silent for a moment then suddenly there was a flurry of interest.

My phone suddenly burst into life next to me. I answered it, knowing it would be Harry. 'What do you mean, "yes"?'

'What do you mean by me saying yes would be the best part of these proposals?'

'You never give me an answer.'

I was thrown by this.

'What kind of answer do you want, would you like me to throw my arms around your neck and scream yes from the top of my lungs?'

He cleared his throat and he took a long time to answer.

'Well, we're trying to find the perfect proposal for you and I don't know if I'm anywhere near. The tiny little heartfelt gestures, the huge spectacular ones, I have no clue what it is you're looking for.'

I stood up, suddenly angry. He was torturing me with daily, empty, meaningless proposals and he wanted me to be happy about it.

'Ok, ok, you want the truth, there's something missing from your proposals.'

'Like what?' He was angry now too. 'Flowers, champagne, chocolates, a fifty carat diamond engagement ring, what's missing?'

'You tell me about this secret blog and I'll tell you what's missing.'

'I don't know what this secret blog is either, it must be something else that Silver Linings are doing on their website and people are getting it confused with ours or thinking they are some way connected.' He was lying again, I knew him well enough to know that.

'Why do I feel like I'm the butt of some horrible practical joke?'

'Oh no Suze, this isn't what that's about.' All anger had vanished. 'No one is laughing at you, I promise.'

I pushed my hair from my face and stared out at the CN tower. Badger was taking me to an ice hockey game tonight. I *was* really looking forward to it. Now all I could think of was how many people there would be laughing at me behind my back. Being apart from Harry was driving me mad.

'Why are you not here? I've apologised, you've apologised. I doubt you've actually gone for that interview, but you're still not here. It's been five days.' I hated how whiny I was.

'I wanted to but Chloe said…' He trailed off, suddenly aware he'd said too much.

'Do you love her?' I closed my eyes against the pain of the expected answer.

'No. I just…'

I sighed with sudden clarity. 'It's ok. I get it. You want to spend time with her. You've missed her. I can't have been much fun to be around lately. Take your time, catch up. Maybe I'll see you in a few weeks.'

He started to protest but I hung up. The phone rang immediately but just then Badger knocked on my door. I ignored the ringing and went to answer it.

'You ready?' I grinned that he was wearing a hockey jersey and baseball cap. He passed me one for my head. I shoved it on and grabbed my bag as my phone rang incessantly on my bed.

'Aren't you going to get that?' he asked.

'Nope.' I closed the door behind me and ignored the pointed stare from Badger as we walked down the corridor. I didn't say anything until the ringing faded completely.

'So who's playing tonight?' I asked.

Badger clearly sensed I wanted to change the subject and rose to the challenge magnanimously. 'Toronto Otters versus the Dallas Demons.'

I smiled gratefully. 'The cute, cuddly Otters versus the mean, savage Demons, sounds like the battle will be over very quickly.'

'I think it will, the Demons' captain, Harrison Flynn, is just amazing…'

I listened to Badger rattle on about the amazing skills of Harrison and steadfastly ignored the huge pain in my heart.

*

I lay on my bunk as the motion of the train lulled me to sleep. Badger had put me on the train to Jasper first thing this morning and I knew he was now flying home back to Jules and Bella.

I hoped I would get a reprieve here from Harry and the proposals. It was nearly three days until I reached Jasper and I had no mobile signal at all. He would be hard pushed to arrange anything on a moving train and I found myself happy about that. I didn't want to be a part of these games that Harry was clearly playing with me. He was obviously up to something and I didn't like it.

The train had left the busy city of Toronto behind, and slowly the landscape had turned greener, more mountainous again. I had sat in the lounge cart all day, staring out at the mountains. It was breathtaking.

Then it had turned dark and I returned to my cabin.

I sighed happily as I put the book I was reading down. I felt contented here. No one knew who I was, or gave me those sympathetic looks. I didn't need Harry, I was quite capable of enjoying life without him.

I closed my eyes and forced a smile onto my face as I drifted off to sleep. If I said it often enough, I might start to believe it was true.

*

A loud knocking snatched me from my dreams and for a moment or two I had no idea where I was. It was completely dark. Then I felt the familiar gentle rocking, the soft noise of the train wheels as it sped along the track.

The knocking came again, louder this time, and I realised it was someone at my door.

I got up and opened it. I was greeted with a huge man towering over me and in my half asleep state I thought it was Harry for a second, until I saw the black bushy beard. He was one of the porters – as I peered through bleary eyes, I could see his uniform.

'Miss,' the man said, his voice was rough like sandpaper with a soft American lilt. 'You need to come with me.'

'Is there a problem?'

'No problem, you need to come with me now.'

I blinked at him, it was the middle of the night. I sighed wearily as comprehension dawned. 'Did Harry send you?'

The man smiled slightly. 'He does this sort of thing a lot eh? Wake you up in the middle of the night? I think the man sounds crazy in love if you ask me.'

I put my camera into the pocket of my hoodie top and shoved my feet into my shoes as the man held the door open for me. 'I doubt that. He's in New York, I'm here on my own.'

He studied me for a moment then gestured for me to follow him. 'I'm Connor by the way.'

'Suzie, though I guess you already knew that.'

I followed Connor along empty corridors – there was not a soul in sight, everyone tucked up in their cabins for the night. We walked through the lounge areas and the dining carriage, until we reached the door leading out onto the observation deck at the very back of the train. He pushed it open and an icy blast of air engulfed me.

'We're going outside? It's freezing out there. Let me go and get my coat.'

'It's ok Miss, we've got that covered. Here.' He passed me a huge sleeping bag.

I stared at it. 'As much as I love Harry, I'm not sleeping out here for him, or for anyone for that matter, not when I have a lovely warm bed waiting for me about a hundred yards that way.'

He laughed and for a moment I was reminded painfully of Harry – it wasn't just Connor's size that was familiar, there was something else that reminded me of Harry too.

'It's just to keep you warm.'

I sat down on the seat just inside the door and climbed into it – with a bit of wiggling around, I managed to zip myself up in it too, making me look like an oversized maggot.

Connor opened the outside door again and although the cold air rushed through to greet me, I was ready to face it now.

With some difficulty, I half hopped, half jumped outside onto the empty observation deck with Connor stifling his laughter behind me.

'Harry didn't really think this through did he?' I said, shuffling carefully forwards.

'Oh I don't know, it's certainly got comedy value.'

Connor pulled the hood up over my head and tightened the cord so it stayed in place then he draped a thick blanket around my shoulders.

I looked up at him as he secured the blanket; even in the darkness I could see his eyes were kind. I had an overwhelming urge to lean into him, my head against his chest, and I had no idea where that urge came from.

'Thank you.'

He smiled, slightly.

'I need to leave you now. I'll be back to collect you shortly.'

It was only as he stepped back that I saw the incredible view. Mountains stretched as far as the eye could see in every direction. The moon was full, lighting up the landscape like a searchlight, bathing the snow-covered hills and fields in a silvery blanket.

'Oh my God, it's beautiful,' I whispered. Why had I gone to sleep when I could have stayed out here for hours just enjoying that view?

I shuffled closer to the rail, desperate to see it all.

'Miss, would you mind not getting so close to the rail, there's a seat here. I'm sure Mr Forbes would prefer you to sit here rather than lean out over the rail and fall to your death.'

I smiled and shuffled into the seat as directed, then Connor left.

I watched the mountains sail past, the train quietly rattling its way through the tranquil, majestic beauty. I didn't want to blink in case I missed anything, it was the most incredible thing I had ever seen and somehow being the only person out here to witness it made it all the more special.

Something gold and orange caught my eye, and I realised as it floated past that it was a Chinese lantern, its tiny candle flame glowing bright in the darkness. Another one joined it, floating gently past and up into the cold night sky. I stood up. It looked magical. Another floated past, but this one had a large black M printed on the side. I could see where this was going and it was confirmed when the next one to float past had an A printed on the side. I smiled, the golden glow set against the inky snowy landscape was beautiful.

I had to get some pictures for the blog. I fumbled round in my pocket and grabbed my camera, but I didn't have enough room to bring my arms up to the top of the sleeping bag. I bent double as another golden lantern floated above me, no doubt the first R. I brought my head to my knees to try to drop the camera out of the hole at the top, thinking I would catch it with my face but as I let go, it hit me in the chin, bounced off and hit the floor. I bent over to get it, with some serious wiggling around, I forced the arm out of the hole at the top, making me look like a unicorn with my arm now protruding out of my face. I leaned down to get it just as the train swung round a corner, making me wobble and land flat on my face.

Damn it, this beautiful proposal was going on right above my head and I was missing it. I wriggled around trying to get some leverage to get up, but with one arm by my face and the other welded to my side, I could hardly move at all. I was just squirming around on the floor, rubbing my nose against the rough wood.

I wiggled and twisted, shifting my hand in front of me and somehow managed to roll over onto my back, with my arm now over my face. This was ridiculous. Connor had done the sleeping bag up so tightly that I could barely move my arm at all. Finally I managed to move it to one side just as a lantern floated over me bearing the letter U on the side.

I looked at it in confusion. 'Marry Me' didn't have a U in it. Unless it was 'Marry Me Suzie', in which case the Z, I, and E would be along shortly. But as I lay there waiting, not wanting to miss anything else, there seemed to be no more lanterns coming. So if the U wasn't part of Suzie, what was it part of?

I heard footsteps approaching and I prayed it was Connor and not someone else who would find this hilarious.

The door swung open and there was silence for a second as I strained my eyes to see over the sleeping bag.

I wriggled around, desperate to be able to sit up, but to no avail. I heard the footsteps come closer and Connor peered over the sleeping bag to look at me. It was clear he was trying to stifle a smile.

'Suzie, are you ok?'

I nodded. 'Except, I fell over and couldn't get back up and I missed half of the proposal, well probably more than half. I saw the M, A and what I assumed was the R, but after that I didn't see anything.'

His face visibly fell.

'You missed the proposal?'

'Well I saw the first part, it was beautiful. Were you helping? I saw the U at the end, but I don't know what word the U was from.'

'It doesn't matter,' his voice was gruff again, almost angry this time. 'Can I help you up?'

I nodded.

He bent down and undid the cord from the top of the sleeping bag, freeing my hand and part of my shoulders.

I twisted about until both my arms were free and then he pulled me to my feet with ease.

I looked out to see the lanterns, there were a lot more than I expected disappearing into the night sky. A quick count revealed seventeen lanterns bobbing like golden stars into the darkness. Seventeen? With the first two blank ones and Marry Me that was nine. What did the other eight say, ending in U?

'What did they say?'

Connor shrugged as he held the door open for me. 'Marry Me.'

'And?'

He shrugged again, obviously annoyed that I had missed it.

An eight letter word ending in U? Or two words?

With one last longing look at the view, I followed, well actually half shuffled inside.

Connor didn't hang around, as soon as I was inside he strode off, whilst I was still struggling to extract myself from the sleeping bag. By the time I was free from my confines, he was gone.

SECRET BLOG

I cannot tell you how gutted I am. I've been planning the latest proposal for days. Because this was the proposal where I was going to declare my love for Suzie as well. I've been trying to pluck up the courage to tell her ever since she left me in New York. I've followed her at a distance, desperate to just close the gap between us, hold her in my arms and tell her I love her. But I couldn't do it. What if she doesn't feel the same? What if she rejects me? I don't think I could take that pain all over again. So I came up with a genius plan. I would do it in my proposal and that way I wouldn't have to see her face when she saw the words. Thanks to Chloe, I was in disguise again, this time as a porter called Connor with a suspicious similarity to Hagrid from Harry Potter. I stood at the front of the train and released Chinese lanterns, each with a letter on the side. I spelt out first the words 'Marry Me', then 'I Love You'.

After the proposal, I hurried to the back of the train where Suzie was to gauge her reaction. But she'd missed it. She'd fallen over and missed the whole thing.

Part of me now thinks that she didn't miss it, but is only pretending that she did so she won't have to turn me down.

I need to talk to her because it's eating me up inside, but Chloe still won't let me go back to her. I think she's worried that I'll get hurt.

I kind of thought I'd be wrapped in her arms round about now. Instead I'll have to stay in my cabin for the next three days in case she sees me.

COMMENTS

Laura Lovelock says: *Tell her, walk straight into her cabin now and tell her. Ignore Chloe.*

Megan Wood says: *I love that you told Suzie you love her with Chinese lanterns, that's so sweet, so romantic. Just kiss her and see if she kisses you back, I bet she does.*

Victoria Stone says: *This is driving me mad, grow some balls and tell her already.*

Erin McEwan says: If she really is your best friend then even if she doesn't feel the same she'll still be your friend.

Kirsty MacLennan says: I agree with Megan, snog her face off, you'll get a definitive reaction then.

*

Jasper was tiny and everybody seemed to be wearing shorts and flip flops, despite the icy weather and the fact that there was snow still on the ground.

I had arrived here the night before and finally spoke to Harry after three days of phone silence. The proposals had arrived daily – after the Chinese lanterns, I'd had a barber shop quartet sing to me in front of a train full of passengers and rose petals spelling out the words on my bed, which was a bit creepy thinking of someone being in my room doing that. But despite the proposals and the effort in arranging them, they were missing one thing. Harry. I missed him like crazy and my heart just wasn't in this proposal malarkey any more. Maybe it was the fact that the proposals were empty, made even more so by the fact that he was in New York while I was alone. He didn't even want to be with me anymore.

I had today to explore Jasper and tomorrow I was heading towards Lake Louise via the Athabasca Glacier.

I'd decided to rent a car from the car rental place opposite the hotel because I had heard about this fantastic waterfall in nearby Maligne Canyon. I'd asked for something little and cheap as I was paying for it. I didn't know if renting a car to satisfy my own whims would be covered by Silver Linings and Sunlounger. After checking the map several times, I set off.

I had never driven in a foreign country before, so I was a little nervous about driving on the other side of the road, but five minutes after leaving the little town the roads were deserted. The roads wound higher and higher as they went up into the mountains, so much so that at one stage I felt my ears pop. Fresh snow had fallen and lay quite deep in places, though they seemed to be a lot more prepared for it in Canada. In England a little snow fall quite often caused the whole country to grind to a halt. New little flurries of snow had started to fall now, but nothing that would cause me any problems.

I could see the town I had left behind far below me and other towns in clusters spread out across the snowy landscape. The road ahead of me remained completely empty, though behind me I caught the odd glimpse of a big red SUV following at some distance. It was oddly comforting to have it there as I headed off into the barren wilderness.

As I straightened out onto a long stretch of road, I noticed the complete lack of barriers that would prevent me from falling to my death and this caused me to drive even slower. It wasn't a sheer drop but the hillside was very steep. But slowly, as I drove along the road without any incident, I started to become more confident.

The beauty of Canada is just something I don't think I will ever tire of looking at; the rugged, jagged cliff faces, jutting out mere metres from where I sat and the lakes and mountains that could be seen for miles in every direction.

Life was good. I turned the radio up and sung along to some dodgy country song.

The air was colder up here, I could feel the chill and I fumbled around to find the heating controls and whacked up the heat.

CHAPTER FIFTEEN

I steered, pumped the breaks and screamed as the car toppled over the edge. But at the last second before gravity took hold and tossed me to a painful death, it stopped and then hung, one wheel on the verge, teetering on the brink.

I'd forgotten how to breathe. I couldn't move, one inch to either side could be fatal. The car rocked gently, trying to decide between my salvation and my death. I had to get out, waiting for help was not an option. I undid my seatbelt and carefully released it but even that tiny movement caused the car to groan and lean forwards even more. My stomach rolled with fear and panic and I blinked away tears.

Suddenly my driver door was flung open, there was someone there – a man – but I was too scared to move to look.

The car was already rocking with this new movement and I wanted to scream out to him to be careful, to move slowly, but all words were stuck in my throat.

The man was not cautious though. There was nothing gentle or slow about his movements. He reached into the car and in one swift, violent gesture yanked me out into his arms. I flung my arms around my rescuer, he staggered back and as we hit the floor I realised with sickening clarity that it was Harry.

'Harry?'

'Hi.'

'Harry, oh God.'

Sobs tore from my throat. Relief, adrenaline, joy and terror surged through me and I wrapped my hands round his neck and kissed him. I didn't understand why he was here, but right then I didn't need to. I felt tears soak my cheeks as he pulled me tight against him, kissing me back. His hands were around my face, in my hair. The kiss became more urgent, needful and a noise escaped from his throat that sounded like a moan. But I couldn't stop.

'Are you guys ok?' came a voice from above and I snatched my mouth from Harry's in shock.

Two policemen were standing on the road, having obviously stopped after they had seen my car teetering on the edge.

I looked back at Harry. I couldn't believe I had just been kissing him.

'I'm so sorry… I just…' I was still crying and shaking. He held my face gently, kissed my forehead, wiped the tears from my eyes and kissed me on the mouth – a short, sweet kiss. Not a proper kiss, not how I had been kissing him before, with my tongue in his mouth. God, had my tongue really been in his mouth? How embarrassing.

'Are you ok?'

I nodded

'Are you hurt?'

I shook my head.

He arched an eyebrow at me. 'Can you speak?'

'Not right now.'

He smiled slightly.

I wanted to get off him, it seemed inappropriate to be lying on top of him after what I had just subjected him to, but my fingers were wrapped tightly in his shirt, and I couldn't work out how to loosen them. Although he didn't seem that bothered by it.

'We'll be right up,' Harry called to the officers, then he returned his gentle gaze to me. 'As reluctant as I am to move from this position, I think we need to get up now.'

I couldn't stop shaking and I was starting to feel numb all over. I couldn't actually move and he seemed to realise that. Harry sat up, shifting me carefully onto his lap and then stood up, with me still in his arms so he was carrying me like a baby.

'One moment,' he said to the men as he approached them.

I heard them talking as we walked past. 'I've helped a lot of women in my time – I've never been kissed like that before,' said one.

'Me neither.'

I blushed and looked away so Harry wouldn't see me.

Harry walked back towards his red SUV which had been abandoned in the middle of the road. He sat me in the driver's seat and wrapped his coat tightly round me. He turned the heating on full blast, kissed me on the forehead and left me alone in the car.

I watched him talk to the men. I wondered what he was telling them about what had happened. There were a lot of hand gestures but the police were laughing now – Harry was working his charm as always. My little car didn't seem to be going anywhere, which made my overreaction even more embarrassing.

I watched as they attached a rope from my car to the police car and, with a little bit of coercion and help from

Harry and the other officer, they pulled my car back onto the road. And after a few more laughs, Harry grabbed my things from the car and came back to me.

'How you doing?' he said, motioning for me to scoot over so he could get in.

'I'm feeling a bit silly.'

'What? Why? It was an accident. Nothing to feel silly about.'

'I thought I was going to die.'

'I thought you were going to die too, scared me half to death when I saw you go over the edge. I literally have never been so terrified before in my entire life.'

I looked at him as he started the car.

Is that why he'd kissed me back, because he'd been scared as well? We should really speak about the kiss. It lay unspoken between us.

'What happened anyway? One minute you were driving along, the next you just went over the cliff. Did you fall asleep at the wheel or something?'

'It was a deer, I just swerved and the next thing I know I'm going over the edge.'

'Pesky deer.'

He was smiling hugely to himself, as if the whole thing was hilarious. He waved his thanks at the police and turned the car around to head back to the town where my hotel was.

'What about my car?'

'The police are going to drive it back, they're heading that way anyway.'

'What are you doing here? You're supposed to be in New York.'

'I wanted to catch you up. I was going to surprise you.'

'You did that all right, I was very surprised to see you.'

He laughed. 'I could tell.'

Oh no, the kiss. How was I going to explain that?

I was still shaking and I buried myself deep in his coat, relishing his wonderful scent that washed over my senses. There was a small tear in his sleeve and I desperately tried to focus my attention on that instead of the forthcoming explanation.

*

Soft voices pulled me from my sleep. I opened one eye and realised I was lying on Harry's chest, his arm clamped tightly round my shoulders. After we'd returned to the hotel, to Harry's room which he had quite obviously slept in the night before, Harry had called the car rental place to discuss insurance – and informed Silver Linings and Sunlounger too in case they needed to know. I must have fallen asleep shortly after that, and now he was here by my side, holding me tight. None of it made any sense; that he was here when he should have been still in New York. And even more confusing was that Chloe was clearly here with him too.

'So she kissed you?' Chloe said. I couldn't see her from where I was lying and I kept very still to listen to the conversation.

'Yeah I know,' said Harry. 'Don't look at me like that, it didn't mean anything, she was terrified.'

'I've been terrified quite a few times in my life, I've never kissed anyone like that because of it.'

'She was just pleased to see me.'

'I'd say.'

Chloe seemed really annoyed by this latest development. I was clearly stepping on toes. She liked him, that much was clear.

'It didn't mean anything,' Harry repeated.

I sat up and looked at Chloe and back down at Harry. 'I'm sorry,' I muttered, moving to get off the bed but Harry stopped me.

'Where are you going?'

'Back to my room.'

'Oh no you're not. Not a chance,' Harry said, vehemently. 'Chloe will sleep in your room tonight.'

This was obviously news to Chloe as she glared at Harry but he just glared back at her.

'Please, I don't want to get in the middle of something. I'm sorry, I really am.' I moved to leave again, but Harry physically stopped me.

Chloe stood up and stalked out of the room.

I stared at Harry and I knew the topic of the kiss just wasn't going to go away.

'Please don't,' I whispered. 'Just don't. I'm sorry I kissed you, I was scared and ridiculously pleased to see you. Please don't read anything into it. Let's enjoy this trip. We're going to travel the world and have an amazing time and I'd like to do that without this awkward cloud hanging over our heads.'

He stared at me and I wished for the thousandth time that I could read his thoughts, it would make everything so much simpler.

'So… we're just going to forget it ever happened and never speak of it again?'

'Yes.'

I willed him to drop it. If he wanted to know why I had kissed him, if he pushed me for an answer, I feared everything would come out and where would that leave our friendship then? If we couldn't be together then I still wanted him as a friend, I needed him as a friend. I wouldn't have been able to get through the last few months without him by my side and I wanted to be there for him too – to see him happy, settling down, maybe having kids. I didn't want to ruin that with a declaration of my undying love.

'You kissed me.'

Oh crap, he really wasn't going to let this go.

'As a friend. We're friends. We hug and stuff all the time, it didn't mean anything.'

'Right.' He seemed angry. 'That's all that was then, a friend kiss? Because it felt like a hell of a lot more than that to me.'

'I was scared, relieved. Please don't push this. It will ruin everything between us.'

He stared at me for a moment, clearly wanting to dig deeper, but he didn't. 'We better get some sleep. We have an early start tomorrow.'

I nodded and lay down with my head on his chest again. He didn't push me off but he didn't hold me either. After a few minutes of me lying there awkwardly, feeling unwanted, I rolled off him. A few moments after that, he rolled over to face away from me.

SECRET BLOG

I'm so confused. After rescuing Suzie from a near fatal car accident, we kissed – well she kissed me and I damned well kissed her back. It was incredible, it was everything I hoped it would be and more. There was real feeling in that kiss. In that moment I knew that she felt the same for me too.

But afterwards she brushed it off, said it didn't mean anything. She said it would ruin everything between us if I pushed it.

I was so disappointed. Chloe was furious that she would toy with me like that. She's gone back to New York and wanted me to come with her. But I've stayed. I need to talk to Suzie about this.

You guys have been brilliant so far with your support and although I don't always agree with your methods, I would appreciate your take on this.

COMMENTS

Megan Wood says: She loves you, definitely. You don't kiss someone like that if you don't have feelings for them. I don't care how scared someone is. That kiss meant something to her and she's denying it because she's scared you don't feel the same way.

Victoria Stone says: I want to fly out there and bang your heads together. You love her, she loves you, just tell her. What's holding you back?

Harry Forbes says: I wish it was that simple Victoria. Issues from my childhood have left me fearing rejection as much as someone with acute arachnophobia fears spiders. I've tried, believe me I have. Many times over the last two years, I've plucked up the courage to give her my heart and every time I've been left a sweating quivering wreck. That was the whole point of these proposals, so I could show her how much she meant to me rather than actually telling her. But I know she needs to hear the words, she said as much herself. I will tell her… one day.

Tilly Tennant says: I'm new to this secret blog but even without reading all the entries, I'd have to agree with the others. She loves you, any fool can see that.

Kirsty MacLennn says: She loves you. Kiss her again and this time don't stop until you're both sweaty and naked.

Laura Lovelock says: *She definitely loves you, what are you waiting for?*

*

Proposer's Blog

Day 31: The Fossilised Proposal. Location: Athabasca Glacier.

A fantastic journey across the Icefields Parkway towards the glacier. We saw moose, elk and a fleeting glimpse of a wolf on the trip through the wilderness. Suzie was like a child as she excitedly pointed out all the sights.

We boarded what can only be described as a 4x4 bus, with huge, thick wheels, to travel across the glacier.

The beauty of the place was staggering. Where before we have viewed the incredible mountain landscape at a distance, today we were literally driving through it, so close to the mountains we could reach out and touch them.

At the midway point we were allowed to step out of the bus onto the glacier, onto the ice and snow that had been there for thousands of years.

Everyone was busy taking photos and touching the ice and the mountains. I tried to guide Suzie surreptitiously towards where the pre-prepared proposal was. Things have been a bit awkward between us today and after sitting on the bus together almost in silence, I think she was relieved to be able to get away from me, even for a short while. Which didn't help the proposal. We only had limited time on the ice before we were to re-board the bus and make our way back to our hotel. I wanted her to find the proposal herself but short of grabbing her and frog marching her towards it, I was at a bit of a loss about what to do.

Suddenly someone else found it, another one of the tourists. And with the screams and shouts from this couple, everyone came running to see what they had found underneath the ice, including thankfully Suzie. It wasn't the discreet proposal I had been hoping for, but the crowd effect is always a good one.

As Suzie pushed her way through the people, she saw it too. In a lump of ice and snow, looking like it had been there for hundreds of years, was the proposal written in stones and twigs. I had asked an ice sculptor to create it and then the Ice Explorer crew had placed it onto the glacier the day before and poured water over it to freeze it in place.

The effect was stunning. Suzie's face, as she looked around for me, was an absolute picture. The crowd realised the proposal was meant for her and as she approached me they all started cheering. I got down on one knee and then there was silence as they waited for her answer. For the first time I honestly thought I was going to get one too.

She bent down and whispered in my ear. 'Get up and hug me or I'll never hear the end of it.'

So I did and the crowd roared, thinking she had said yes. Not the romantic ending I was hoping for, but still she was smiling all the way back to the hotel, which was definitely something.

Proposer's Blog

Day 32: The Chainsaw Sculpture Proposal. Location: Lake Louise.

We had the day to explore Lake Louise so we hired a car and drove round the lake, the small town and into the mountains. The lake is the most gorgeous turquoise colour and it just looks startling against the backdrop of the mountains.

But I wanted Suzie to see something else. Max Cordwain is a chainsaw artist who lives nearby. With the use of chainsaws and other power tools he can quickly and skilfully produce the most magnificent sculptures and works of art.

As we drove up, great wooden horses and bears adorned the driveway to his house, accompanied by tiny intricate fairies and birds. The man clearly had loads of talent.

Unfortunately he was the best looking bloke I had ever seen in my entire life. This man literally had a square jaw, his muscles were huge, dark curly hair that fell over his eyes as he worked, thighs like tree trunks. If I had been gay, I would have been fawning all over him too.

Yes, as he carved my proposal into this deep red wood, Suzie couldn't take her eyes off him for one second. It didn't help that halfway through the carving, he took his top off, and stood half naked as he tore manfully through the trunk of the tree, gliding his tools with ease – like a knife through butter. To say Suzie was turned on would be a massive understatement. She barely noticed the proposal come to life under his hands, she only had eyes for him.

I'm a big man but as she stared at him with lust filled eyes, I have never felt so inadequate and small before. I don't think she even noticed I was there. I felt like getting back in the car and driving off and leaving them to it.

Finally he produced the finished piece and handed her the beautiful plaque with the words carved in big chunky letters. She barely gave it a glance.

I was not impressed.

My advice my dear would-be proposers: if you enlist help in your proposals, make sure the people helping you are as ugly as sin first.

I felt bad about that proposal, of course I did. Max had been gorgeous, I admit that. He was the first person other than Harry that I'd imagined doing wicked and dirty things to for over two years. I was surprised to feel such an urge when I met Max. It probably hadn't helped that since I had kissed Harry, he had started to pull away from me. I could feel him distancing himself from me. We talked and things were still sort of friendly on the surface but there was this... awkwardness between us now that had never been there before. He obviously knew how I felt and was trying to push me away. So I suppose I appreciated Max a bit too much to try to show Harry I wasn't really interested in him. Harry had been quite annoyed.

What I hadn't expected was the reaction of the followers on the blog. Since Harry had posted the chainsaw proposal the day before, the followers' comments had been quite nasty and I had received five rather hurtful emails from followers telling me what a cow I was.

'Harry is lovely and beautiful, you don't deserve him you bitch,' said one.

'I can't believe he is going to all this effort to show how much he loves you and you would rather spend your time ogling the woodcutter, what a complete and utter cow,' said another.

Talk about completely misunderstanding the situation.

'You're either blind, gay, stupid or just an attention seeking slut, which is it? Either way I don't think much of Harry's taste in women.'

'So your brother dies, Harry spends months helping you pick up the pieces, he takes you around the world and proposes to you in incredible and beautiful ways and you take a shine to the first person who flashes a bit of flesh. You ungrateful, stuck up tart.'

'Harry deserves so much better than you, you make me sick. You fuc-'

Harry walked into the hotel room, distracting me from the laptop. I quickly closed the screen so he wouldn't see the emails. He was obviously cold from being outside as he rubbed his hands together to get warm.

He stopped when he saw me. 'What's wrong?'

'Nothing, just answering emails and stuff, nothing important.'

He tilted his head. 'You look upset.'

'No, I'm fine.' I was annoyed with how not fine my voice was. They were right, I was a horrible person.

Harry was still not convinced and I cursed that he knew me so well. He moved to take the laptop off me, I held onto it, but he was stronger and he forced it out of my grasp.

He opened it up and started reading. His face turned to thunder.

'What the hell is this?'

'It doesn't matter.'

'Of course it matters. How dare they write those things to you?'

I sighed. 'It doesn't help, though, that you write these blog pieces like you're in love with me and I end up looking like the bad guy because I'm not saying yes to any of these proposals. I know that's what Silver Linings wants to see, all romance and flowers and birds singing but that's simply not the case at all. We're just friends and I think our followers need to know that.'

He stared at me for what seemed like an eternity. 'Just friends?'

'I don't mean just friends, you're so much more than a friend to me…' I trailed off. Oh what a tangled web we weave. 'You've been incredible after Jack, through all of this, you mean the world to me and I…'

'I'm going to take care of this, don't think about it again. Get yourself ready, we need to leave in half an hour.'

With the laptop under his arm, he stormed out.

Our nice relaxing trip on the lake this afternoon wasn't looking so promising now. I had hoped it would be fun and we could somehow recapture the cosy bond between us. As the door slammed behind him, that prospect was looking less and less likely.

*

Harry's mood hadn't improved at all by the time we stood on the shores of Lake Louise an hour later. He wouldn't tell me what he had said to the people who had emailed me but evidently it wasn't nice.

We had hired two canoes to take us to the furthest shores, and a half hour's walk from there was a log cabin we were going to spend the night in. I couldn't imagine anything more romantic, even though the mood hanging between us at the moment was anything but romantic.

Harry took off, his powerful arms ploughing through the water, whilst I seemed to struggle to go in a straight line. The lake was big but the people who had rented the canoes seemed hopeful we could traverse it in about half an hour. I wasn't hopeful that we could reach the other side before nightfall and it wasn't even lunchtime yet.

Somehow I managed to get into a rhythm, and pointed myself in the right direction. But after a few short minutes my shoulders and back were screaming with the exertion of using muscles I hadn't even known existed, let alone used before. I stopped for a breather. When Harry had mentioned it to me the day before, I'd imagined it would be fun. I was sweating, aching, out of breath and I'd barely crossed a third of the lake.

Harry seemed to realise I was struggling and within a few minutes he was back by my side.

'You ok?' He glided effortlessly through the water towards me.

'It's a lot harder than it looks.'

'Nah, it's easy. Come on, we're nearly there.'

We were not nearly there, but the thought of sitting by the fire in that little log cabin kept me going.

Harry turned and headed towards the far shore again, and soon there was a huge gap between us. As hard and as fast as I was trying, I didn't seem to be moving at all.

Harry came back for me again. 'Let me tow you.' He offered a rope.

'No, I'm fine, you go on ahead. I'll be there soon.'

He sighed. 'Just come a little closer.' He was clearly still angry, either at me or our followers but I knew when not to argue with him and this was one of those times.

I reluctantly admitted defeat and tried to steer myself towards him, but I missed his hands by a good metre. As he leaned out to try to grab the end of the canoe, it toppled with his weight and dumped him into the lake.

'No, Harry, oh my God, are you ok?'

'Shit!' he muttered. 'Crap, that's freezing.'

His canoe had turned upside down and I paddled towards it to try to help turn it over.

'Don't,' Harry said through gritted teeth. 'You'll only bloody well fall in as well.'

I watched helplessly as he flipped the boat back over and hauled himself out of the icy water. 'Crap, that's so frigging cold.'

'Let's go back, we could be back in our hotel sooner than we can get to the cabin, and the hotel has hot showers.'

'No, it's fine.'

It clearly was not fine, he was shaking so much.

With fumbling fingers he tied the rope to the front of my boat. 'Harry, please leave it, just get yourself to the cabin, I'll catch you up.'

He ignored me and soon he was powering through the water, dragging my canoe in his wake.

As we approached the shore I could see a fire blazing away; a picnic blanket, hamper and champagne bucket had been left for us. Harry was nothing if not prepared.

He quickly moored his canoe on the small sandy beach and pulled mine in alongside his. He got out and helped me out too. He was freezing – bunched up and trying to protect himself from the cold as he staggered a few feet to the fire and dropped to his knees by the flames.

'Let's leave the picnic,' I said. 'Let's just go straight to the cabin and get changed. We can come back and do this later.' All our stuff was either already at the cabin or on its way. But even if it wasn't there, we would be inside, out of the cold, and we could light a fire.

'It's half an hour from here, I need to warm up first before I make that walk, I'll be hypothermic otherwise.'

Hypothermia. Oh God, no. Should I call an ambulance, should I run back along the track to the hotel to get help?

He must have seen me panicking because he forced a smile onto his face.

'It's fine, don't worry. I'll be fine in a minute.'

To my surprise, he started to strip. His coat, trousers, boots, hoodie, T-shirt, all came off in quick succession and even through my panic I couldn't help but stand and stare at his glorious body. He wrapped a blanket round himself so he was covered toe to neck and lay down by the fire.

'What can I do to help?' I said, hopping from foot to foot nervously.

'You can get your clothes off and come and join me.'

Of course. Survival 101. Body heat was one of the best ways to help someone with hypothermia. I didn't hesitate. I stripped as quickly as I could, only leaving my underwear on. The cold mountain air was like knives to my bare skin, but I quickly climbed under the blankets with Harry and lay on top of him, trying to cover his enormous frame with my body.

I tucked the blankets in around his shoulders, took my hat off and pulled it over his head, knowing that a lot of the body heat escaped through the head, then lay still, hoping somehow that I was making a difference to him.

He was cold, but not icy cold – maybe we had caught it early enough, maybe me being with him helped.

'Suzie.'

I looked up at him.

'I was actually joking when I said get your clothes off. I kind of expected you to tell me where to shove it.'

'What?'

'I never thought for one second you would actually do it.' His eyes shone with mischief.

'But… you were hypothermic, I was trying to give you body heat.' I could feel my cheeks burning red.

'I'm cold, honey, but I doubt very much whether I'm hypothermic – I don't think I was in the water for that long. I am very touched though that you would strip off for me so readily.'

I stared at him. 'You arse.'

He laughed so loudly, so deeply, I could feel the vibrations of it against my body.

I moved to get off him but he held me close. 'Not a chance, Miss McKenzie. There's always a possibility that I might be hypothermic after all.'

He laughed again and I joined him. Just like that, the awkwardness of the last few days just vanished.

Proposer's Blog

Day 33: The Near Death Experience Proposal. Location: Lake Louise.

The wooing is a big part of any proposal, you can't just pop the question whenever you feel like it. So I arranged a picturesque, tranquil trip across the water of Lake Louise, a romantic picnic by a roaring fire on the shores and then a walk through the snowy forests, past the proposal in front of the log cabin where we were to spend the night.

What I hadn't accounted for was me falling in the lake and nearly dying of hypothermia. But Suzie came to my rescue, stripping off and lying with me under the blankets to give me some much needed body heat.

When I felt warmer, we decided to abandon the picnic and make a run for the log cabin, wrapped only in our respective blankets. It was the fastest sprint we have ever done in our lives. I led the way, as I knew where the cabin was, but I could hear Suzie giggling uncontrollably as we ran through the trees.

We barely looked at the proposal of a snowman on his knees proposing to a snow woman just outside the cabin, we just flung ourselves through the door and out of the cold. There was a roaring fire burning in the main room and we dragged the couch in front of it and curled up on the sofa together, under the blankets.

Her heart was beating so fast, I could feel it hammering against her chest as I held her in my arms.

That's when I asked her to marry me.

She told me that, despite everything going wrong, this was the best proposal so far. I asked her if that meant yes. I felt her smile against my neck, one of the best feelings in the world. She said 'I'm lying with you naked, in front of a roaring fire, I'll let you make up your own mind on that one.'

I decided it was a yes.

*

I was shaken awake and I blinked in the darkness. The fire had long since gone out and as I stretched on the couch, I realised Harry was no longer with me.

'Suzie, you need to get up, now.'

I could see Harry's huge shadow looming over me.

I stuck one arm out from the blanket, but the cold of the room sliced though me and I tucked it back into the warmth of the blanket again.

'It's cold,' I mumbled sleepily.

'I know, the fire went out, get up.'

I held up the blanket for him. 'Come back to bed, we can keep each other warm.'

I blinked. Had I really just said that? There was a silence from Harry, so I guessed I had.

When he spoke there was a gruffness to his voice. 'I want that, believe me I do, but you need to get up and get dressed. Now.'

I looked at him and realised he was getting dressed quickly. There was a sudden sense of urgency from him and I quickly threw back the blanket and stood up. 'What's wrong?'

He held out some clothes for me and I quickly pulled them on.

'I'll be outside.'

He marched out. I pulled on my boots and ran after him. He was standing on the decking looking out over the mountains. Lake Louise was below us, glinting in the moonlight. I hadn't appreciated the magnificent view when we had run naked through the trees earlier.

He turned, smiling when he saw me and pulled me into his side.

'Look,' he whispered, pointing at the gap between the mountains.

'What?' I blinked at the clear sky, at the stars peppering the mountain landscape and the moonlight that seemed to be almost as bright as the sun. But I could see nothing. The sky wasn't black here, it had that greyish inky tinge of very early morning.

We had barely moved from the couch all day, apart from to throw some more logs on the fire. Although it was clear to both of us that Harry had quickly thawed out, neither of us had been willing to leave the confines of the couch and our half naked embrace. Of course nothing happened, but the intimacy of him holding me, of playing with my hair as he watched the flames, was hard to ignore.

We had eaten on the couch, and I'd even sent a few emails and he'd blogged about our proposal and still he had lay with me, half naked, under the blankets.

In all other circumstances, it would have been incredibly romantic.

It had grown dark and we had fallen asleep together.

But now it was early hours in the morning and I was standing outside in the freezing cold staring at the mountains. It was beautiful, with the moon over the water, but I couldn't help but wish I was back wrapped in his arms in front of the fire.

Then I saw it, and my heart leapt in my chest.

Far off, at the furthest point of the horizon, was an eerie green glow that shimmered and danced in the sky.

I gasped. 'Is that…?'

I looked up at Harry who was grinning hugely. 'The Northern Lights.'

'No! We're not supposed to see it down here, we're too far south.'

'They get occasional displays, the odd glimpse at this time of year, but supposedly nothing spectacular.'

I looked back at the green trails that moved like smoke in the distance. 'That looks pretty spectacular to me.'

He wrapped his arm round me and pulled me in tighter and I felt him nodding in agreement.

After a few minutes, Harry disappeared back inside and brought out the blankets. He cleared the bench of the snow and we sat down to watch the show, cuddled up against each other.

Although it was far away, it was still an incredible sight to see the light trails playing in the night sky. It almost looked like the shadows of people dancing as the lights rippled against the clouds.

'Thank you,' I said into his shoulder.

He looked down at me. 'For what? I didn't arrange the Northern Lights kid, I'm good but I'm not that good.'

I smiled. 'For everything, for being there for me, for my proposals, for all of this.' I gestured wildly with my arms, making the blanket slide off my shoulders. He pulled it back up, tucking me back in. 'I'm sorry things have been weird between us, I'm not sure why we've fought so much over the last few weeks, when we never have before. I guess I'm scared I'm going to lose you.'

He smiled down at me. 'That will never happen Suzie, no matter what happens, no matter where we are in the world, you will always be my best friend.' He paused and frowned slightly. 'Right?'

I nodded vehemently.

He kissed me on the forehead, then looked away over the mountains.

'I should have told you before. I'm damaged goods and I guess I didn't want you to know how completely messed up I am.'

I was very still, sensing that everything that I wanted to know and everything I didn't was about to come pouring out. And I was right.

CHAPTER SIXTEEN

'I was a horrible baby, just didn't stop crying from the moment I was born till I was about three years old.' I wrapped my arms tighter around him. 'Mum and Dad had never had a happy relationship. Abigail, my sister, was six when I was born and she said even before I came along they were always arguing and shouting at each other. I was an accident, that much was clear, they argued a lot about how they didn't want me even before I came into the world and so Abigail hated me as well. I don't suppose the constant crying endeared me to her either. My parents put me in her room as they couldn't put up with the crying. Looking back now on what Abigail told me, they were just rubbish parents.'

He looked down at me, probably to gauge my reaction. Whatever he saw in my expression made him continue.

'The crying stopped, I guess, well according to Abigail it did, but I had terrible night terrors. Still do sometimes. I'd wake up in the night screaming. Every night, sometimes two or three times a night. Though I have no memory of my parents ever coming in to see if I was ok. I do remember my dad shouting at me to shut up. That is pretty much the only memory I have of him. I was nearly four when he left. Just walked out and I never saw him again. I have almost no memory of him and no idea even if he's still alive. My mum drank herself into a stupor almost every day for the next four years. My sister raised me, made sure we both had food – we lived off sandwiches and cereal mostly. She took us both to school. I'm surprised no one noticed anything. My mum would occasionally come out of her catatonic state to wash our clothes and go shopping, to claim her benefits, to occasionally show her face at school, maybe it was enough so that the authorities didn't notice our neglect.

'One day, when I was eight, she took us out. Loaded us and two big suitcases into the car and drove us for hours. I was really excited, we had never been out before and suitcases clearly meant we were going on holiday. We pulled into this park and there were loads of kids playing with their families. And I think then was the first time I truly realised how our little family was so different to everyone else's. The love that was clearly shown in every single one of the different families that day was glaringly missing from ours. I mean, I loved my mum, I knew she was a bit rubbish but I loved her unconditionally. I think for the first time I saw that she probably didn't return those feelings. She told us to get out, which we did, and she drove off. I've never seen her again either.'

'Oh Harry.'

He looked down at me. 'Don't pity me Suzie, that's the last thing I want.'

'Of course I'm going to feel sorry for you, you were a child and what you are telling me is awful.'

'I'm not telling you because I want your sympathy, that's exactly why I never told you before. I just want you to understand me, all of me. Why I am like I am.'

'One of the most beautiful people I know.'

'Urgh. I may look ok on the outside, I mean I must do because I get quite a lot of female attention. And it's nice, that girls want to be with me. I spent my whole life not being wanted and suddenly I hit my twenties and the girls were all over me. It's hard to turn them down when I've never had that before. But they don't really know me and to be honest I don't want them to.'

'I meant that you're beautiful on the inside.'

He let out a hollow laugh. 'I'm bitter, angry, emotionally crippled. I fell in love with the most incredible woman and I could never tell her for fear of rejection. What kind of woman would want a man like that?'

He had no idea.

I put my hand over his heart. 'This is beautiful. You're kind, generous, smart, funny.' I smiled. 'Really funny. Protective, supportive. Any woman would be lucky to have you. We all have issues and baggage. Don't doubt that what you have is a pretty incredible package.'

He stared down at my hand then wrapped his hand around it but kept it over his heart.

'I can't lose you,' he said, so quietly that I barely heard him.

'There is nothing that you can say that will push me away from you. You're my best friend.'

'The job, in New York…'

'Oh Harry.' Suddenly all his anger and upset over the job made sense. 'I thought we could move to New York together.'

'But… you never said.'

'You never gave me a chance.'

He leaned his head back and laughed with relief.

I shifted closer to him, not wanting to push him but not wanting the dam to close just yet. 'Did they find your mum?'

He shook his head. 'She flew to France hours before we were taken to the police by some family who realised we were alone in the park as it was getting dark. She must have got on a plane as soon as she dumped us. They tracked her to South America after that but there's been no sight of her since. We lived with my gran after that – who spent every day telling us how much she hated us and how we had ruined her life. Thankfully she died two years later. After that, we were in and out of foster care for the next few years – but Abigail was a nightmare, causing trouble at school, trashing the house, she was rude, aggressive. My night terrors continued. There wasn't a single family that wanted to put up with that – her moods, and me screaming at early hours in the morning. No sooner had we been placed in one home they were sending us back a few days later. I learned very quickly that I couldn't trust any of them.'

My heart was breaking just listening to this.

'There was one family that stuck with us, when I was about fourteen. They weren't particularly nice but they weren't horrible to me either. Though I found out later it was only the extra cash incentive the state threw at the family that kept me living with them for so long. It was there that I met Chloe, another waif that the family had taken in.'

'But… you said you dated, that she was an ex.'

'She was, we did for like two weeks when I was fifteen. Before she dumped me for Isabel Carmichael.'

'She's gay?'

He nodded.

I supressed the smile of relief. So she really did love him like a brother. He was her foster brother.

'Anyway, my foster family. I was with them for four years. Abigail had already moved out to live with a boyfriend and I kind of felt I had a real family. It wasn't a great one, admittedly, but I still figured that they would always be there for me. At eighteen, the funding stops for any children in care. Literally on my eighteenth birthday they told me that I would have to find somewhere else to live. I was practically kicked out on the streets after that. I vowed then that I would never put my trust in anyone again.' He gripped my hand tighter. 'Except you. I trust you.'

I smiled.

'And do you trust me too?'

'Yes.'

'I would never hurt you.'

'I know.'

'So now you know everything there is to know about me, and you're still here holding my hand. Shall we talk about that kiss?'

I felt my face fall.

Oh no. He had trusted me with his biggest secret, now he was expecting me to do the same. As much as I trusted him not to stamp all over my heart if he didn't feel the same way, I still didn't want it to be weird between us, not when things had just started to go back to normal for us. And there was no escape from him either, we were going to be together for the next two months as we travelled the world, two months of weird awkwardness. And I couldn't forget how he had pulled away from me in the days immediately after the kiss, distancing himself from me. And the negative comment he'd made about me being naked in his bed – although it had been weeks before, the night I had covered myself in noodles, it still echoed in my head. But then… The way he was looking at me now, if he did feel the same way then we could be back inside our little log cabin within a few seconds and he could make love to me in front of that fire. My gut clenched with desire and need. I was so confused.

'Harry. I...'

His eyes filled with fear and it was enough to stall me in my tracks. He didn't want things to change between us either.

'The kiss, what it meant to me, what it meant to you, can we talk about it when we get back? This, what we have now, I don't want to spoil that. We have the whole world to see and I want to do that with my best friend – not with an awkward cloud hanging over us. We are going to have an amazing time.'

He frowned slightly then nodded. 'We will. There's so much of the world to see, so much to do, I can't wait to share it all with you. But we do need to talk, though I'm happy to wait until we get back. I don't want to spoil this either.'

I knew that talk was coming – ever since we'd kissed, I knew he wasn't going to let it go. But I had just earned a two month reprieve. We would talk. I'd tell him everything. I had to know one way or another.

I leaned into his shoulder and returned my attention to the sun that was just rising in the east, sending pink tinged clouds across the sky. 'Ok,' I said.

He pulled me tighter against him and looked out over the mountains too. 'Good.'

*

Proposer's Blog

Day 40: The Fire Proposal. Location: Prince Rupert, British Columbia.

We were supposed to be flying from Vancouver to Japan today but I've delayed it until tomorrow. When I asked

Suzie if she had seen everything she wanted to see in Canada, she said she was disappointed not to see any bears. Khutzeymateen Sanctuary is a bear sanctuary just north of Prince Rupert where you can view the bears by boat, so I couldn't resist changing our plans to incorporate a quick visit up the coast. Plus we had heard that Prince Rupert does the best seafood for miles around. So we had taken a small sea plane up to spend the day in Prince Rupert.

I thought Suzie might get bored of Canada – we have spent over three weeks looking at mountains, lakes and forests – so I was keen to take her to Japan where the landscape is completely different, especially with the bright lights of Tokyo. But there is a peaceful quality about being here, undisturbed by city noises. Suzie loves it and I don't think she is in any rush to leave.

With only a few hours to rustle up a proposal with this last minute change of plans, I wasn't hopeful of creating anything spectacular. But my would-be proposers and followers of this blog, you guys are truly magnificent. I put out a plea for help earlier this morning and within minutes I had the number of a local fisherman, David Whittaker, who was more than happy to help me put something together at the last minute.

The sea plane came in low over the little islands and rivers as it prepared to land in the bay. I think Suzie was a little nervous about landing on the sea and not on solid tarmac, so I tried to distract her by pointing out the incredible views of the iced rivers and snow-capped hills. That's when she saw it.

As we swooped over the snow covered shores of Smith Island, flames licked the sky and Suzie gave a little scream before she realised that the flames were arranged in the shape of the now familiar words, 'Marry Me'. Six foot high letters in golden flames set against the backdrop of the snowy beaches, even I had to admit, it was bloody impressive. I don't know how David had done it in such a short amount of time, but he had.

Suzie was silent, her face pressed against the glass and I could see the wonder in her face. Although that wonder quickly turned to fear as the plane touched down on the water and the waves engulfed the sides of the plane. Then she was screaming for an altogether different reason.

Thanks David.

Proposer's Blog

Day 46: The Symphony of Lights Proposal. Location: Hong Kong

Hong Kong is an incredible city – the tall skyscrapers, the forests on the hills beyond, the mists rolling in off the harbour, the pagodas, the bridges, the insane views over the city, the people, the dragon boats, the beautiful junk boats. It's such a thriving, buzzing place. And for me there's nowhere that epitomises Hong Kong and all its splendour more than the Symphony of Lights display in Victoria Harbour. Over forty buildings are involved in the show on both sides of the harbour, so the best place to view it is from the boats.

Music blares out over the harbour as the skyscrapers light up in a kaleidoscope of colours, with laser beams and searchlights that pierce the night sky. It is all timed beautifully with the music as the sky swirls with red, gold, green and blue. It is an incredible sight.

I have to say, this proposal was the hardest to organise of all the proposals so far and one I started preparing at the very beginning of this trip. I have spent hours on the phone, and sending emails to co-ordinate this but as we have gained more followers, more people were willing to help.

But even standing there on the boat with my arms round Suzie, I still wasn't sure if it would work or even happen at all. What if it only partly worked and Suzie was left looking at the letters UZ MR ME?

I had a back-up, a snow globe of the city of Hong Kong which had the words 'Marry Me,' in lights above the city when it was shaken. If all else failed I would present her with it at the end of the light show, though I wanted the big spectacle – and after almost a month of planning I was so excited to see it pulled off.

The lights lit up the sky taking us through the huge finale and as it came to an incredible end, the buildings were momentarily plunged into darkness.

Then selected lights lit up the sides of the buildings for just three seconds, 'Suzie Marry Me,' blazed through the darkness, and sparkled over the water. People around us screamed with excitement and then it was gone, the city in darkness again. But as I closed my eyes the words still danced in front of my eyes, and I knew Suzie would be able to see it too. Slowly the city came back to life as if it had never happened and people on the boats cheered at the unexpected finale.

Suzie was shaking in my arms and she didn't say a word as the boat went back to the dock. In fact she has barely said a word since. We came back to the hotel and apart from to say goodnight she hasn't spoke to me at all.

Not sure if that's a good reaction or a bad one.

Proposer's Blog

Day 58: The Air Ambulance Proposal. Location: Nepal

Hi, Suzie here. Harry's fine by the way, now. He wasn't looking so good a few hours ago. As you know, we are hiking through the Himalayas for a few days. Harry has been so looking forward to this. He didn't think we would get as far as the Everest Base Camp, but he just wanted to be in the foothills of this great mountain and it's all he's talked about for days. We stayed in Monju last night and we got up early this morning to head towards Namche. This was as far as Harry wanted to go as he was worried I might get altitude sickness. Oh how wrong was he.

No sooner had we left Monju Harry started feeling ill. He complained of a bad headache and dizziness and he was really short of breath. I kept saying we should turn back but evidently my proposal was up ahead and he wanted to keep going. As we started up the steep hill to Namche, Harry had a bad nose bleed and passed out.

I have literally never been so scared in all my life.

Luckily one of the porters who was taking some equipment up to one of the other camps was passing and he spoke fluent English. He explained that altitude sickness was very common, even in the fittest of men. He said he would summon help. I expected him to run to a nearby village and bring back some kind of local doctor who would shove herbs under Harry's nose. But the porter whipped out his mobile phone and called an ambulance.

Harry and I were airlifted to the nearby Lukla airport and from there taken to the nearest hospital. Harry had come round by this point but he was very incoherent. The helicopter stayed close to the ground as we made our way back, not wanting to aggravate his condition.

And that's when Harry proposed to me, when he was barely conscious he just grabbed my hand and muttered the words. I told him if he survived I would marry him, the very next day.

By the time we arrived at the hospital Harry was sitting up, talking and laughing with the doctors. The doctors say altitude sickness normally passes once you return to a lower height. They are keeping him in overnight just in case, but they're not too worried. I think Harry might still be delirious. He keeps talking about our forthcoming wedding.

But I wouldn't rush out and buy a hat just yet, blog followers, I'm sure he will come to his senses in a few days.

Proposer's Blog

Day 64: The Tattoo Proposal. Location: Dubai

We dined in the dunes tonight, at a secluded hotel resort, surrounded by sand and sky. Suzie looked stunning in a long satin silver dress she had bought from the market and her hair swept back with sparkly clips. I couldn't take my eyes off her for a second. There were belly dancers and other entertainment from lots of beautiful exotic women, but Suzie was the most beautiful woman there and everyone knew that. Everyone, that is, except Suzie. I told her, I told her several times throughout the night but she didn't believe me. That's one of the things I love about her, she just doesn't get how incredibly beautiful she is. With the stars, the heat, the amazing food, the incense burning, it was all a heady combination. I wanted to kiss her tonight, I wanted her so badly it actually hurt.

There was sword fighting and horsemanship to watch and Suzie was enjoying herself immensely, even though I was creepily staring at her all night.

The henna tattooists came round and as Suzie got her hands painted with beautiful intricate spirals, curls, geometric designs and flowers, I too had my own tattoo done.

Afterwards, I showed her the back of my hands and she laughed at the pretty flowers that I'd had done. I took her hands in my own and as I entwined my fingers with hers that's when she saw the proposal. The lines on the back of her hands were just that, lines, nothing of any particular shape – but when combined with the lines on my hands, when our hands were connected, the henna clearly spelt out the words 'Marry Me'.

Her eyes lit up in the glowing flames of our surroundings. We sat for ages with our hands entwined. It was my favourite proposal yet.

Proposer's Blog

Day 83: The Spider Proposal. Location: Kenya

We have had an amazing few days on safari here in Kenya. We have seen elephants, lions, rhinos, hippos and the highlight so far of our entire trip – giraffes galloping across the plains. Suzie has not stopped smiling for one second.

We were staying in a large tent last night. It's one where you can walk around inside and it even has a little stove.

I thought I would have some fun and play a little joke on her, which I totally thought she would realise was a joke straight away.

She has a thing for creepy crawlies, she hates them. Though I didn't realise quite how deep that fear ran.

I placed a fake spider in her bed. It was bigger than her head and I figured she would see it and laugh straight away.

She didn't see it. She climbed into bed and only when she was getting comfortable did she brush against it. She lifted the sheets, saw the beast lurking in the shadows and leapt out of bed screaming and crying. She grabbed one of the sledgehammers we were using earlier to tighten the tent pegs and attacked the spider. She completely destroyed the bed and I had to pull her off to stop her hurting herself in the struggle.

She was actually sobbing.

Worst proposal ever.

When I managed to get her to calm down, I picked up the fake spider and showed her the proposal underneath.

She didn't speak to me for the rest of the night and she's still not speaking to me this morning.

Proposer's Blog

Day 97: The Firefly Proposal. Location: Springbrook National Park, Australia.

I was worried about this proposal probably more so than any of the others. Although most of the proposals have relied on outside help, relying on animals is something completely different.

We had gone to a cave, underneath the plunge pool of a waterfall. The waterfall had eroded the land underneath and formed a cave with a hole in the roof where the water tumbled through. It was here that the fireflies lived.

I was told this special fruit juice was something the fireflies loved – but what if they weren't hungry, what if they were too tired, what if the moon wasn't in the right place in the sky? Never work with children and animals they say. So this was either going to work or it wasn't.

I squirted the juice onto the walls in the shape of the words 'Marry Me', then asked Suzie to open her eyes. Nothing happened. Long seconds stretched on. Still. Nothing. Then a few of them obviously caught a whiff of the juice and flew over to it, then a few more. Slowly, slowly, as they feasted on the juice, the words 'Marry Me' were clearly seen on the cave walls.

Suzie was stunned and she was clearly thrilled by the beauty of it. I do love surprising her with something beyond the normal proposals.

She said there was still something missing. I'm running out of time and I don't know what else I can do to get the answer I want. Three more proposals and it's over.

I read the blog and smiled. The followers of our blog adored the loving comments Harry made about me, they lapped it up and Harry's blog posts had become more and more loved up as the weeks went by. They were all big romantics and wanted to see me and Harry married off with a whole football team of babies by the end of this trip.

I didn't know what we were going to tell the bloggers when it was all over, but they would be desperate for some satisfying conclusion and it was never going to end in the way they hoped it would.

I scrolled through some of the older blog entries while we waited for the boat to leave.

It had been one hell of a ride over the last three months. Initially, I'd had reservations about how I was going to protect my heart. A hundred proposals from a man who didn't love me was a cruel and unwanted punishment but

I had become adept at shrugging them off now. And a lot of the proposals had been fun. In trying to find the ultimate proposal, Harry had taken me to the most amazing places and we had done some incredible things. We had stood on top of the world's tallest buildings, seen the most beautiful beaches and forests, swam in the bluest oceans and eaten the strangest food.

But now there were just three proposals left and my torment would be over.

Harry slid his arm around my shoulders as he sat down next to me in the booth.

'I'm so hungry I could eat a moose,' he said, nibbling my shoulder playfully.

'We may have to go back to Canada for that, not too many moosies round here.' I deliberately got the word wrong so he would focus on that and not how my whole body had just erupted in goose bumps at his touch. Even now after so long, he still affected me in ways which were mostly X-rated.

Harry laughed, 'Moosies?'

'Moosi?'

He scrunched up his nose, knowing I was teasing him.

'Moss? Mosses? Moses?'

For a split second his eyes scanned down to my lips before he looked away. What was that? He had become a lot more tactile over the last month or so and, coupled with the looks I sometimes caught him giving me, I often convinced myself on an almost daily basis that he returned the feelings for me. But the holiday, our trip together had almost put a block on me telling him how I felt. How awkward would it be to throw myself into his arms after one of his proposals, for him to turn me down? I'd then have to spend every day with him with that horrid awkwardness hanging over us. Plus I kept on waiting for him to utter the words himself. Harry pouring out his heart about his past had been a small but vital turning point in our relationship. Harry had told me everything, he trusted me completely and I loved him all the more for taking that risk and telling me. Surely now he trusted me he could trust me with his heart too. If he felt that way. But there had been nothing from him, no words of encouragement at all.

Part of me was really looking forward to the conversation I'd promised Harry we would have at the end of the trip. Finally I would find out once and for all whether he returned the feelings for me, though part of me was dreading it with an all-encompassing fear.

'Come on, the boat is leaving, we should go out on the deck.' Harry stood up and pulled me to my feet. I closed the laptop, slipped it into my bag and followed him out.

We were heading out to spend a few days at the beach resort of Tangalooma on Moreton Island. It was a convoluted boat trip, not taking the most direct route but the one most likely to encounter whales and dolphins.

'So three more proposals,' Harry said.

I stared out at the waves, hoping to see some kind of whale, tail, or dark shape. 'Yep.'

'We need to do something big for the last one, a spectacular finale. The followers of our blog will be expecting it.'

'You know I like the small gestures as well as the big ones. What are you suggesting?'

'Well, a wedding would be a good ending, they'd like to see that.'

I saw the humour in his eyes. 'I should marry you to keep our followers happy?'

'Just imagine it. The vicar waiting at the end of a candlelit aisle, you walk up and I ask you one final time, "do you want to marry me?" and you say "I do". That's pure gold right there. The followers would love that.'

'And then?'

He was teasing me, I could tell that. 'We get married, then we have amazing honeymoon sex.' He waggled his eyebrows, saucily. 'That's the law.'

'And we'd put that in the blog too, all the ins and outs.'

'Well we want to give our followers a complete picture.'

'Ewww.' I swiped him and he laughed. 'It seems a bit... far-fetched to go to those lengths just to give our followers what they want.'

'We need to give them something, it can't just be another no like all the others.'

'I've never said no.'

He looked at me. 'You've never said yes.'

'Maybe you're just not asking the right question.'

'It's "Marry Me" Suzie, it's pretty black and white, yes or no.'

'It's not how you say it, with all the bells and whistles, it's what you say that's important.'

'So you want a huge declaration of love for the last one? Then I'll get a yes? The followers will just go mad for that.' He grinned at me. He wasn't taking any of this remotely seriously. 'We could invite all the followers there to see the last one. Then there can be a big kiss, and you can lean in on one foot like they do in the movies.'

A flash suddenly went off in our face and we both turned to see a Japanese man we had spoken to briefly as we were getting on the boat. He was waving a camera in our direction.

I looked back at Harry in confusion. 'Did he just take our picture?'

'Probably not, he must be taking it of the view.' Harry guided me out of the man's shot but weirdly the man took another photo of us before he disappeared through the crowds of people.

A shout rang out on the other side of the boat. En masse, a whole boatload of people ran to where the shout came from. I could feel the boat tipping under the weight of such a force. Harry grabbed my hand and ran to the other side too.

We stared at the waves, some of the tourists taking pictures of water swells, but if there was a whale there it was concealing itself well.

Another shout rang out from the other side and the boat almost groaned in protest at the mass exodus as we ran to the opposite rail. In a minute the boat would pitch us all into the sea in revenge. There was a definite dark patch this time but it could just have been a patch of seaweed. The beauty of the sea was incredible. The turquoise waters, the sun glinting off its surface. In some parts you could see right down to the sea bed.

A message was announced over the loudspeakers.

'We have a sighting out the rear of the boat, it seems like a humpback is following us.'

I felt the boat pitch as everyone ran towards the rear. Harry nudged me in front of him and with his hand at my back he guided me through the throng.

People were laughing and clapping and I hurried to see the great humpback myself. As I fought my way through the crowd, I saw what it was that everyone was laughing at. The humpback sighting was in fact a large inflatable whale being towed by the boat. Out of the top was a blue ribbon, supposedly representing a spray of water, and emblazoned onto the material were the words 'Suzie, Marry Me.'

I smiled. The whale was cute and dorky with googly eyes that rolled in its head as it bounced along in our wake. I quickly pulled my camera out and started firing off shots.

Just as people were turning away to head back to the front, a huge real life humpback whale breached the surface as it leapt out of the wake, twisted in the air and flopped back into the waves – sending a deluge of water over the deck of the boat.

There were shouts of excitement as everyone rushed to the barrier to take pictures. But although the whale followed us for a while, giving the passengers ample time to take some shots through the waves, he didn't breach again.

A quick check on my camera revealed I had taken two winning shots. My proposal endorsed by a real humpback whale.

I turned to go back inside but Harry was there smiling at me.

'You really do pull out all the stops, don't you?'

'You wait till the last one, I have big plans.'

*

Tangalooma was like stepping into a Bounty advert. The long strip of golden sand nestled into the sea of emerald palm trees was a tropical paradise. The only thing missing was the beautiful girl shipwrecked on the island with her incredible non-melting bar of chocolate. If that had been me, the chocolate would have melted all over me before I'd managed to take the first bite.

Our hotel room looked straight out onto the beach. From the open window I could see the fat pelicans waddling up the shore, flapping their great wings as the sun set into the rosy waters beyond.

We had missed most of the beauty arriving on the island after dark the day before, and today we had left early to tour the area and go sand tobogganing – which was easily one of the most exhilarating experiences of my life. Though I had brought most of the dunes back with me. It was in my clothes, my hair, my shoes. I managed to clean most of it off me in the shower.

I nibbled on a piece of pineapple but the fruit lodged in my throat as Harry stepped out of the bathroom, soaking wet with only a towel wrapped round his hips. Harry had no problem with his nudity or with me seeing him practically naked. I had seen his fine, beautiful bottom many times and I knew I would never tire of seeing his half naked body. It was a glorious daily treat now. Yes it was wrong to perv over my best friend like that but nothing was ever going to happen between us so the odd appreciative glance didn't do anyone any harm.

As Harry dressed, I quickly diverted my attention to the spectacular view but his reflection was very clearly displayed in the glass in front of me. I tried to focus on the sea and the sky rather than the vision of naked loveliness that was parading around the room behind me.

In the glass, I saw the towel drop as he pulled on a pair of boxer shorts, the tight black kind, that left very little to the imagination. A white shirt was next, covering that beautiful tanned body of his.

I focused on the sea.

I'd not had a proposal today, so I presumed Harry was going to whip one out of his pocket tonight when we went for our meal.

We weren't going anywhere fancy tonight, just some beach bar that was having a barbeque and served the best burgers and cocktails for miles around. At least that's what the posters advertising the place said.

I'd worn a sea green floaty sundress, it was one of Harry's favourites. I loved the way he looked at me in it.

Seeing he was dressed, I turned around and saw that his eyes were already on me. I smoothed out my dress then met his gaze, arching an eyebrow at the way he was unashamedly admiring me.

He smiled. 'I do love that dress.'

'It's a pity they don't come in your size.'

He laughed as he scooped up my pashmina and carefully wrapped it round my shoulders. 'Let's be very clear. I love *you* in that dress.'

I looked up at him as he arranged the pashmina, unsure what to say to that. He offered me his arm and I took it.

'Come on then Suzie, let's see what all the fuss is about with these amazing cocktails.'

'I want Sex on the Beach.'

Harry cleared his throat. 'That can be arranged.'

My stomach clenched unnecessarily. It was ridiculous to be excited by the dark implied threat in his voice but for a few seconds I let myself enjoy the fantasy – the waves crashing on the beach, the incredible passionate sex – until I realised Harry was speaking.

'Sorry, what did you say?'

'I said I prefer the Sloe Comfortable Screw up Against the Wall.'

I laughed. 'So that's your plan, get me drunk and take advantage of me?'

'I was talking about the cocktails, what were you talking about?' Harry looked at me innocently and I laughed again.

*

'You know your trouble,' I waved my hand theatrically through the air to make my point as Harry steered me along the beach back towards the hotel. I was very drunk, I knew that, and my mouth had somehow disengaged itself from my brain and was talking without any consent from me. 'You don't realise how bloody amazing you are. How lovely, how kind, how scrumptious, how sweet you are. You just don't get it. You are just gorgeous. And not in a fit way, inside you are gorgeous. I mean you are fit, very fit, freaking sexy hot fit. But that's not what makes you beautiful – you are beautiful Harry, inside and out. Where are we going?'

'I thought we'd sit on the beach for a while.'

I'd thought that Harry was perhaps a bit more sober than I was, despite the fact that we had drunk the same, but he didn't seem that steady on his feet either.

With his arm round my shoulders, he guided me down the beach to a dark patch near the end, where the lights didn't shine. Moonlight licked the waters but other than that it seemed to be pitch black.

I shivered a little in the cool night air.

'Here, sit down. I'll build a fire.'

'Oooh you're such a man.'

Harry smiled and I sat down watching him as he moved amongst the trees gathering sticks and bits of wood. I looked up at the stars and then lay back on my hands to study them more closely. There were thousands of them, millions, all filling the night sky, shining so brightly that the sky no longer looked black but a sparkling blanket of charcoal grey.

Orange flames distracted me and I sat up to see a fire burning strongly. I was impressed.

'That was quick, did you rub two sticks together, or use a flint stone?'

Harry showed me the lighter in his hand and I laughed.

The flames turned through green and blue, the heat igniting the salt water that had dried on the bits of driftwood. It was beautiful.

Harry looked up at the tops of the trees and I followed his gaze.

'Fancy a coconut?' he asked, leaping lightly to his feet.

I looked at the pair of coconuts hanging from the tree like a large pair of green testicles. 'You'll never get them, they're too high.'

But Harry was already running off into the trees. I heard him stamping around for a few minutes and he returned triumphantly with two coconuts in his arms, one small hairy one which had obviously come out of the green husk, and one still in its large green outer shell.

'Here,' he passed me the small one. 'Crack this open on the rock.'

I scooted over to the rock excitedly, and smashed it down hard. To my surprise it cleaved open in two neat halves, but there was no milk inside at all. Instead, in the light of the fire, I could see letters on the inside of the shell. I brought the coconut back towards the fire and held it up to the light to see the words 'Marry Me' branded onto the inside of the shell in black burnt writing.

I squealed in delight and looked up in surprise at Harry as he watched me.

'How did you do that?' I had asked that question so many times in the last few months. I looked back at the coconut and could see the shiny glue on the rim of the two halves. Clearly the coconut had been cut in half, branded and glued back together. Very sweet.

This was number ninety-nine. I had one more to go.

'Thank you.'

Harry scooted over to the rock and smashed the other coconut on the side of it. Nothing happened, the green hard shell stayed resolute and unbroken. He brought it down three more times and then suddenly milk spurted from a small crack and he quickly brought it back for me to drink. I licked up the side and sucked over the hole. The milk was warm and watery rather than an actual milk. There was a definite coconut flavour but it didn't taste great. I passed it to Harry and I watched as he licked round the sides too, then closed his mouth over the crack, closing his eyes in what looked like sheer bliss. There was something incredibly intimate about having his mouth over the same spot my mouth had been seconds before – almost as if we were kissing. Harry let out a tiny, involuntary moan and a bolt of desire slammed into my stomach. He was tasting me.

I shuffled closer and he eyed me over the coconut, his eyes dark with lust.

'Can I have some more?' I whispered.

He stopped drinking and passed it back, holding it for me. My hands joined with his as I licked along the crack, and I watched him, his eyes burning into mine as I drank. I barely tasted the coconut this time. I could taste him, his dark, sweet, sensual taste. I could smell his spicy, clean scent. I wanted more but the shell was now empty as I lowered it to the ground. I ran my fingers over my lip and sucked the last residue off them, longing to taste him again.

'Tastes so good,' I said, his eyes still on mine.

His voice was strangled when he spoke. 'What did it taste of?'

'You.'

I heard the breath catch in his throat and suddenly he launched himself at me. Or I launched myself at him. Our mouths met, hard, but as he cupped my face he tried to turn it gentle – holding himself back.

CHAPTER SEVENTEEN

The heat, the zing of need for him, ripped through my heart, and sliced straight down to my groin. His tongue invaded my mouth, the taste of him exploding on my tongue. Oh his taste, the acute, pure wondrous delight of feeling his tongue against mine.

His arms wrapped round me, cradling me against his body as the kiss continued. The kiss became urgent, desperate, filled with want and need.

His hands were everywhere, as his mouth didn't leave mine for a second. He pulled at my clothes, sliding my pashmina off my shoulder. The feel of his skin against mine was electrifying.

We fell back into the sand, Harry pinning me with his delicious weight. His kiss, his taste, his smell, the feel of his body against mine, it was a complete sensory overload. Kissing had never been like this before, this insatiable desperate need for more. An urgent frenzy of hands and mouths and lips.

The fire cracked loudly and Harry snatched his mouth from mine in shock.

'Sorry, God I'm so sorry. You're drunk and I'm an ass for taking advantage of you like this.'

'You're drunk too, I could be taking advantage of you.'

He smiled slightly, as he stared down at me, his moral conscience warring with need and desire. 'I want you so much.'

I reached up to hold his face, tracing my fingers over his lips. He kissed my thumb, closing his eyes, then softly kissed my palm and then the inside of my wrist, leaving his mouth there as he felt my pulse race against his lips. He opened his eyes and they were almost black with desire as he kissed me again.

His hand gently pushed the strap off my shoulder, reverentially trailing kisses along my neck to my breast.

Suddenly a flash went off, followed quickly by another.

We both looked up in shock to see the Japanese man from the day before standing a few feet away taking our picture.

'Crap,' Harry hissed, moving his hand quickly over my breast to try to hide my modesty but the Japanese man took another picture of this too. 'What the hell?'

'Harry and Suzie, yes?' the Japanese man said, smiling inanely as he fired off another shot. 'One Hundred Proposals? She say yes?'

Harry quickly got up and I grabbed my pashmina but the Japanese man was fast. As Harry moved towards him he sprinted off down the beach in a blur.

I stared after him in horror because he was taking with him very personal, private photos.

Harry stood torn for a moment between staying with me or chasing after the man, but in the end he chose me. He knelt by my side, wrapping the pashmina round my shoulders and then pulling me to my feet. He could hardly bear to look at me, his lips were thin with disgust.

I found I was shaking. It was such a huge invasion of privacy, coupled with the desire and need that was quickly fading to be replaced by shame.

Harry didn't say anything as we walked up the beach – the worst thing was he didn't even touch me or look at me. It was just a drunken fumble and one which he was now deeply regretting.

We approached the bright lights of the hotel and he stopped me. By blocking my way, not by touching me as he would normally. 'I'm sorry. That should never have happened.'

I folded my arms across my chest 'What? Some pervert taking our picture whilst you had your mouth on my breast or you drunkenly groping me on the beach?'

He looked horrified and I instantly felt bad. 'I'm sorry I kissed you, like that. And you seemed to be enjoying it as much as I was, so don't make out that I forced myself on you.'

'I was enjoying it until you looked at me as if kissing me made you physically sick. Then it kind of lost its shine a bit.'

He stared at me then laughed. He moved his hands to my shoulders and leaned his forehead against mine. It was such a sweet gesture and almost all of my anger just faded away. 'You really have no idea how much you mean to me. I was angry with myself for kissing you when we're both too drunk to appreciate it properly.'

My head was swimming. He was right, I *was* drunk – and this argument made almost no sense. Harry was simply not the drunken fumble sort of man, and I was angry that the kiss had been thwarted rather than at Harry. I pulled out of his embrace, still unsure what the kiss had meant.

We walked back to the hotel, still in silence but the tension seemed to have gone – leaving behind only confusion.

Once back in the room, we both got changed for bed. I slipped under the covers and probably more out of habit than anything else, Harry curled himself around my back, tucking me in to his chest with his arm round my waist. I considered removing myself from his arms for a few seconds but he was breathing deeply a few moments later and I didn't want to disturb him.

*

I woke the next morning to an empty bed, which didn't make me feel any better about the kiss. I sat up to see if he was there but I was alone.

Next to my bed was a jam jar with a note inside. Curious, I unscrewed the lid and tipped the note out onto the bed.

It wasn't a long note but what it said made me smile, hugely.

'*You are my best friend and I have never regretted a single moment in your company, when you've shouted at me, laughed with me, slept with me, or kissed me, being with you has always given me the best moments in my life.*'

I hugged the letter to me when I noticed another jam jar by the door, again with a note inside.

I climbed out of bed, unscrewed the lid on the second jar and tipped the note out.

'*Breakfast will be served to you by the pool under the tree canopy at the far end. Please stay by the pool until you're called sometime this afternoon. I don't want you*

*to see anything you shouldn't. I have to prepare your final
proposal. I'll see you later.*

   Love Harry xxx'

I smiled. I quickly showered, dressed and went down to
the pool. I was nervous about this proposal. Just what did
he have planned for the final one? And how would I feel
when it was finally over?

Would we return to being two friends sitting in our
office or had this trip irrevocably changed us?

I lay on my sun lounger replying to the huge volume of
work emails, hoping I would catch some glimpse of Harry
before the proposal, but there was no sign of him all day.
I watched the sun glinting off the water of the pool and
found myself drifting off.

*

I woke with a start as a hand slid down my back. I was
lying on my front and the sun had moved round so now my
head and shoulders were caught in the rays. I was wearing
a hat but my shoulders felt hot. The hand stroking me was
Harry's, it had to be, it was too overly familiar otherwise.

'You'll burn if you're not careful,' Harry whispered in my
ear as he slathered more sun cream into my back and neck.

I arched my back slightly into his expert touch. His
hands stilled. 'But then you get to rub after-sun into my
back too.'

The hands were gone and a second later I saw him sit
down on the sunbed next to me.

Talk about mixed messages. His attitude after the kiss
still hurt but the way he had kissed me was permanently
etched inside my brain – a glorious, vivid image that
I would replay again and again and again.

I sat up and looked at him. He must have seen the question in my eyes.

'When you flirt with me like that, I never know whether it's a genuine "I want your hands on me" flirt or just friendly banter.' Harry looked down. 'I just think a gesture like that means something very different to me than it does to you.'

'You flirt all the time. How do you think that makes me feel?'

'I never flirt, not with you.'

I felt my mouth fall open. 'How can you say that, you're one hundred percent flirt – every move, every word, every look is flirty. You flirt with everyone – strangers, Chloe, me. Trust me when I say you're even harder to read. I have no idea where I stand with you.'

'Seriously! You have no idea? None at all? Have I not given you any clue on this trip?'

I stared at him and like a flashback in a movie, my mind played back how many times Harry had told me I was his best friend. Is that what he meant, we were friends and nothing more? But then if that was the case, that kiss was nothing more than a drunken fumble and it certainly didn't feel like that.

'You kissed me.' I said.

'You kissed me.'

'Oh Harry you're such a child.'

I stood up to leave but he stopped me.

'And you storming off every time we get into a fight isn't childish?'

I stared down at his hand in mine and felt myself smile. 'I'm a woman, that's what we do.'

He laughed. 'Please let's not argue about this.' He pulled me down onto the sunbed next to him. 'It's our last day and

I have something beautiful planned for tonight. Just tell me one thing and I promise I'll say no more about it. When I touch you like that, when my hands are on you, do you like it?'

I stared at his gentle brown eyes, at the lips I so wanted to kiss again and I answered automatically. 'Yes.'

He nodded, more to himself than to me, then he stood up. 'Come on, we need to get ready.'

'Wait, I just told you something…' I gestured vaguely, '…about us, are you not going to give me anything in return?'

He smiled – his gorgeous, winning charm-the-birds-from-the-trees smile. 'Tonight, I promise. But let's get through this pantomime first. We have a show to put on. But I think you'll like it.'

I felt uneasy about that. I sort of wanted our last proposal to just be the two of us, but it sounded like he had a huge spectacle planned. He rubbed away my frown I didn't even know I was wearing.

'I bought you something.' He handed me another jar. There was a large flower inside, almost filling the whole jar, its petals the palest pink. But as I took the jar I realised it was filled with water, sea water judging by the tiny bits of sand that were also floating around inside. As the water swirled, tiny sparkles of gold twinkled inside too.

'Harry, it's beautiful. What's it for?'

'It's a clue for what tonight will hold. And because I love seeing you smile.'

I smiled as I leaned into him. Whatever he had in mind for tonight, it was going to be ok, I knew it.

*

The dolphin feeding, so Harry had told me, was one of the main attractions in Tangalooma. A wild bottlenose dolphin pod visited the shores every evening to be hand fed by the tourists.

There was a storm on its way in and the air had got a lot cooler. The waves were getting slightly choppy and we had been told that the dolphins might not stay for long.

I put the jam jar that Harry had just given me down on the sand – this one was filled with a cuddly dolphin – and walked into the shallows with Harry. The night sky had long since arrived but we could see clearly thanks to the lights that lined the edge of the pier and reflected off the water.

My heart was thudding with what tonight may hold, but all thoughts of that almost vanished when the dolphins arrived. The marine biologists in the water with us easily recognised which dolphins had visited that night and as they drew closer they introduced them to us as Echo, Silhouette, Rani, Zephyr and Bella.

I was so excited. It was the weirdest feeling of wanting to do this all over again and I hadn't even done it yet.

We watched as the dolphins swam around us – some of them, we were told, were hunting food for themselves as the fish we provided only gave them a small percentage of their daily diet. Their sleek bodies cut through the water like flashes of silver. Some were rolling on their backs, or poking their heads out of the water. As a few got closer, some of them started blowing air from their holes – spraying water over us.

We were told to hold the fish in the water and let the dolphins take them. As a fish was gently pulled from my hand by Silhouette I glanced across at Harry who was grinning inanely at the wonder of it. It truly was one of the most exhilarating and moving experiences of my life.

But all too soon the fish were gone and the dolphins started to drift away. I watched them until I could no longer see them. It was really getting dark now and the wind was getting up. I became aware that Harry was no longer with me.

I glanced around and then turned to look back at the beach. Harry was waiting for me and I sensed this was only the beginning. He offered me his hand and I sploshed through the water to reach him.

Without a word he pulled me down the beach, away from the lights and the pier until it was just us, standing under the trees in the dark. This is what I wanted, just us, no grand gestures, just simple words. Just three little words.

'We have to wait here a minute, they're not quite ready,' he said, and for the first time I realised he was wearing a hands-free earpiece.

I quelled the tiny stab of disappointment that it wasn't going to just be us after all. But later, there would be time for us to be alone. And we would talk. I was damned sure about that.

'I have to blindfold you,' he said, looking into my eyes to see if I was ok with that. I nodded. He pulled a scarf from his pocket and wrapped it round my head, plunging me into darkness.

I felt his hands on my arms, his warm breath on my face, and desire erupted through me.

'Are you cold?' he asked quietly, as he ran his hands over my goose bumps.

'Not one bit.'

His hands stilled on my arms as he understood my meaning, and then I felt them move to my waist as he pulled me in gently towards him. Was he going to kiss me as he did the night before? My heart was thundering against my chest. He held me against him but nothing else happened. The tension was almost unbearable. I leaned in further, leaned up ever so slightly and felt his lips faintly brush against mine, so soft it was barely a whisper.

'They're ready, come on.' Harry took me by the hand and guided me gently down the beach. We walked for a few minutes and I could hear whispers of people, then Harry stopped me and removed the blindfold from my eyes.

Hundreds of people stood in front of me lining the beach, all of them holding a jam jar with a candle inside. Flowers formed a path between them and beyond up onto the hillside. We followed the path of flowers, walking between them, and they all smiled and nodded at me as we passed, but none of them said a word. I noticed the candles in the jars were fake, little battery-operated tea lights, and a feeling of immense sadness resonated in me. None of this was real. We walked through the crowd and up the hill – I looked back and realised they were in some kind of shape, though I couldn't see from this angle what shape they were in. We continued walking until we reached the peak of the small hill, Harry holding my hand the whole time.

I watched Harry carefully as we stopped. Then looked back at the people on the beach below. The candlelit message was vividly scrawled across the sand. 'I Love You, Marry Me.'

I gasped as I whirled round to face Harry again. He was already down on one knee. But bizarrely he was wearing a head mic, making it look like he was a pop star about to launch into a song. Surely he wasn't going to sing to me.

'It's show time,' he muttered, then he switched the mic on and somewhere down on the beach I heard speakers squeak into life.

'Suzie McKenzie,' Harry said, and I heard his voice echo across the beach for all to hear. 'I love you.'

The crowd cheered.

My heart was in my throat. The words I finally wanted to hear. But unease settled in my gut and refused to go away.

'I've always loved you – from the first moment we met, I knew I was in trouble. I remember you standing there in your stained dressing gown and hippo slippers and I fell head over heels in love with you then. I love your laugh, your beautiful smile – and when you turn that smile on me it's one of the best feelings in the world, like you're smiling just for me. I love your freckles on your nose, I love the way the wind blows your hair, I love your smell, I love your little bouncy walk, the way you wrinkle your nose when you think. I love how you close your eyes when you eat. I love lying next to you in bed, holding you in my arms.' The crowd whooped at this and I heard a few wolf whistles. He really was putting on a show. 'I love the person I've become because of you. I love you.' The crowd collectively 'ahhhhed' as if we were in a pantomime. 'Every day I'm with you makes me so happy, but you would make me the happiest man alive if you would do me the honour of being my wife. Marry me?'

My head was buzzing and the people on the beach cheered again. Harry laughed at their response. I looked at him and he was grinning up at me, his eyes filled with mischief and humour. This was all for show, every single word. It was as fake as the candles on the beach. Disappointment flooded through me in great waves.

'Well?' He grinned up at me.

My carefully reined in emotions snapped. I held my hand out for the mic and he passed it to me. I yanked the cable out from the headset and the speakers squeaked before going silent.

'What is it you want from me, Harry? You're putting on a show for them. None of this is real. One hundred empty, meaningless proposals.' I watched his face fall at my venom, but I didn't care. How could he hurt me like this when he knew how I felt about him? 'I didn't turn down greasy kebab boy because he proposed to me over a greasy kebab in a vandalised bus shelter, I turned him down because I didn't love him, because he certainly didn't love me. I know I shouldn't be saying this considering the line of business we're in, but there's really only one thing that gets women excited about proposals. It isn't the ring, the location, the fireworks or flowers, it isn't even the words the men find to ask the big question. It's the man they love wanting to spend the rest of their life with them. Because after the proposal comes marriage, the happy ever after. And *that* is what's been missing from every single one of your proposals. You could have asked me to marry you on the back seat of the number thirty-seven bus on a rainy day sharing a bag of chips and I would have said yes.' I dashed angry tears from my eyes and Harry's face went all blurry. 'I didn't kiss you last night because I was drunk and horny. I kissed you because I love you, because I've always loved you. Every single one of your proposals was perfect because it was you doing the asking. Perfect apart from one tiny detail. The man I love, the man asking me to marry him, doesn't actually love me.'

I turned and walked away. When he called after me, the walk turned into a run.

*

I stood on the beach as the rain lashed around me. I was soaked to the skin, my hair clinging to my head, but it was a warm rain so I didn't really mind. Dark clouds rolled above me, lit up periodically by flashes of electric blue. Forks of lightning ripped apart the sky with foreboding cracks and rumbles of thunder. Wind roared across the sea, throwing white crested waves onto the sand.

I loved a good storm. I much preferred the beauty and power of a storm than a sunset or sunrise.

I couldn't find it in me to be angry at Harry any more. He really hadn't done anything wrong. He had never given me any false hope or promises. We had started this trip as friends and it was me that had moved the goal posts. He had made it clear all along, we were friends, best friends, nothing more. Yes he had kissed me but more likely I had kissed him first and being drunk he had simply kissed me back. I should expect no less from someone who attracted women like a jar of jam attracted bees. I couldn't hate him for not returning my feelings. He had showed me the world and I could never be ungrateful for that.

It was going to be weird between us from now on. I didn't know if we could get past this now.

Surprisingly, given the noise of the storm, I knew he was suddenly there behind me. I turned to look at him.

'Hello,' he said, stepping closer. He was wearing his big coat. I loved that coat, especially as he had given it to me to wear on countless chilly occasions. I doubted he would be chivalrously handing it over today, he hated the rain. Though I supposed that him coming to look for me in this weather rather than waiting in the warmth of our hotel room spoke for something.

'You're soaked.'

'It's raining.' Wow, this was awkward.

To my surprise, he suddenly started unbuttoning his coat and then held it open like he was a flasher.

One step better than giving me the coat was sharing it with me. I hesitated for a moment, then stepped up against his warm body, leaning my head against his chest as he fastened the coat around my back.

I closed my eyes as I felt his heart beating against my ear. If we could do this, maybe we would be ok after all.

'What are you doing out here?'

'Watching the storm.'

'Don't your eyes have to be open for that?'

My eyes snapped open and I realised he was looking at me.

'So we need to clear a few things up –'

'No we don't, we can just pretend that my little outburst back there never happened.'

'I liked it, finally one of my proposals caused some kind of reaction. Though you shouting at me wasn't really the reaction I was hoping for.'

'What were you hoping for? I couldn't let myself get excited about them – '

'I was hoping you would say yes.'

My heart leapt and Harry felt it because he was suddenly smiling down at me. He wrapped his arms round my back and pulled me tighter against him.

'I realise I've gone about this arse about face. I should have told you I loved you before, that I've been in love with you since the first day I walked into your house. I should have told you every day. But I didn't. You know why I didn't. I couldn't risk losing you like I'd lost and been rejected by everyone else I've ever loved.'

'But…' He really loved me? That was so not what I was expecting to hear. I looked around for the crowds but we were alone. 'You couldn't tell me in private, when we were up in the mountains and you were pouring out your heart, you couldn't tell me then but you declare it here in front of everyone?'

'Weirdly it seemed easier that way. They already knew, I'd told them in the secret blog how I felt for you.'

'What was the secret blog?'

'It was my declaration of love to you. I couldn't tell you, I was so scared of losing you. But I wanted the followers of our blog to know what was really happening, how much I loved you, why I was doing all of this. I will show you every single comment I wrote on there and you'll end up thinking I'm some weird stalker when you read how I like to stroke your hair, how I watch you sleep. I'm sorry that I told them first instead of you and I'm sorry that the first time you heard the words was in front of a crowd of people. I thought that's what you wanted, the huge declaration. You said that back in New York, that the woman wants the all-consuming "shout-it-from-the-rooftops" kind of love. I wanted to give you that.'

I had said that and he'd taken me literally. Maybe I would have appreciated the proposal more if I'd only heard the words before.

'I meant every word I said back there. I do love you. I love the way you make me feel when I'm with you: safe, like I've finally found a place to call home.'

'Oh, Harry.'

Tears welled in my eyes and he brushed them away.

The lump in my throat was huge, my brain willing to understand whilst I desperately wanted to throw myself into his arms. I'd lived with the doubt and the uncertainty for so long I was finding it hard to accept the truth. He'd loved me all this time – but then what about the women he'd been with? How could he sleep with these women when he loved me?

'But all those women…'

Harry looked away, clearly embarrassed. 'I never wanted to fall in love with you, with anyone. I couldn't let myself get hurt again, so it was just easier to pretend I didn't feel that way about you and carry on as I've always carried on – moving on from one woman to the next, never staying long enough for either of us to form any attachments. But every day I spent with you, I fell further and further in love with you. I didn't cancel my job in America because of Jack, but because I was in love with you and I couldn't bear to leave you.'

I was the woman he fell in love with. All this time and I never knew. He never said, but I understood why. I'd never told him either, for fear of losing him, and he had so much more to lose than I did.

'I rejected you, in front of thousands of people.'

He grinned. 'You told me you loved me, it was the best kind of rejection – believe me. After one hundred proposals, to finally hear those words was the best moment of my life.'

I felt so sad all of a sudden. 'One hundred proposals, one hundred missed opportunities.'

I buried my head into his chest, screwing my eyes up tight. Every time he'd proposed I'd felt my heart breaking a little over the emptiness of the gesture – but each time he had been hoping I would say yes, each time he had been disappointed. And every day he had come back for more, more heartache and pain. I wanted to sob for him.

He tipped my chin up to face him again. He trailed his hand down my cheek, grazing my lips with the softest of touches. 'I love you so much Harry.'

He leaned his forehead against mine, his grin splitting his face.

'Which one was your favourite? The big ones, the small ones? I'll recreate it again and ask you properly this time.'

'The one where I said yes.'

'But you never said yes. I would have remembered that.'

'It was a stormy night, we were standing on the beach alone, wrapped in each other's arms…'

He grinned. 'Oh! That one.'

I nodded. It was a big ask. He'd asked me a hundred times and I'd never said yes before, but I needed him to ask me one more time.

Harry looked around. 'Here, really? This is your perfect proposal?'

'I don't need all the bells and whistles, I just need you.'

He gathered me in tighter against him. The sky lit up around us and thunder filled the sky. He pushed a wet tendril of hair out of my face and my heart roared in my chest.

He grew serious as he looked down at me.

'So, I have no gimmicks or flowers, I don't even have a bag of chips to sweeten the deal, but… I love you, I will always love you and I will spend every day trying to make you as happy as you make me. Will you marry me?'

Sheer joy coursed through me and I leapt up to wrap my arms round his neck. Caught up in his coat, the movement caused him to take a step back – unfortunately he took me with him and we toppled over into the sand. As we hit the floor, my mouth was already on his, picking up where we left off the night before with that incredible, passionate, needful kiss. I moaned against his mouth as he rolled on top of me. He tore his mouth from mine, trailing kisses along my neck.

'I'm taking that as a yes,' he murmured, in between his kisses.

I laughed. 'It's a yes. Yes, Yes, YES!'

I felt him smile against my throat. 'Why don't you save the shouting for when we're back in our hotel room?'

I pulled his head back up to look at me and for a few seconds we just stared at each other. The meaning in that look was very clear. Suddenly there was a mad scramble to get up, but being trapped in the confines of his coat made it very difficult. Harry quickly undid the buttons and released me and we staggered to our feet.

He took his coat off and wrapped it round me, doing up the buttons as he got soaked himself.

'Harry you're getting wet.'

But he was still grinning inanely. 'You have no idea how crazily happy you've just made me. The rain can soak me to the bone and I still wouldn't care.'

He swung me up into his arms and started running back towards the hotel.

I laughed. 'What are you doing?'

'I think I've just found my perfect proposal – the one that ends in sex.'

'Oh, I'm pretty sure all proposals end that way.'

'Well, you've got a hundred proposals to make up for then.'

'I'll see what I can do.'

I laughed again as he ran even faster.

We approached the hotel and I could see our bedroom window was already lined with the jam jars filled with candles. We burst through the door and I could see the other jars filled the room, sending flickering lights across the wall and ceiling.

Harry put me down, instantly kissing me again as he peeled me out of my wet clothes and I helped him out of his, then he scooped me up and lay me down on the bed, lying down with me, kissing me so softly.

'Are you sure you want to do this now?' he asked. He looked around the room. 'I could make it more perfect for you, flowers, music…' He trailed off as I kissed him.

'Are we going to be disturbed by a barber shop quartet leaping out of the cupboard?'

He laughed and shook his head.

'An overzealous Japanese photographer?'

'No, it's just us, I promise.'

'Then it is perfect.'

Harry kissed me again and as he rolled on top of me he showed me just how damned perfect it was.

Proposer's Blog

After one hundred days, sixteen different countries and a hundred and one different proposals, Suzie McKenzie finally said yes. I'm not allowed to say what it was that happened in that last proposal. Suzie thinks it might damage our business if people knew she succumbed without so much as a bag of chips or a greasy kebab. But I can give all you would-be proposers one piece of advice. Tell her you love her, tell her every day until she knows it and believes it. Then tell her every day anyway. If you're incredibly lucky she'll love you back. I wish every single one of you reading this a very happy ever after.

And if words are not enough, then you know where we are.

Also from
CARINA

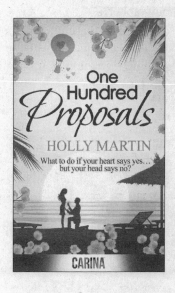

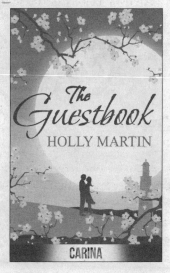

Also from
CARINA

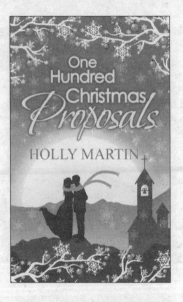

Did you enjoy reading this book?
If so, why not leave a review…we'd love to hear your thoughts!

WWW.CARINAUK.COM
Facebook.com/UKCarina
@UKCarina